HOT DAYS,
HEATED NIGHTS

What Reviewers Say About Renee Roman's Work

Where the Lies Hide

"I like the concept of the novel. The story idea is well thought out and well researched. I really connected with Cam's character..." —*Rainbow Reflections*

"[T]his book is just what I needed. There's plenty of romantic tension, intrigue, and mystery. I wanted Sarah to find her brother as much as she did, and I struggled right alongside Cam in her discoveries." —*Kissing Backwards*

"Overall, a really great novel. Well written incredible characters, an interesting investigation storyline and the perfect amount of sexy times."—*Books, Life and Everything Nice*

"This is a fire and ice romance wrapped up in an engaging crime plot that will keep you hooked."—*Istoria Lit*

Epicurean Delights

"[*Epicurean Delights*] is captivating, with delightful humor and well-placed banter taking place between the two characters. ...[T]he main characters are lovable and easily become friends we'd like to see succeed in life and in love."—*Lambda Literary Review*

"Hard Body"

"[T]he tenderness and heat make it a great read."—*reviewer@large*

"[A] short erotic story that has some beautiful emotional moments." —*Kitty Kat's Book Review Blog*

Visit us at www.boldstrokesbooks.com

By the Author

HOT DAYS, HEATED NIGHTS

by

Renee Roman

2021

HOT DAYS, HEATED NIGHTS

ISBN 13: 978-1-63555-888-3

This Trade Paperback Original Is Published By
Bold Strokes Books, Inc.
P.O. Box 249
Valley Falls, NY 12185

First Edition: August 2021

Credits
Editors: Victoria Villasenor and Cindy Cresap
Production Design: Susan Ramundo
Cover Design By Tammy Seidick

Acknowledgments

There's a never-ending list of people to thank. Some for hours of their time. Some for a perfect sentiment when it's needed most. And some for being a beacon in the midst of darkness. My humble appreciation to you all.

Special thanks to Radclyffe, for continuing to have faith in me as a writer and nurturing the BSB family by providing a safe space for us all.

Sandy Lowe, you never cease to surprise me by your words of wisdom when it comes to writing and knowing what will work…and what won't. (P.S. Keep writing your own stories…please.)

Victoria Villasenor, you continue to teach me the finer points of craft and the error of my ways, and I am grateful for your patience. Cindy Cresap, for putting the finishing touches on each story and making it better (though you probably want to shake me over the present participle thing).

And for those who beta read, proofread, and help produce a story I can be proud of…your efforts do not go unnoticed.

Readers everywhere, please know that you are the lifeline in the moments of struggle. Thank you for your loyalty and for cheering me on.

Dedication

To everyone who struggles with finding their authentic self,
be brave, be persistent. Most of all—be happy.

CHAPTER ONE

Cole Jackson's hair ruffled along the edge of her vision as she stared out the open bay and watched the puffy clouds meander across a vivid blue sky. Rain wasn't forecast, but she didn't have to be a meteorologist to know there was a storm brewing. She didn't feel it in her bones. It was inside her—a foreshadowing of sorts that was just as reliable as her grandmother's knees.

After pivoting military style, Cole shook her head, refocused. She'd gotten used to having conversations with herself over the years. Most of the time she didn't mind being alone because she wasn't actually lonely, it was merely her body waking from self-imposed hibernation and she wanted someone to share it with. Lesbians were few and far between in her sleepy little town of Inlet, New York, though she loved the slow pace and open spaces so much, she'd rarely considered leaving.

Even Dixie, her old beagle, played possum and barely raised her head when Cole came home. Long gone were the days when she'd bring her to the shop. Her hips had gotten bad and lying on the concrete wasn't good for her. Cole missed her company and the sound of her nails clicking on the concrete floor.

"Time to get to work," she said out loud in the cavernous, high-ceilinged garage. Wishing and hoping were a waste of time, and she didn't want to waste hers. Her father's unexpected departure had thrown her into a tailspin at the time, but she was older now and hopefully wise enough to make decisions about her future, though each time she went down that road she always came back to the promise she'd made to him, and she dismissed the idea she'd be happier doing something else. Lying on her back on the mechanic's creeper, she slid under the carriage of the rusted Mercury. She didn't trust it on the lift and would rather avoid the chance it could fall on her. The idea of not being found for hours while waiting for her demise had no appeal. The vehicle was older than Cole and well past its heyday. It shouldn't even be on the road, but she didn't have the heart to tell Glen Falcon that the car wouldn't pass inspection, even if she bothered to do one. He was the farmer she still bought her vegetables from, same as her father had and his mother before him. Glen only drove it a mile or so to the grocer's, then home again. Every town member knew he crept along at no more than twenty miles an hour—hardly a menace on the road. In fact, he drove so little he never bothered to stop for gas. Glen would call when he ran the ancient muscle car dry, and Cole would drop by with a five-gallon can. It would be months before she'd get the familiar call again.

She never minded and never saw it as a hardship. That's what neighbors did. Cole had been raised to consider the entire population of three hundred, give or take a dozen, as part of her family. She might not want to invite every one of them into her home, but it wouldn't stop her from lending a hand wherever there was a need.

If only she didn't have to use her own hands for sexual gratification. A change of pace would be nice, unlikely as that might be. Maybe she'd go for a ride tonight. Embrace a familiar fantasy to get herself off. Familiar wasn't bad, but variety wouldn't be unwelcome either. She stilled the wrench in her hand. If she were to dwell on it, she'd have to admit to a different kind of craving she couldn't name, but it had been gnawing at her for a while. Cole tightened the bolt and slid out. On her feet again, she rolled her shoulders and ignored the unease.

❖

Lee Walker hauled her weary body out of the truck and strapped on her tool belt. Monday had come a little too fast since she hadn't gotten to bed until well after two in the morning. A few hours ago, she'd been tangled in the sheets with a woman she'd talked to a couple of times at the local bar she frequented on Sunday afternoons when she would shoot the shit with some of the crew she worked with. Janice had asked if she could join them, and the guys had welcomed the buxom blonde with open arms. When she slid in next to Lee, there'd been no mistaking her preference as she moved her warm hand along Lee's thigh.

Janice was pretty enough and a good conversationalist, so Lee had invited her back to her place while her co-workers smiled and shook their heads. They'd harass her the first chance they got about her womanizing, though they never seemed surprised when she left with someone on her arm. Lee had a charming, easygoing disposition in bed that came naturally. If she had to be someone other than herself, she was just as happy leaving the woman behind to head home alone. She never did anything to impress others for impressions' sake and had never understood why men put on airs to get women into their beds. Strike that. She pretty much knew why men struggled in that department.

Sex was great as long as it remained casual because she had no interest in emotional entanglements, and sex with Janice had been spectacular. A little edgy, a little kinky, and a whole lot of sweat. She could still taste Janice's spicy flavor and pictured her sparkling eyes when she'd let Janice do whatever she wanted to her. Lee hadn't come that hard in a long time.

"Lee." Sam, one of the men who'd been at Rusty's last night, hustled over to her as she leaned against her truck and drank the last of her coffee. "Have you heard?"

She tossed the empty container into a garbage bucket she kept in the bed of her truck. "Heard what?" The rumor mill was often rampant in the construction business and she rarely bothered listening.

"Charlie was robbed last night. Some punk beat him up and left him lying in an alley."

Sam looked worried. He and Charlie went way back. Last Lee had seen him, Charlie was more than three sheets to the wind. "Damn. That's a shame. He was toast when I left." She stretched out her back and walked gingerly toward the building. Janice was a contortionist if she'd ever met one, and some of the positions they'd engaged in had been more acrobatic than Lee was used to, but she hadn't complained.

Breaking routine every now and again was good for her and provided a few new ideas to spice up the bedroom, albeit temporarily.

Sam strode beside her. "I told him to get his ass home, but you know Charlie. His wife complains about everything, so why bother. Not like she'd give him a break for being back early." He swiped his timecard.

Lee had trouble focusing. She was used to getting at least six hours sleep a night. Four was pushing it, even at twenty-nine.

Sam reached around her then swiped her card. "Late night, stud?" The knowing look in his keen eyes leaned toward admiration rather than envy.

She laughed. "You could say that." Lee glanced around. "Is the coffee truck here? I could really use another cup."

He clapped her on the back. "Come on. I'll buy you an extra-large one and you can tell me all about what kept you up so late."

CHAPTER TWO

I'll never get tired of your cooking," Cole said as she dragged a piece of homemade bread through the savory gravy covering her roast beef. Her grandmother had been cooking dinner twice a week for as long as she could remember, and the tradition had continued after her father died. It was one of the constants in her life that helped her through the most difficult time she'd ever experienced. There'd been no warning signs and no way Cole could have prepared for her father leaving her so young. She was grateful he hadn't suffered and almost glad he'd died while doing what he loved, but knowing all that wouldn't help her face the fact that her aged grandmother would likely follow in the not-so-distant future. The inevitable was coming, but it didn't make her heart hurt any less.

"You know I like having you around to cook for."

"I like to cook too, like you. Sometimes I think I would have liked to do something different. You know, other than work on cars."

"What are you waiting for?"

"A few years after Dad died, I thought about it, but I'd made a promise. I keep my promises." And she had. To her father, to herself. On occasion though, she became melancholy when the prospect of doing more, *being* more chased her until she finally pushed the nagging idea away. "Besides, I may be past the point of a new career. There are other things I want."

Her grandmother was quiet for a moment, and she put down her fork to wait. "It's time you think about making a family of your own."

Cole took in her wrinkled face. Her grandmother had earned each line by hard work in the fields and years in the sun when she was young, but it was the softest skin Cole had ever touched. Her light brown eyes still sparkled with life, and her snow-white hair gently framed her face. "We've had this conversation before, Nana. There's no one I want to settle with." That was true enough, but it didn't mean the notion hadn't crossed her mind every now and again, just like changing occupations. She couldn't though.

"You're never gonna find a good woman if you don't leave this cracker box of a town. I know you love it, but I think it's more because it's all you've ever known." She sat back. "Hell, it's even slim pickings for straight folk."

She laughed. "All the more reason to stay single." Cole reached for her hand, gnarled with arthritis. "I'm okay with the way things are." She wasn't about to tell her grandmother her thoughts had wandered off the beaten track of late. The idea that her restlessness had to do with wanting a different life would likely take her away from everything that represented home, and home was where she needed to be. "If I have to go looking that hard it's not meant to be."

Her grandmother shook her head. "At least tell me you're having sex?"

"Nana," Cole said, not at all surprised by the direct question. She'd come out to her grandmother in her early teens, and she hadn't batted an eye, saying she always knew. *Just because they came up with a newfangled name for it doesn't mean the concept of women loving women is new.* They'd laughed over chocolate chip cookies and milk. Cole smiled at the warmth of the memory.

"Well?"

"I do okay."

She scoffed. "Is okay some code word for your own hand doing overtime?"

Cole felt her face heat. How did her grandmother always know when something was on her mind? Hadn't she just been thinking along similar lines last week? She stared at her plate, unwilling to put into words her feelings of unrest.

"A woman as handsome as you shouldn't be alone." Nana placed her hand over Cole's larger one. "I worry about what will happen to you when I'm gone."

She drew a sharp breath. "Don't say that. Don't even think it, Nana." Cole blinked away the tears. "You aren't going anywhere."

"I'm not planning on it, but we both know I'm not getting any younger and the time for me to rest will be here someday, whether you admit it or not." She lifted Cole's chin with her fingers. "Promise me you won't live out your days alone."

"Nana, I—"

"Cole Anne Jackson, you promise me. I don't want to go to my grave knowing I've left my eldest grandchild with no one to love."

"I've never lacked love. I've always had yours."

Her grandmother's eyes softened. "That's not the same. Promise."

Cole sighed. Her grandmother was the most headstrong person she'd ever known. She wouldn't let it go until Cole agreed.

"I promise. Someday I'll have a love of my own." In the back of her mind, she doubted that would ever happen, especially if she stayed in Inlet. No one interesting ever came to the sleepy little town. But the promise would give her grandmother a sense of relief, and really, Cole *did* hope she'd find a partner someday. Cole was good at keeping promises. She just wasn't going to hold her breath waiting.

Her grandmother smiled and patted her hand. "Good." She stood and picked up their plates. "I hope you saved room. I made a peach pie this morning."

She groaned. Stuffed or not, she'd never say no to homemade pie.

❖

The crew milling around the trailer that served as the mobile office for the job site were restless. Low grumbles and heated shouts could be heard among them. Sam stood on the makeshift stairs shaking his head.

"What's going on?" Lee asked.

Sam stepped out of the way. "Read for yourself." He pointed to a sign taped on the scratched and muddy plexiglass pane.

"Due to unforeseen circumstances, R.J. Contractors has permanently closed," she said out loud more to herself than to Sam, then turned to him. "What the hell does that mean?"

Sam shook his head. "Whatever it means it isn't good. Today is payday. One of the guys overheard the secretary on the phone yesterday saying she wasn't telling any of the crew 'that morsel of news.' No one's seen her today, so I doubt she's coming in." Sam looked around at the disgruntled faces. "I think we're done here."

She ran her hand over her face. She had bills to pay and the entire crew had already been waiting weeks for their money. It wasn't uncommon in the construction business for delays with insurance companies notoriously waiting until the last possible minute to pay for repairs on commercial property, ensuring they were getting what they were paying for. Other times, the down payment was used for materials, and workers were always the last to receive their due. Until now she hadn't thought twice about waiting. Her gut churned at the notion of even more devastating news.

"What about our retirement plans?"

"I haven't a clue, but if they were being managed by R.J., who knows."

Lee swallowed around the knot in her throat. She'd deposited ten percent of her income into the retirement plan her employer had promised was backed in full by the company. Now she wasn't so sure. Last she knew, there was over twenty thousand in her account. She didn't even want to think about what it would mean if she had to start over.

"Fuck."

"No, more like fucked." Sam watched as despondent co-workers headed toward their vehicles. "I think it's all gone." He clapped her back and walked off to join the others.

Over the years, she'd financially struggled. Even in construction where the pay was above average, there were times she wasn't working due to the economy, or her lack of seniority, or uncooperative weather. Any number of reasons could throw her into emotional despair and financial insecurity. Lee wondered how something like this could have happened to her again. What had she done to deserve a worst-case scenario? She thought she'd left her troubles far behind. Once again, she'd been wrong. No wonder she had trust issues.

Days later, Lee drummed her fingers in a relentless beat, the rhythm hypnotic. She'd been in the same position too long and the problems facing her were still unresolved. Her insistent tapping served no purpose. Neither would punching the wall, though the vision was somewhat satisfying in a strange kind of way.

As word spread, the grim news reached all the employees of R.J. Contractors. Bankruptcy. Splicing together the bits and pieces of intel she'd discovered, the owner and his wife, who just happened to also be the bookkeeper, had a serious gambling problem. Not only had they cashed all the advance checks and lost the money to their habit, but everyone who had a retirement fund was now at a zero balance. All assets were frozen while the court decided what to do with the charges being filed against her former employer.

She had most of her money tied up in those shattered promises, and the little she had on hand would have to keep her afloat until she found work again. Then there was the issue of delinquent rent. With little in the way of options, Lee swallowed her pride and picked up her phone.

"Hello."

"Hi, Uncle Dan, it's Leanna. How are you?" Lee hadn't talked with him since last Christmas when he insisted she be with family for the holiday. She hadn't known her mother would be there, but she'd let herself hope things between them would be different this time. She needn't have bothered and should have known better. Dan had called a few days later, apologizing for not telling her ahead of time, saying he thought maybe his sister had come to her senses about her only daughter. She didn't blame the strained visit on him, but she hadn't talked to him since. Maybe she resented being blindsided without realizing it, but that wasn't good enough reason to stay away, and she'd used the physical distance as an excuse to not reach out sooner.

Her uncle lived in a tiny town in upstate New York and she was living, for today at least, on the outskirts of Atlantic City, not far from the ocean. Anger twisted around her like a boa constrictor intent on stealing her air. With a silent growl, she pushed it away. Being mad at the world for something out of her control was a waste of energy.

"Well, well. It's good to hear from you. How you been?"

She could hear the smile in his voice. After her father had disowned her for being a disappointment, among other things, and her mother's continued silence on the matter, Lee had been left to her own devices. Moving out while he was at work, she'd taken what she could manage to fit in her best friend's car. There should have been tears. Some outward demonstration of the loss and the connections being severed, but she'd been numb. Her father had never shown her love, only the need to control her. Even as a child, Lee had never been someone easily manipulated, and her stubbornness fueled her father's rage.

"I've been better."

"Tell me all about your woes. I could do with more than staring at the TV for hours."

With his kind encouragement, Lee told him everything that had transpired over the last week or so. Loss of her job, overdue rent, and bills to pay. When she was done, she let out the breath she'd been metaphorically holding since she'd read the notice on the trailer door. Relief flooded her at being able to share her troubles with someone who actually cared.

"Well, it's settled then. You pack up your stuff and head my way. It's not a mansion, but I've got that extra bedroom. You can have the bigger room with its own bath."

"That's very kind of you, but..."

He chuckled. "Isn't that why you called? For a place where you could sort yourself out and figure where to go from here? It's not Atlantic City, but you know the people are friendly."

Lee chewed the inside of her cheek. She hadn't known she'd made any decisions about the immediate future. She'd called her uncle because he was the only living relative who'd ever given two shits about her. "Okay. When will you be ready for a roomie?"

"Tomorrow?" Uncle Dan laughed with gusto. "You come when you can. I'll have keys made for you. Let me know what you like to eat and drink so I can stock up."

She'd have to notify the landlord and change her address with the post office. It would take her a day or two to pack up what she wanted to bring with her, the rest she'd have to put in storage. Another expense she didn't want, but she wasn't about to get rid of her furniture. Most of it was only a couple of years old if that. When she landed somewhere permanent, she wouldn't have to lay out more cash she didn't have.

"Would Friday be okay?"

"That's great. Looking forward to seeing you."

"Thanks so much for letting me crash with you for a while." Lee wasn't sure what she'd done if her uncle hadn't offered to take her in. She would never go back to the loveless home of her parents.

"Now about the fridge stuff—"

"You don't have to bother. I can pick up groceries. Besides, I'm not fussy." She'd have to figure out what she could afford to chip in. There was no way she was going to be a freeloader.

"Till Friday then. Safe travels, Lee."

The screen on her phone dimmed. Lee hadn't had an actual plan when she'd reached out, unsure she wanted to dump her frustration on anyone else since she was used to handling things on her own, not that she'd been given much of a choice. The ease of the conversation and knowing she had somewhere to call home, even if temporarily, gave her something to look forward to.

In a show of appreciation, she'd do something special for him. At least she didn't have to worry about where she was going to sleep.

When she called her landlord to tell him she'd be moving, she promised she'd pay her arrears as soon as she could. He told her to consider it a gift for being a great tenant, but he counted on the income to pay his own bills, and he wanted the place re-rented as soon as possible. Of course, she understood his position.

Tomorrow she'd pack up boxes with whatever she could fit in her truck. Not that she needed a lot. Depending on how long it would take her to find a job and recover the two-plus months' pay, she wanted to bring some of her favorite things, like her skates and her bongo drums. She couldn't think about her retirement right now. The class action suit most of the employees had filed was unlikely to recover any money, but R.J. would never be able to form another construction business. It wasn't much, but at least it was something.

CHAPTER THREE

Cole stared through the steam rising from her mug. The day promised to be a hot one with the heat already building as the morning dew burned off the bright green expanse, sending low-lying fog across the gently rising hills. The scent of freshly cut grass from a nearby field reminded her of the day she'd fallen in love with the smell as a child. The first year her father let her push the old manual mower when she was barely tall enough to grip the handles. How he had laughed while shouting encouragement from this very porch. She finally got it moving, fascinated by the spray from the cutting blades and the trail it left behind, not a little of which stuck to her, too. It had been a messy, exhilarating experience, one she'd repeated every week until she started working at the garage where the smell of grease and gasoline took its place.

A glance at the sky provided a sense of time and she headed inside. As the owner and sole employee of Jackson's Repair Shop, Cole had the responsibility of opening and closing the business. She swapped out her T-shirt for a tank top followed by a work shirt and her shorts for uniform pants. Both were the typical dark blue of her profession, able to hide the various stains that refused to be washed away. It was a dirty business, but she never regretted following in her father's footsteps because all she wanted was to keep him close for fear of losing him, too. Though now that she was older and realized he'd done nothing to keep her mother and sister around, the idea of doing something different wasn't as far-fetched. Would her father have discouraged her if she'd chosen another way to earn a living? She couldn't imagine it. Her father had unerringly loved her and supported her in following her passion.

After high school, he'd asked if she wanted to go to college and she'd seriously considered the idea of heading off somewhere to explore the world and see how the other side lived. In the end Cole couldn't leave the only home she'd ever known. Besides, she loved working with machines, taking apart engines, and figuring out how to put them back together. She had a knack for it—a natural born talent. There'd never been a motor she couldn't reassemble and have it run better than it did before. There was no reason to leave. Aside from a few lean years when gas was scarce in the US and money scarcer, they'd still managed to make a fair living. It helped that investments meant they didn't have to rely on the garage to live well.

Her father's side of the family had made a tidy sum selling off huge tracks of land to various buyers and investing wisely for the future. He'd made sure commercial businesses remained on the outskirts of the property and their lawyer assured him the remaining tracts would always be available for generations to enjoy. The land provided more than open spaces. It was the anchor on which Cole found security whenever her quiet existence became quicksand, threatening to pull her under. The homestead had been there through it all. Cole took in a full, centering breath.

She would always be comfortable though never rich, something she didn't want or desire. Money changed people. Made them forget that just one mistake, one unforeseeable loss, could drop them down a peg or two on the social ladder. Cole didn't mind being lower on the ladder where she'd have less distance to fall if that happened to her. She was careful with the money she spent, though she'd been a bit less conscientious with the house renovations. She didn't want for material things. Besides, what was money when there wasn't anyone to enjoy it with?

Zipping her fly, Cole's hand brushed her center, making her moan. She'd fucked herself last night, burying a dildo deep inside while playing with her clit and fantasizing of someone doing those same things to her. She'd fallen asleep thinking the hard orgasm would end the constant restlessness she'd been fighting. *Wrong.* She swiped her hair off her forehead and sighed. She would have to make the trip to another town and find a companion for the night.

She grabbed her thermos and lunch, then patted Dixie's head. Two droopy eyes glanced up at her and a couple wags of her tail were the best she could hope for. "Have a good one, Dixie girl." Dixie flopped onto her side with a groan.

The farmhouse always remained cooler in summer because it sat among old growth maples, pines, and oaks. The huge weeping willow out back gave a sense of privacy that wasn't necessary. The closest house was her grandmother's and that was almost a mile away. No one could see her home from the end of the curved road, and the deep covered porch hid her from view. She often sat unseen until visitors, few that they were, approached the front door. She'd scared her share of unwanted folk, too. In the waning light of approaching nightfall, Cole felt like a phantom when her presence was suddenly noticed, and the uninvited visitor's eyes widened in surprise. It always made her laugh.

When Cole hit the brick walkway, the sun's heat seeped through her shirt. Soon her tank top would be soaked with sweat. The light breeze was warm but welcome, nonetheless. She settled into her seat and turned the key. The Chevy Silverado rumbled to life and the vibration beneath her was another reminder her body was already on high alert.

Driving on autopilot for the few miles to the shop gave her an opportunity to come up with a solution to her growing urges. Perhaps *this* was the storm that had been brewing the last few days and it had nothing at all to do with the weather. Like it or not, the choice was easy. Continue to suffer or give in and find someone to take the edge off. Cole wasn't sure why she was fighting a need so natural it was akin to breathing. She wanted sex and to feel another's warm body pressed against hers. So what was holding her back? She'd never hesitated to scratch that itch before. Desire tightened her lower belly, curling in on itself and making her center throb like the pulse in her neck.

She swiped her shaky hand over her forehead. Something had to give soon. The approaching storm was already at her door and it wasn't going away.

❖

Lee pulled up to her uncle's house and wished she were someplace else. She ought to be thankful she had a place at all, but God, moving from the city had been harder than she thought it would be and represented one more place she'd been forced to leave. The front door opened, and Dan hurried down the steps to greet her. When she stepped onto the driveway, he pulled her into a fierce hug.

"You're a sight for sore eyes. Welcome home, Lee."

Home. Emotion choked her, unexpected and unwanted. Estranged from her parents for the last dozen years, Lee relied on her closest friends and a few sustaining but casual lovers for an occasional hug. They were nice but couldn't compare with her own blood being so glad to see her.

"It's good to see you, too," Lee mumbled into his neck as she tried to get control. She wasn't normally someone who felt sorry for herself and had learned survival meant keeping emotions in check, but her feelings were running close to the surface these days, and denying them would be foolish. "I can't thank you enough for letting me stay."

"Nonsense. You're my niece." Dan pursed his lips and studied her. "Are you thirsty? Hungry?"

She grinned. His generation was known for plying people with food and drink as a way of making them feel welcome. It was still true. "I could definitely use a drink."

"Great. Let's grab some of your things. No sense going in empty-handed."

Lee looked up at the crystal blue sky. Rain wasn't in sight and the morning forecast promised sunshine for the next two days. The stuff in the bed of the truck would be fine. Except if someone decided to help themselves to it. She glanced nervously along the quiet street.

"No one will take it." He clapped her on the back. "Small towns have definite perks." Dan winked.

"A fact that will take me some time to get used to." She opened the passenger door and handed him a stack of her folded sweatshirts and sweaters, not sure why she'd been compelled to be prepared for an apocalypse. Likely because she was living in one. A heavier box sat in the footwell, and Lee hefted it before following him inside.

Dan cleared his throat. "I hope you like blue," he said over his shoulder as he headed down the hallway.

For a man in his sixties, he moved gracefully, and she wondered once again why he'd never married or spoken of a love interest. "It's one of my favorites." She thought the question odd until she stepped into the room. Her jaw dropped. The former bland beige walls had been painted a beautiful shade of cerulean blue and the bedding and curtains matched with a pattern of paintbrush marks in various shades of blue on a white background. The black leather armchair held throw pillows that matched the walls.

"The paint smell should be gone. I've had the windows open for two days." He looked shy, almost apologetic for having done it without asking first. "There's no central air, but if you want an air conditioner, just let me know. There's an extra one in the basement. I have one in my bedroom. It helps me sleep at night when it's beastly out, but I'm old, so..."

She set the box on the floor and took the stack he was still carrying. "Uncle Dan, this is such a nice surprise." Lee kissed his cheek and he blushed. She chuckled. "Aww, you look so cute all red-faced."

She gave her a playful nudge and laughed. "Come on. Let's go have a cold beer, then I'll help you finish unloading."

They sat across from each other at the kitchen table and she stared at the bottle of Guinness in her hand, unsure what to say or do without a label to peel and play with. Dan must have sensed her unease.

"How was traffic?" he asked.

"Once I got away from the coast it wasn't too bad." She gazed out the back door. Mountains nestled among pines in the distance. There were open skies along the ocean, but the view here was different, almost majestic in its soaring height. "I'm not sure where the town is in relation to your house."

"Our house." He tipped his bottle at her. "Go to the end of the driveway and turn right. If you blink too long you'll miss it." Dan smiled.

Lee laughed. She'd driven into a foreign land. Ocean City, where she'd spent her college years and apprenticeship before relocating to nearby Atlantic City, had been her playground for the last ten years. Having to fill her days with the mundane would drive her crazy. The sooner she found work, the better. "I'm surprised you've stayed here as long as you have. You always seemed like a very social person."

"My lover was here. The choice to stay was easy."

She sat back, surprised by the revelation. "I never knew. Were you and she together long?"

A smile played on Dan's lips. "Not she. He. Mike was my everything for a few years. He loved this town and I loved him. We bought this house together, but we never lived together. It was a different time then." Dan stared off, perhaps reliving memories of happier times.

The shock of not realizing her uncle was gay wasn't nearly as shocking as discovering the real reason he and her mother rarely spent time together. Lee had made the trip by bus several times as a teen and had enjoyed their visits while she was still figuring out her sexuality. He'd always been kind and his tone gentle. Now she knew why she'd been drawn to him. She would have asked more about Mike, but something in Dan's eyes conveyed he wasn't ready to dig up old memories and she let it drop. "Is that why you and mom rarely spoke?"

"Your mother and I used to be close. Then she married that..." he shook his head. "Married your father and listened to him when he told her I was *not* someone he wanted around his family."

Lee finished her beer. She'd always thought it strange her mother and uncle's relationship was nothing like her friends' families. But then again, her own relationship with her parents had been strained even before she came out to them. "Is that why you stayed away too?"

Dan took her empty and rinsed the bottles, then brought two more to the table. "I never cared for the man, and your mother refused to stand up to him. I missed her, but I'd be damned if I was going to pretend to be someone else just to please him." He took a healthy swallow. "I figured that was the reason you moved out."

She nodded. Knowing her family, especially her father, didn't accept her being a lesbian still hurt. She'd gotten over the sting as she grew older, but being estranged from her parents had left her questioning if she could have done anything differently to change their mind, right along with thinking she wasn't someone another person could love.

"When I told them, I never expected to be looked at as though I had a contagious disease and that they'd want nothing to do with me." Lee didn't even realize she was crying until hot tears landed on her chest. She swiped them away. "I'm sorry. I don't know where that came from."

"Don't you apologize for having a bruised heart. If I'd have known what happened back then, I would have come for you. When you came to visit those few times, you were always polite and inquisitive. Then Anne told me you'd been sent to a school for headstrong girls. It sounded fishy to me, but legally there was little I could do. I should have tried to find you and brought you here. I don't know a thing about raising kids, but we would have made it work." His head moved side to side, gaze downcast. He looked sad. "I knew you were gay, and I figured when you hit your teen years you must have gotten a wild streak and they didn't know how else to handle you. Then when you went off to college and I didn't hear from you, I thought I'd been wrong…that maybe you felt the same as your parents did about me." He shrugged.

Lee considered the gaps between contact with him. Her life had been busy with courses, followed by training with an experienced mentor and, of course, partying and women. She rarely thought of anyone but herself, and now she regretted not staying in touch. "I'm sorry I didn't. I was into myself more than I should have been. I wish I hadn't wasted opportunities to know you better."

"Water under the bridge, Leanna." He finished off his brew and smacked his lips. "Let's get the rest of your things, then I'll make you dinner."

She took her bottle to the counter. "I've got it, Uncle Dan. I could use the exercise after sitting on my ass for most of the last two weeks."

For a minute he looked like he was going to protest. "Okay. You unpack, take a shower or whatever you want. Dinner will take about an hour or so. Is that long enough?"

"That sounds great."

❖

Lee hauled the last of her boxes into the garage and added them to the neatly stacked piles along the wall. She'd found a storage unit twenty minutes from her apartment in New Jersey and managed to move all her furniture in three trips, the last two with Sam's help. The seventy-dollar a month fee would be automatically withdrawn from her account. The last thing she needed was to lose what she had by forgetting to pay. If luck was on her side, she'd be in her own place in a few months…six at the most.

What had remained in the apartment filled a dozen boxes and few totes. Books, DVDs, some mementos, pictures, and a few souvenirs were among her treasures. One large tote held footwear for all seasons, including her beloved inline skates that sat on top. After using the edge of her tank top to wipe the sweat dripping down her face, she nodded in satisfaction, then grabbed a bottle of water from the old refrigerator her uncle said to help herself to. She sat on the tailgate and considered her life right now.

She'd had a job she enjoyed, a retirement nest egg, and health insurance. They were all gone. The queasiness from the prior weeks returned, but the edge had dulled, at least for the time being. What bothered her the most was how gullible she'd been believing her boss when he said he was waiting for another check in order to pay the workers.

Still, the situation wasn't as grim for her as it was for others. She only had herself to worry about. Co-workers like Sam had families to take care of and mortgages to pay. What was he supposed to do? If she managed to get on her feet any time soon, she planned on sending what she could his way. He'd shown her the ropes when she first started, and he'd never considered her less capable than any of the guys. She'd appreciated his camaraderie.

Lee tossed the empty bottle in the return bin, then scrubbed her hands over her face. She'd done enough thinking for one day. The sun had moved lower in the cloudless sky, but the heat of the day lingered. She was hot and sweaty. A shower would ease the tension from the drive, and she was looking forward to a home cooked meal. Things were looking up and she had to focus her energy there.

After unpacking some of her clothes and showering, she sat down to a comfort meal of meatloaf, mashed potatoes, and steamed broccoli. Lee was midway through her plate before she thought about asking if there was Wi-Fi. Her uncle chuckled.

"We're small town, not back woods." He pointed his fork at her. "Keeping the look of panic on your face was almost worth me pulling your leg though."

"Not funny, Uncle Dan. How do you expect me to get back to work if I have no way of searching for a job?"

"Hang on there. You just got here and you're already sick of me? I'm wounded."

Lee swallowed her food. "No, no. But I'm sure you didn't plan on taking in an orphan at this stage…" Her face heated and she sighed. She was making her staying with him sound worse by the minute.

Dan laughed out loud. "It's okay, Lee. I know this whole situation must be messing with your head. I'm in no hurry to see you go. You can stay here as long as you like, no matter when you find a job, and I know you will."

❖

Cole sat at her desk in the small office and looked out the plate glass window. Most people paid by card at the pump, but even when she was in the three-bay garage, she kept an eye on things, though she didn't worry about stolen gas. Her father had been a trusting but practical person and had put a few video cameras in when the security system was installed. One monitor hung in the corner of the shop while another hung above the entrance across from her and visible from where she sat. The last one was in the room behind her.

She pulled the small stack of bills to her and logged into her business account. It didn't take her long to pay them, noting each with the date and amount paid before filing them away in the June folder. Then it was time to send out payment due notices to her customers. She clicked her Square Invoices program and opened the folder of grease-smudged work orders. Sometimes she got into a repair only to discover more issues, and Cole always called a customer, relayed the additional work needed, then noted if they gave approval to proceed.

She and her family may have always been small town residents, but they ran their business the same as a franchise might, with a detailed paper trail. The familiar task had become monotonous, but necessary. One she didn't have to think about, like the routine in her life.

The processing of the last invoice was interrupted by the familiar chime alerting her a customer was at the pumps. She glanced out as an older model gray Ford F-150 rolled to a stop. She almost turned back to her screen, but something about the driver caught her eye as the door opened, and a dusty construction boot perched on the side rail before the owner jumped out. The blond hair cut close on one side and longer on top wasn't all that remarkable, but the form-fitting ribbed purple tank top that clung to her full, firm-looking breasts certainly was. Cole's belly tightened in response, the instantaneous reaction catching her off guard. She repositioned to relieve the pressure in her crotch and watched the woman glance around as she walked to the other side of the vehicle. Her camouflage pants hugged her ass and a large earring in her left lobe called to Cole for a closer look.

The customer slid her sunglasses to the top of her head before inserting her card in the credit card slot. When she lifted the nozzle, muscles rippled along her arm and shoulder. Cole's nipples tightened and pressed against the fabric of her shirt. Confused, she pulled her gaze back to the invoice. The woman wasn't her usual type. While she had curves, she looked anything but soft. This woman was carved, and Cole off-handedly pictured that body pressed against hers. Her desires had always been predictable, so why it wavered now left her questioning what was different. The constant edge of wanting a woman's body moving beneath her was the obvious answer.

Cole returned her gaze to the window and fixed on her as she used the squeegee and balanced on one foot in the open door so she could reach farther, stretching and extending over the windshield. She didn't have to have binoculars to see her buttock muscles tighten. Her clitoris swelled and wet heat trickled between her thighs. Cole stood. She could go say hello, ask if the woman needed anything else. Her face was handsome, androgynous. A strong jaw, high cheek bones, and smooth skin came together for an enticing look. The woman replaced the nozzle, slid her sunglasses back in place, and got in the truck. Before Cole could fully register a missed opportunity, the woman pulled away.

She could replay the video if she wanted, but what difference would it make? She was likely just passing through on her way to somewhere much more interesting than Inlet. Sighing, she dropped into her chair, turned back to her computer screen, and adjusted her constricting clothes. She needed to stop putting off the inevitable. Tonight she'd head out of town, no longer able to ignore her body's demand for satisfaction. Sex was her best outlet for getting her head back where it belonged.

CHAPTER FOUR

Lee had only been in town a few days, but already she was restless. Aside from work, there was always something to do in Atlantic City. So far she'd cut the grass, arranged her closet and dresser, and gone for several walks. She'd thought about putting on her skates, but she was too preoccupied to be careful, and she needed to be. The roads here were foreign, and she didn't have muscle memory to keep her safe from unexpected dips or bumps. Besides, the heat during the day had been oppressive, even though the nights were comfortable. Dan had brought her a fan to pull in the cool air, and sleeping nude helped. She'd hated living in the apartment building without the option of opening windows to escape the constant air conditioning. The song of crickets and peepers became a soothing sound rather than the annoyance of car horns blaring and people yelling in the streets, even at night. The convenience store she'd found in town boasted three area newspapers, each one the length of only a section of her previous town's. *At least there's internet.*

"Damnit," Dan said.

He'd set her up at the small desk in the screened in porch at the back of the house, and she'd put her laptop there, along with a stack of papers to review regarding her former employee benefits package. Whether or not she was eligible for unemployment was still a mystery. Neither she nor Sam had been able to find out if R.J. had paid for the mandatory coverage. She'd been through them once, but the legal jargon was hard to understand, so she needed to read it again. Lee went to the doorway of the kitchen.

"What's up?"

Dan grumbled. "I'm making Cobb salads with garlic bread for dinner, and this fucking heat has mold growing all over the Italian bread I picked up a couple of days ago." He shook the loaf in the air before setting it aside. "I have to go get more."

Lee chuckled at his colorful language. "I'll go." She could use some fresh air after the dismal employment opportunities she'd glanced at in the papers that covered a fifty-mile radius.

"You don't mind?"

She reached around him and snagged a grape tomato. "Of course not." Lee grabbed her keys from a hook by the door. "Anything else?"

He leaned against the counter with his finger to his chin. "Do you want ice cream with your blueberry cobbler?"

Lee groaned. "You're going to make me fat."

"Ha, not likely. You're carved lean and you're young. Two factors in your favor. Take my car though, and gas her up for me." He handed her two twenties.

"I can put gas in your car."

"You could, but you won't." He shoved the money into her hand. "I expect you back in thirty minutes, so don't dawdle."

After easing the SUV out of the garage, Lee headed for the only gas station she'd found in town, though there might have been more in the other direction. With the radio on and the warm breeze coming through the open windows, she could almost forget her troubles.

Jackson's Repair Shop appeared on her left, and she cruised to a stop beside one of the regular pumps. A few months ago, she'd unwittingly pumped a couple of gallons of diesel in her truck before noticing. Lucky for her the tank had been close to empty and it had been diluted enough it hadn't caused any issues. She was out of the car and standing at the pump before realizing the gas tank was on the other side. Lee swore under her breath and repositioned the vehicle.

The smell of gasoline wafted around her, and she wrinkled her nose as she stood in the last of the setting sun. The temperature had steadily climbed throughout the day, but with evening approaching, it was starting to abate. A sign on the pump caught her attention. "If paying by cash, please stop on the dollar." She chuckled. *Small town indeed.* When the readout neared twenty-five dollars, she eked out the last few cents and hoped it was close enough to full. She replaced the cap and strode toward the only door, but when she looked inside no one was there. Not about to drive off without paying, she decided to try to find someone in the garage.

"Hello?"

A head popped out from under the hood of an old car at the back of the shop. "Hey there." The mechanic set down a tool, grabbed a rag, then headed toward her. "Sorry. I didn't hear the chime go off. What can I do for you?"

The alto voice reminded her of aged, fine whiskey. The kind meant for all-day drinking. The woman smiled at her as she continued to wipe her hands. Lean, a few inches shorter than Lee, and dressed in dark blue uniform shirt and pants, she was handsome in a roguish sort of way, but that might have had more to do with the smudges on her face rather than her sharply carved features.

Lee studied her for a long beat and thought about the combination of deep and sultry in her voice until the woman cocked her head, and she stopped staring. "Gas." Christ, she was pathetic. It hadn't been *that* long. "I need to pay for gas."

The woman looked where her uncle's car was parked before turning back, concern etching lines around her mouth. "If I'm not mistaken, that's Dan Burke's vehicle." Her tone wasn't accusatory, but it held an edge of suspicion.

Small town chivalry. "Yes, it is. He's my uncle. I'm staying with him for a bit." Lee held out the money. Something about the woman's scrutiny made her uneasy.

"He's not ill, is he?"

"No. Nothing like that." She wasn't about to share her personal business with a complete stranger.

"Good." Her face relaxed and she stuck out her hand. "I'm Cole Jackson."

The tension in her shoulders eased. It wasn't like her to jump to conclusions regarding what others were thinking. She was more on edge than she thought. "Lee Walker. Nice to meet you." Cole's hand was firm, slightly rough. Cole looked down at the bills in her hand.

"How much change do you need?"

"Fifteen." She laughed. "Do you trust all strangers to tell you the truth?"

Cole studied her as a small smile lifted one side of her mouth. She produced a wad of bills and pulled out a couple. "Not all," she said as she swapped the twenties for a five and a ten. "I guess I'll be seeing you around."

"Most likely." Lee slid the change into her back pocket. "Have a good one."

"Will do. You too."

The open intensity of Cole's gaze followed her like a heat-seeking missile as she turned away, and she couldn't help wondering what Cole was thinking. What were the chances there were more than two lesbians in a town this size? There she went, being presumptuous again. Cole hadn't shown anything other than curious interest and genuine concern for her uncle. Still, she fought the urge to see if Cole was watching her walk away. It was safer if she didn't. She wasn't going to be in town long enough to get to know her, even if she was batting for her team.

"Damn." Cole's cousin, Michael, swore as her dart found the bull's–eye.

"Aw, don't be upset. You're out of practice is all."

"And when was the last time you played?" he asked, then handed off the beer she'd won.

"I don't know." She took a swig. "Maybe six or eight months."

Michael harrumphed. "Once you master something you never lose your touch. Why is that?"

She forced herself not to smile. "Dyke power."

His eyes widened before he broke into a fit of laughter. He clapped her on the back. "I've missed hanging out with you, cuz."

"Same here. What's new? Any women on your horizon?" Michael was a good guy. He worked hard and played hard. A couple years older than Cole, he was still looking for Mrs. Right.

His pale cheeks took on color. "You know me. I can't just drop into bed with a woman for bragging rights."

Cole's back stiffened at what felt like a barb.

"I wasn't referring to you. Even if it's only for a night, I know you have to have a connection with the women you sleep with." Michael took a drink. "Guys tend to be a little slack in that department, but that's not who I am, and probably the reason I haven't gotten laid in a very long time."

"I'm sure I have you beat."

"Stop."

"I'm serious." Cole pretended to be figuring it out, but she knew exactly when the last time was, since she still hadn't made the search for relief. Lately, it felt like too much trouble. Or maybe casual had lost its appeal. "November of last year."

"No." Michael shook his head. "Seriously?"

She set down her empty. "It's true. I wish it weren't, though." Having someone to talk to about her sexuality and her desires was something she sorely missed at times. The vision of Lee's aquamarine eyes flashed before her, and her body reacted. Even now her clit twitched as though it had a mind of its own. Cole rose from the stool and smoothed the legs of her jeans while pretending to remove the wrinkles when what she was actually doing was getting her equilibrium back. She needed to get home and take care of her immediate need, then she'd force herself to find a real solution to the throbbing that had moved so deep inside her, she was afraid no one would be able to touch it.

"I'm heading out." She gave Michael a hard hug that was returned. When she stepped back, Cole placed a hand on his shoulder. "Don't sell yourself short. Wait for what you want. She'll come along when you least expect her."

He glanced down at his feet, then nodded. "It's good to see you. Let's not make it so long before the next time."

"You got it." Cole said over her shoulder. She made it outside before stopping short. Why was she thinking about the woman she'd just met with the quick smile and mesmerizing eyes? And why did she continue to wonder what sex with her would be like? What would having that hard body pressed to hers feel like? Her chest tightened when she couldn't get enough air in her lungs. Cole focused on making it to her truck. She'd left the windows down in hopes the cab would be bearable when she got in. She leaned her head back and looked around the open lot. She was parked in the back, the entrance blocked by a number of other trucks. She snaked her hand down the front of her jeans until her fingertips swept through the slipperiness, eliciting a groan. A minute later, she was on the road.

Tonight would call for something special. Jerking off wouldn't satisfy the level of fevered yearning that gripped her. The traffic light gave her a brief respite to close her eyes and will her body to relax, but all she could see was Lee, standing with her back to the sunlight, her broad shoulders silhouetted against the bright outside, her wide stance begging for Cole's focus.

Five minutes later, she slammed the front door behind her and began to peel off her too tight clothes. The upstairs master bedroom served as her safe haven. The faster she strode, the farther away it seemed. By the time she reached the door, she was trembling, like a stallion preparing for a hard run. Naked, she pulled the round exercise bolster from the closet, attached the black dildo with her homemade harness, and slicked her fingers over her distended knot. A few hard strokes and she was ready. Cole straddled the bolster and impaled herself on the cock, raising up and down in a steady rhythm as she attempted to dispel the emptiness that never truly left as she tugged at her clit. She closed her eyes, searching for one of her favorite fantasies, but instead saw the tall blonde with the let's fuck sex appeal and a mouth that looked capable of being a lethal weapon wielded with skill and precision.

Cole cried out, riding the waves of her orgasm until she collapsed. Believing she'd quieted the beast, Cole sat up and the base pressed against her, once more stirring her tight bundle of nerves to life. When was the last time her body demanded more? What had brought on such wanton desire? Slower, without the abandon of her first ride, Cole eased back and forth. Rivulets of her excitement coated the surfaces beneath her. She squeezed her distended clit, sending a jolt through her. Close. So close. Her harsh pants echoed off the walls while she imagined the sound wasn't coming from her at all. Instead they belonged to the focus of her newest fantasy. This time when she cried out, a name tumbled from her lips.

Chapter Five

Y ou're like a cat in a room full of rocking chairs." Dan wiped his hands on a kitchen towel while leaning against the doorway.

"What does that even mean?" Lee asked as her leg jangled in perpetual motion.

"It means you're restless as hell. You need to find something to do with all that pent up energy." His crystal blue eyes, so much like her mother's, focused on her for a minute before he turned away. The refrigerator door opened and closed several times. A few minutes later, he returned and set a small cooler next to the desk. "You've been here almost a month. Have you explored at all? Been to the nearby towns? Taken in the scenery?"

In truth, she'd thought about doing just that, but with watching every penny she spent, Lee couldn't justify the waste of gas. "You mean there's more than the ten blocks I've seen a dozen times?" Her tone was uncharacteristically sarcastic.

Dan eyed her suspiciously. "Aren't you sick of staring at the four walls yet?"

"What's the rush? I've got time." She couldn't help the edge of discontent in her voice. Prospects for work were basically nonexistent.

"What you've got is ants in your pants."

Lee laughed. It broke the tension she'd been holding inside since she arrived. If she were back home...no, this was her home. At least for now. There wasn't any reason to refer to her former place as home. If she were somewhere that didn't have more livestock than people, she'd bed down with a woman, or two, for the night until exhaustion overtook her and her body was spent. That wasn't an option at the moment. She could only think of one woman nearby who might be interested but that was likely more wishful thinking than actual interest. Her life was complicated enough without chasing a woman. Maybe Dan was right. A long drive might clear her head and give her a chance to sort herself out. One thing was certain, her uncle was aware of her restlessness…and he loved her.

She tipped her head at the cooler. "What's in there?"

"Staples. Water, a couple beers, sandwiches, snacks."

"How long do you expect me to be gone?"

Dan pushed off the doorway. "As long as it takes."

❖

If social distancing became a thing, this would be the perfect location. Traveling along Route 28, Lee had passed less than ten cars over the last thirty minutes. After reviewing the laminated map her uncle had provided of lakes and hiking trails, she'd decided to try to find Indian Lake. She needed a break from the heat, and sitting beside calm water would be a good way to reconnect with her life, and to figure out whatever was bothering her, aside from the obvious. A few days ago, she filed for unemployment and received notification the case was pending until verification of her employer paid benefits. Lee had laughed, though there hadn't been any humor in it. If he hadn't paid into her retirement fund, how could she rely on his having done so for anything else? Until she heard the outcome, she'd continue to live as frugally as possible. She'd searched the internet for construction jobs nearby, but no one was hiring.

Main Street, USA, covered several blocks with quaint shops, a few restaurants, and a couple of bars. Not in the mood to shop, Lee kept going until she was directed by a fading hand-painted sign stating, "Lakeside access this way," and she eased the truck onto a narrow road. She moved slowly along the hard-packed dirt and gravel lane, vigilant of wildlife that might dart out from the underbrush. The overhanging foliage provided welcome shade from the bright sun. It wasn't long before a bend in the road opened to a pristine view of calm, dark water that reflected sparse white clouds and was surrounded by pines and deciduous trees.

Lee pulled off the road after spotting a scattering of big logs near the water's edge. With the cooler in hand, she picked out a dry log and straddled its length. Birds sang in the nearby trees, a calm, welcoming sound she hadn't been attuned to until she moved here. She closed her eyes and took time to let the clean air fill and expand her lungs.

Recalling her childhood, there'd been times when her father had stared her down as though trying to bend her to his will, even back then. Moments when she'd been afraid of his wrath and his overbearing demeanor so she'd done what he wanted her to. When she was older and her body began to change, she'd seen something sinister in his gaze. She refused to show her terror and forced herself to become hard as steel—her fists clenched at her sides. At fourteen, she began to wonder why she'd been sent away to stay a few nights at her friend's home or put on a bus bound for her uncle. What would have awaited her if she hadn't gone. What reason did her mother have for not trusting her father around her? That was when she began to do things for herself. There was no one else to take care of her, and Lee began to live on the edge between doing what she wanted rather than what was in her best interest.

Unfortunately, she'd had no say in being drawn into her current situation. How had she been so naive? It's not like when she was younger and just learning the ropes of how to maneuver through life. She'd been forced to learn how to survive during her developmental years. Had she gotten complacent to details she viewed as unimportant since her carefree life seemed to be going so well? No. It wasn't like all the other workers hadn't been screwed, too. It was a crappy situation that she couldn't have foreseen. The question remained: what now? There was no crystal ball to provide answers, but the hope lingered she'd figure out what to do so she could move forward. Her stomach rumbled, and she opened the cooler to see what her choices were.

Two bottles of beer poked out of the top of the ice, and she almost reached for one before thinking better of it. The heat would intensify the effects of alcohol, and she had to drive back at some point. She opted for one of the flavored seltzers Dan had introduced her to. She'd always drunk her share of water while working, but there were times when she'd grown tired of the lack of flavor, and she welcomed the change. After rummaging some more, she uncovered a couple of sealed sandwiches and opened the zippered bag to pull one free. In a separate compartment there was a small bag of chips, a container of watermelon, and a few homemade chocolate chip cookies. She snagged a cookie since there was nothing wrong with having dessert first. It was gone in four bites, her hand smudged with chocolate. There was a roll of paper towels in her truck and she was about to get up when she noticed the outer pocket on the cooler and peeked in. A few napkins, a fork, and a Wet-Nap were tucked inside. The cache made her smile. Her uncle was proving his innate ability to pay attention to details that mattered. He would have been a great parent.

Lee took a bite of her sandwich and chewed the contrasting textures of hand carved ham, Swiss cheese, and crunchy lettuce on multigrain bread smeared with mayonnaise. It was delicious. She washed it down with her drink as she gazed out over the placid water. Two ducks dove beneath the surface, webbed yellow feet kicking in the air. A large green dragonfly darted to and fro, its path determined on a whim. Off in the distance a large fish jumped, sending out rings in an ever-expanding circle. Life out here, away from the concrete and steel, *was* simpler, and not a bad thing. It just wasn't *her* thing. At least, not for the long haul.

Dan had recognized her disquiet, but she hadn't been able to tell him it stemmed from needing some intense physical relief. Maybe she *should* tell him. Sex centered her. Made her feel in control when nothing else in her life did. Her release would serve as a welcome distraction. He'd probably be able to point her in a direction where she could find someone to enjoy for a night. She'd have to stop for gas. She'd have to see Cole again. The sandwich was halfway to her mouth before the vision of Cole materialized. Not just her face, but her strong hands and slender hips. What was her story? Did she work for a relative at the garage? Was it a family business? The easy smile, intelligent eyes, and lean body sent her mind in other directions, ones she should let be. Cole was friendly and might have looked her over, but that didn't mean she was interested in sex, or anything else. Reasoning did nothing to tone down the hum in her body. *Christ.*

Unemployed, horny as fuck, and always on edge was a dangerous combination. With no job to wake up for, she could prowl for a willing partner and disappear for the entire night. She just had to make sure a night stayed a night and didn't turn into something longer. She wasn't about to hope for anything. With luck, she'd be gone before too long.

She picked up her trash and shoved it in the cooler pocket, then turned sideways to finish her drink and another cookie. Dan had been right. She needed to find a semblance of normal to dispel the tension that had accosted her every day since she'd arrived. To help her further cope, she started listing the good that had come from moving.

First and foremost was reconnecting with Dan. His open arms and big heart had been exactly what she needed when she needed it most, and the care with which he'd decorated her room had touched her deeply. There'd never been anyone she'd dated who'd put her first. The feeling of having somewhere to call home was a respite from her mindless walk through life. Missing her crew and the work they did wasn't a surprise. She'd grown to love witnessing the transformation she helped to create on each project. Whether it was from fire or water damage, or a need for remodeling, seeing the pristine finished product was rewarding. Maybe that's what she missed most.

Lee strolled back to the truck and stowed the cooler in the wheel well. Her options were limited though she didn't think she should go back yet. Dan would likely tell her she was back too soon, and she still wanted to find him a special gift. Remembering the pottery shop sign she'd seen in the village earlier, that's where she headed. The truck gently bounced along the dirt road, forcing her to slow down, and the metaphoric meaning wasn't lost on her. She took in the lush greenery and quiet calm that let her breathe a little freer without the hustle and bustle of the fast-paced city she was used to dealing with on a daily basis.

Even the town itself, what there was of it, lent a sense of warmth and sedate energy. The people were a close-knit group, evidenced by Cole's wary inquiry as to her uncle and his car. She was an enigma if Lee had ever met one. Older, though it was hard to tell how much, and the small lines at the corners of her eyes were almost invisible. She'd mistaken Cole's slender build for physical softness, but when she looked closer, the rolled sleeves revealed muscled forearms and heavily veined hands, a sign of repetitive use and strength. Working on engines had to be physically taxing, much as construction was. Lee's own body had adapted to the constant demands to lift and hammer and climb ladders while balancing materials.

Cole seemed self-assured without being cocky and had an open, friendly manner once her suspicions were put to rest. Her entire countenance was unhurried—likely due to living in Inlet for a long time. Her dark brown eyes reminded Lee of pools of smooth chocolate, and she imagined herself immersed in them. Cole came across as a trusting, kind person who took others at face value.

The familiar pulse beat between her legs. Her gaydar was usually spot-on, but these days she doubted everything about her perceptions. Attraction was a reaction she normally tuned in to quickly, but the recent weeks had been anything but normal and relying on what had always been her metric wasn't serving her very well. Still, the familiarity of the look had gotten her attention, if only fleetingly.

Oh, well. Best to leave the questionable alone and concentrate on things she could be certain of. The last thing she needed was to bed down with someone who might put expectations on her for more than a good time. With her situation tenuous at best, there wasn't room for complications, and a woman could be a big one if she slept with the wrong one.

Tomorrow she'd submit her application to a few of the online employment services and troll the newspapers again for any new listings. Maybe she'd make up a flyer with "Handyperson for Hire" on it and hope to land some local repairs or remodels she could handle herself. She didn't have a lot of her own tools because the employer usually supplied them. Maybe her uncle knew someone she could borrow a few from. Anything to keep her busy would be a plus.

A couple of minutes later, she parallel-parked a few doors from the pottery shop. She didn't have much extra money, but as generous as Dan had been, she could splurge a little to show her appreciation. When she stepped inside, her gaze fell on a beautiful vase displaying an array of summer flowers, just like the ones her uncle cut from the fields out in back of his house and placed on the kitchen table where they ate meals or talked. It was perfect. She checked the price tag before bringing it to the counter. The salesperson asked if it was a gift and wrapped it in beautiful floral paper with an impressive bow. With all the padding inside the box, she was confident it would make it to her uncle in one piece.

Cruising down the road a short distance from the edge of town and listening to music, Lee sang along at the top of her lungs, carefree for a change. It all came crashing down when her truck began making a horrible knocking sound. Loud bangs came from under the hood. With few options, she prayed she could make it to the garage before it died. *Shit.* Just what she needed. One more thing to go wrong. She babied it until she was in front of one of the open bay doors and killed the engine. It sounded like it was dying a slow and painful death. Swearing, Lee exited the cab to find Cole standing with her head cocked to one side.

"You borrowing vehicles on a daily basis?" Cole's lopsided grin would have been alluring if the situation didn't involve her only mode of transportation, though it didn't stop the tingle that started low.

"I wish. This one's mine." The tension she'd dispersed lakeside returned ten-fold. "It's making a horrible noise."

Cole's expression became serious, as though sensing the angst she was feeling. "Let me take a listen. You mind?" She gestured toward the cab.

She stepped back to give her room. "You're the expert." Lee watched Cole fluidly jump in and turn the key. A loud series of knocks and bangs began.

"I'm going in the garage with it so I can get a better look," Cole said, her brow creased.

Lee watched as her beloved truck limped into the vacant stall. Cole popped the hood and leaned inside. Before long, she reappeared and shut the engine off. Lee held her breath.

"What I thought," Cole said as she wiped her hands on a rag. "It's a cracked crankshaft."

She shoved her hands deep in her pockets to keep Cole from seeing them shake. Why was this happening? "What's it gonna cost to fix?" Lee wasn't sure she wanted to know.

Cole thought for a moment while she finished removing traces of grease from her hands. "I'll have to get the engine out to know for sure, but two grand, give or take. I'll have to order the parts either way, so it could be a few days before I can start on the repair. If it needs an engine rebuild it's likely not worth the expense."

"Fuck." The word left her lips before she could sensor it. The more she tried to get ahead the more behind she got. She met Cole's gaze and recognized the empathy in them. "Sorry."

Cole shrugged. "Not like I haven't heard it, or said it, a million times."

She ran her hands over her face. She needed time to think and come up with a game plan. Maybe she'd hear about her unemployment claim in a day or two, though it wasn't likely to happen. "Can you keep the truck here and wait on ordering the part?"

Cole nodded. "I've got room out back. It'll be safe there until you decide what to do."

Her reassurance helped loosen the knot in her gut. Not a lot, but for some reason she trusted Cole to take care of her beloved vehicle. "Thanks." She should have explained about the delay, but the idea of Cole seeing her as unable to take care of herself or lacking the ability to pay for necessities left her feeling exposed. Up until a month ago, she'd been on pretty solid ground. Now bad news seemed to be following her everywhere these days and her footing was off. The sympathy in Cole's eyes wasn't helping.

CHAPTER SIX

Cole raised the back bay door after Lee cleared out the cab, piling her things outside the entrance, and drove the noisy truck around the building. Back inside, Lee approached her, and she looked so lost, something inside of Cole tugged at her compassionate side. Lee was obviously going through a rough time.

"I'm closing up for the day. I'll give you a ride home."

"I can call my uncle."

"No need. It's really not a problem."

"Isn't it a little early?" Lee asked as she stared at her.

She quirked her eyebrow. "In case you missed it, I'm not overrun with customers at the moment. It's one of the perks of small town living. If there's nothing going on, and I don't have a backlog, I close shop. If anyone needs me, they all know how to find me, but there's nothing that can't wait till morning." Cole dropped the bay doors and locked them, then went to the office to set the alarm before exiting. Lee stood with a small cooler at her feet and a beautifully wrapped present in her hands.

"Aww, you shouldn't have." She grinned and picked up the cooler. "Come on. Mine's the red one." With the remote, she unlocked the doors, then set the cooler on the floor of the back seat. Lee set her package down carefully behind the passenger seat, her large hands gentle on the delicate paper. Cole's heart rate picked up speed.

Lee got in beside her and fastened the seat belt. "Nice truck." She looked around and ran a hand over the gleaming surfaces. "How do you keep it so clean?"

Cole glanced at her profile. Strong chin, sculpted cheeks, perfectly shaped brows. "It's not easy, but I try to get off as much crud as I can before getting in it." She pointed to her seat cover. "This helps. I wash it once a week and take it off when I'm not in work clothes."

Sweat trickled down the side of Lee's face. A drop followed the line of her chin and fell onto her chest, disappearing beneath the dark tank top. When she brought her eyes back up, Lee was watching her.

"I've gotten used to the heat. I'll put the air on for you." She reached for the control and Lee caught her hand.

"I don't mind sweating."

Lee's fingers were strong, warm against her skin. Her belly tightened. "Good to know." What else were those hands capable of? How would they handle her body? She inhaled sharply. Why was she thinking about a virtual stranger having sex with her? She silently laughed. Weren't most of her sexual partners strangers? Very few were more than acquaintances. Cole had always been the one to lead when engaged in sexual forays, and thinking of letting Lee take her somewhere she'd never been caught her off guard. Was this the harbinger she'd felt for the last few weeks, or was it her own inner turmoil about seeking sexual gratification no matter where she could find it? While she didn't have steady dates, most of the women she slept with were familiar to her, and though she always kept things casual, the idea of wanting something different played in the back of her mind. She'd never hesitated before when the urge had been this strong, yet she'd resisted time and again, not questioning the reason, but accepting she wasn't looking for the usual one-night stand. Cole flexed her thighs and shifted her weight as they hit the road. "I was going to have a beer and a burger on the way home." She faced Lee. "Join me?"

Lee stared out the window. "I don't think so."

She should let it go. Clearly Lee wasn't interested in what she was offering, but she wasn't dissuaded. "I'll accept no for an answer only if you have other plans."

Lee laughed. "Hardly." She made eye contact. The sheen of sweat on her face made her all the more desirable. "It's not that. Funds are a bit low these days. Being frugal, you know?"

Cole breathed a little easier knowing she wasn't the reason Lee hesitated. "I believe I asked you, so that's not an excuse. Small town etiquette means when someone asks you, they pay. It's a rule."

Her features changed from somber to relaxed. "A rule, huh?" She was quiet for a minute, looking deep in thought. "Okay. It's not like I'm going anywhere without a vehicle." Her grin was wry and heart-stopping at the same time. "But if you don't mind, I'd like to drop off my stuff at my uncle's and change my clothes."

"No problem. Dan doing okay? I haven't seen him in a while."

The appearance of a loving smile helped Cole ease back from her protective nature and chased away the last of her concern Lee was there to take advantage of Dan.

"He's great." She tipped her head toward the back. "The present is for him. He..." She swallowed, then went on. "He's given me a home when I didn't have one."

There was more to the story, but she didn't want to make Lee uncomfortable by asking a lot of questions. "That's nice of him, and you."

"He lives—"

"Yes, I know." Cole smiled. "Everyone pretty much knows where everyone else lives in town."

Lee's eyes held hers. "Will I be front page news as the newcomer in town?"

No. You'll make news by being another lesbian in town. Cole almost laughed out loud. She didn't think Lee would see the humor. "Don't worry. I'll make sure everyone knows you're okay." She pulled into Dan's driveway and turned off the truck.

"Do you want to come in?"

"Maybe another time. Don't rush on my account."

Lee gathered her things and went in through the open garage with Dan's vehicle parked inside. She could see rows of neatly stacked and labeled boxes and wondered how long Lee planned to stay. Why was she here in the first place? She got out of the truck and leaned against the side to wait, legs crossed at the ankles and hands in her pockets. Cole recalled the look on Lee's face when she'd given her the news about the truck. Something more than the heat of desire had stirred her. She wasn't sentimental regarding most things in life.

Each day came and went as it was intended and out of her control except for her reaction. She'd spent too many years in a reaction mode, and the wasted energy could have been used elsewhere. But that too, was in the past, and she'd chosen to move forward one minute, one hour, one day at a time instead. Maybe she could help Lee see the worry pinching her handsome features wouldn't change the outcome of whatever was going down. The closing door jarred her into action.

Lee strode more confidently and got in. Her hair was wet, and the pink glow of her chest wasn't just from the sun. The idea that Lee had showered for her pleased Cole, maybe more than it should have.

"Thanks for waiting." The flirtatious smile playing on her mouth suited her much better than the earlier consternation.

Cole backed out. "Like I said, I've nowhere else to be."

"Does that mean I'm your only choice of entertainment?" Lee asked with a questioning lilt.

"No. You're my first choice." She refused to look over and let Lee see how much her smile affected her, or how surprised she was by her body's reaction to Lee's presence. Her blood raced through her veins, heating her skin. Lee didn't say anything, and Cole was glad to escape further inquiry. Lee's closeness made her crazy. Even on opposite sides of the truck, she was too close for Cole to think clearly, let alone talk. The internal conversation she was having did nothing to quell thoughts of Lee's generous mouth on hers.

"Here we are."

Lee wasn't sure what she was doing. Today had been another lightning strike to her armor. The shell she'd built against being disappointed, or hurt, or pissed as fuck normally withstood the occasional battering. Everyone suffered in some way over things out of their control. But today—today had been close to her breaking point. She hadn't allowed herself to cry in ages, so she wasn't sure why she was on the brink of letting her guard down enough to open the floodgates.

Maybe it was Cole's easy, open, friendly nature. Strangely, she felt safe around her. Sliding into the booth, she admired Cole as she laughed with the bartender while he poured two drafts. Moderate shoulders and a narrow waist gently flared into slightly wider hips that were perfect for holding on to. Cole was a couple of inches shorter than her five foot nine height, though the rest of the details were hidden beneath the uniform. When Cole turned she quickly glanced away.

"Here you go." Cole set two pilsner glasses down. "Milk stout," she said, pointing to the dark ale. "And Belgian wheat." She produced a couple of coasters and tossed them onto the table before sitting across from her. "I should have asked what you wanted."

Cole's gaze held hers for a beat before Lee turned her attention back to the beer. "What's your favorite?" she asked. Cole continued to study her, and Lee wondered what she saw.

"Both." Cole shared a lopsided grin. "That's why I ordered them. No matter what you choose, I'll be good."

When was the last time she'd been given a choice in anything? Lee picked up the glass of wheat beer and took a long swallow. It was ice cold and soothed her dry throat. "Perfect."

Cole drank some stout. "That's why I come here. Ice cold beer, air conditioning, and decent food." She reached for menus and handed one over. "What are you in the mood for?"

"I have no idea." She didn't. Not about food, or her future, or whatever else Cole might be offering. Or maybe it was all conjecture and imagination on her part.

"You may not like what I like."

Again, she felt as though the topic wasn't about food. "Try me."

Cole gazed from her eyes, to lips, throat, and downward where her breasts pressed against the fabric of her tank top. Her nipples tightened. Cole got up and went to the bar where the waitress scribbled and laughed, then disappeared into the back where she imagined the kitchen was located.

"Do you mind me asking a personal question?" Cole settled against the booth.

"Go ahead." She sipped more beer, the sharp fermentation waking her taste buds.

"Do you know how long you're staying in Inlet?"

She set the glass down when her hand began to shake. She might have turned to sex to get over tough times before. Cole was easy on the eyes, and her initial impression of Cole batting for her team seemed to be more likely by the minute. But she hesitated because she didn't want to be hit on just because local options were scarce. "I'm not sure. Why?"

"You're shaking. What's wrong?"

Lee shrugged, unwilling to admit her desire and the sudden need to flee the potential complication of it not ending well. "I'm okay. Tired, I guess."

"I don't know where you're from or if you've been here before, but there's some interesting sites around, historical and others. I could show you if you wanted."

Lee was trying to make sense of the energy of Cole's nearness, the offer of friendship, and the possible innuendo of more. "Why?" The word was out before she could sensor it.

"Small town hospitality for someone new in town." Cole's mouth twitched. "You're under no obligation to accept my offer of friendship."

She didn't have many friends. Aside from Sam, even the crews she'd worked with were more casual, often temporary, acquaintances. People she had a beer with. Women she slept with. None were friends. The kind of people she'd randomly hang out with, or text, or call on a whim. She rarely gravitated toward people for simple friendship. "I don't know how long I'll be here." She didn't miss the flicker of disappointment. Perhaps Cole didn't have many friends either, but that seemed unlikely. "Sounds like fun, though." Cole would be temporary, too. She was okay with that.

Cole's easy smile returned. "Okay. You let me know what works for you and I'll play tour guide."

Lee snorted. "Without a job, much money, or anything else on my dance calendar, it depends on what you want to do."

The waitress came over and set a number of plates on the table, along with silverware and a wad of napkins. "Another beer?"

"Why not."

Cole nodded to the waitress, then gestured to the food. "When left to making choices, I tend to go overboard, so that's what I did. Help yourself."

She took in the assortment in front of her. Onion rings; waffle fries smothered in cheese, tomatoes, chives, and black olives; a burger that was thick and piled high with so many toppings—mushrooms, onions, bacon, cheese, lettuce, tomato—there was no way she'd be able to take a bite. A triple-decker sandwich with turkey rounded out the selection.

"How'd I do?" Cole snagged an onion ring.

Her clit twitched. Hard. *Christ.* "Great," she said, but the word came out hoarse and rough. She cleared her throat. "My favorites."

Cole nodded, took a wedge of sandwich, and slowly took a bite. She thought of those lips on hers before chastising herself for letting her mind wander. An offer of friendship was a far stretch to having sex.

"Order something else if you like." Cole sipped her beer, took another bite.

"What's here is good."

"So…" Cole appeared unsure if she should ask any more about her situation.

She took a breath, held it, then let it out. The bite of burger she was about to eat didn't seem as appealing as it once did, and she snagged a fry instead. "The company I worked for went belly up and took most of what I had with it." Even with feeling like an utter failure, sharing the reason she'd landed at her uncle's place was cathartic. She didn't share things about herself with everyone, but Cole seemed curious rather than nosy.

"That's rough. If I can help with anything, just ask." Cole's warmth came through her expressive eyes. They spoke of genuine caring and she could use a bit of understanding right now.

"Thanks." She was about to say she was good and stopped. She didn't think Cole would appreciate the lie, even if it wasn't a big one. She reached for the ketchup at the same time Cole reached for a fry and their hands brushed. Lee saw Cole's pupils dilate along with desire so naked Lee's entire body felt the impact. The shiver that followed raised gooseflesh over her uncovered arms.

"Is that why you asked me to wait on your truck?" Cole drank deeply and her gaze cooled, allowing Lee to resettle her thoughts.

"Partly. I've filed for unemployment and I'm waiting to hear back before I commit to an expense I may not be able to afford."

Cole was quiet for a minute. "Where were you living before?

"Atlantic City."

Cole whistled. "Big change coming here."

"That's for sure. What about you? You're a native of this thriving community, right?" When Cole nodded, she went on. "I'm surprised we haven't met before this. I visited my uncle several times when I was younger." She hadn't recognized her own sexuality until later and perhaps a grease-covered girl would have gone unnoticed. "I did visit again this past Christmas."

"Born and bred. I was in school during the day when I was a young girl, and as a teenager. Then later…well, let's just say I had plenty to keep me busy at home and at the garage." Cole gave her a quick smile and looked back down at her food. "Though I'll likely be the last of my family."

"Never had the urge to have children of your own?"

Cole chuckled and shook her head. "It's not that. I'm into women, which makes it logistically more difficult though not impossible. I'm probably too old now, anyway."

She understood the reasoning but doubted it was true. "You can't be that old." Cole waved her hand in dismissal and she let it drop. "The day I discovered I liked girls…" Pain shot through her gut and she was glad she was sitting. She thought she'd gotten over her abandonment issues long ago. Cole was a stranger, and she didn't share her ghosts with random people. Lee stared at her food, unable to meet Cole's gaze and unwilling to go on. Cole must have sensed her pulling back, holding on to her secrets.

"What about you? Kids in your future?" Cole asked.

Her laugh sounded sarcastic, even to her. 'I'm not even relationship material, let alone into parenting, so that's a no."

Cole studied her for a long time before going on. "How is the heat here compared to the city?"

Lee welcomed the change in topic. She was so tired of trying to figure out what tomorrow would bring, all the while knowing most of it was up to fate. She went with the small talk and slipped into her old habit of picturing what the woman she was talking to looked like naked even as they talked about weather and food. Anything to keep from touching on deeper subjects.

CHAPTER SEVEN

The next morning, Lee lay in bed letting the warm morning breeze brush over her naked body. She hadn't been sure what to expect when Cole had invited her for dinner. Lee hadn't trusted anyone in an awfully long time, and even more so since R.J. had fucked over her and the entire crew. But there'd been more between Lee and Cole than simple comradery. Unless she was sorely mistaken, there had been a distinct undercurrent of sexual tension. Attraction wasn't unusual for her, and the range of women who attracted her varied greatly, and a woman with Cole's physique was hard to miss. Having a few hours to decompress was a wonderful ending to a day of mixed emotions.

When Cole dropped her off, she'd felt a bit like a teenager coming home after a hot date, which was weird since they hadn't *done* anything. Not to say she hadn't thought about it, because she had. A lot. Dan hadn't asked much beyond the usual and that he was glad she'd gotten to relax. But when he asked about the truck, she'd been vague. He was kind enough to give her a nice place to lay her head; she didn't want him to give, or even lend, her money with no idea when she'd be able to pay him back. She'd find another way. It was time to ask around to see if anyone needed household repairs or yardwork. Word of mouth likely worked better than any other form of advertising in a place like this.

In fact, since she no longer had a gym to go to and doubted there was one in town, she could use a bit of exercise. Lee smiled. A workout with Cole would be nice, but the mixed messages had left her unsure how to interpret them. One minute there was the just friends vibe, followed by flares of seductive gazes and intentional, or unintentional, innuendos that left her skin tingling. Her eyes fluttered and she yawned. She turned over onto her stomach, scrunched a pillow against her, and pictured Cole there instead. How would it feel to wake up in her arms, or vice versa? Those were the images that followed her as she drifted back off.

❖

The day had turned rainy and the rumble of thunder echoed in the distance. Lee parked Dan's car alongside the building out of the way of customers. She was just about to get out when the skies opened up with a deluge. Lee thought about waiting it out or driving around to the front, but she didn't want to take advantage of…she wasn't sure what to call what she and Cole had. An acquaintance, maybe. Anyway, she didn't want to take up customer space, even though she technically was one. She scanned the back seat for an umbrella, but didn't see one. Lee jumped out and ran, but she may as well have walked. There was no way to avoid being soaked to the bone before she made it inside the open bay.

"Shit."

"Even us country folk have umbrellas. If you needed a shower, all you had to do was ask. I would have given you the key." Cole moved closer, wiping her hands.

She saw that Cole's gaze had moved to her hard nipples beneath the thin shirt that clung to her. "Very funny," she said, swiping away the water dripping into her eyes.

"Come on. Let's get you dry."

She made it as far as the office doorway and stopped.

"What are you doing?" Cole asked as she pulled a couple of towels off open shelves.

"I'm dripping all over."

Cole rolled her eyes. "It's a fucking garage, Lee. There's grease and grime everywhere. Water is an improvement any time." She held a towel well out of Lee's reach.

The harsh tone surprised her. "I can come back another time." She didn't drop by on people unexpectedly and she wasn't sure what had possessed her to do it today.

"Sorry," Cole said as she pinched the bridge of her nose. The storm in Cole's eyes revealed frustration rather than anger. "Here. Come on in."

After running the towel over her hair and ruffling it until it no longer dripped, Lee held the towel around her. The office was damp, and the cold began to sink into her bones.

"Take your clothes off," Cole said.

Staring in disbelief, she glanced through the plate glass window. "I hardly think this is the place." Her belly tightened as she glanced at the desk and pictured herself sprawled across it.

Cole stepped closer. "I said give me your clothes." A fire ignited in her eyes. The command almost sent Lee to her knees. Another step closer. "Do you think anyone would be foolish enough to pump gas in the torrent raging outside?"

Lee stood her ground. Every nerve ending in her body was firing, her muscles strung tight, ready for the challenge. "What about the storm inside?"

Like a gentle breeze crossing a field of tall grass, Cole's expression morphed from predator to willing prey. "The building is fortified. We're safe enough."

Cole's finger traced her jaw, down the column of her throat, stopping short of touching her breasts. Lee bit back the edge of desire, ignored the hard press of her clit against her wet jeans.

Cole took her hand and pulled her through a short hallway to another room that appeared to be a mini apartment of sorts. Stackable washer/dryer, couch, small table, microwave, coffee pot, and a refrigerator.

"Give me your clothes so I can dry them."

"What about customers?" Lee asked.

Cole closed the door and pointed to the TV hanging in the corner near the ceiling that displayed two views. One of the pumps, another of the garage bays. "I'll know if someone comes by."

Lee's fingers trembled as she worked the buttons. Whether it was from the chill or the fact she was about to strip down in front of a stranger, she couldn't tell. Cole watched her reveal her bare chest, then the rest of her as she peeled her pants and underwear down to pool on the floor. The evidence of her desire was on display, and her pulse beat hard in her ears.

Cole licked her lips.

Her center was heavy with desire. Cole stirred her whenever she saw her, and now that she was nude the draw was undeniable.

"Your body is magnificent." Cole gathered her things and tossed them into the dryer, giving the compliment almost like it was an afterthought.

Lee moved closer. "You have me at a disadvantage. Do you have anything I can put on?"

Cole opened a narrow door then handed her a flannel shirt and sweats.

After dressing, she sat on the couch. "Thanks for the compliment."

Cole laughed. "You probably get a lot of compliments. Coffee?"

"Coffee would be great." She wasn't self-conscious about her body, but they weren't having sex and she'd felt oddly vulnerable, a feeling she'd never been comfortable with. She glanced at the screen, glad there wasn't any customers. The last thing she wanted to do was cause a scandal at Cole's business, and even fully dressed, she knew how quickly a situation could change. The rain continued to obscure the gas pumps behind a watery curtain, turning puddles into small ponds. The distant rumble of thunder vibrated along the floor beneath her feet.

"So, to what do I owe the pleasure of your visit?" Cole handed her coffee. "Did you miss me that much?" she teased her.

Lee wrapped her hands around the mug, grateful for something to do with them. Cole's scent enveloped her like the steam from the mug, cloying and sweet. Lee shook her head. This was a temporary infatuation. Her yearning for Cole would fade, just like everything else that was good in her life. "I came to get tools out of my truck." She took a breath, unsure how to proceed. "It's going to be a few weeks before I can tell you to go ahead and fix it. If you don't mind the wait."

"It's not a problem. Just let me know when you're ready." Cole leaned against the table and blew across the surface of her cup, then sipped.

"I put an ad in the penny saver in case anyone needed a handyperson, but the new issue won't be published until next week." Her uncle had always had a copy lying around and she was surprised to see it was still in print.

"It going to be hard to work without a vehicle of your own, but I wouldn't recommend running yours." Cole pushed off from the table. "Come on."

Lee shoved her feet into her wet shoes and followed her into the garage until they stood shoulder to shoulder looking out the back bay door. Cole pointed to an older model Ford Ranger XL. "She's a little beat up, but she's reliable. You're welcome to use it for however long you need it."

"I appreciate the offer, but I can't take your truck." Even as she said it, she began to work out the logistics in her head.

Cole faced her, grinning. "Why not? She's just sitting there feeling neglected."

She chewed on her lip. She hadn't expected Cole's generous offer. Lee hadn't relied on anyone's help since leaving her parents' house, and now she found herself relying on the kindness of others on a frequent basis. She wasn't sure she liked it.

"No strings attached." Cole handed her a keychain with a mini gas pump.

Lee's eyes welled up. She didn't deserve Cole's friendship, and she had so little to give in return. "Thank you isn't nearly enough." She swallowed around the lump in her throat.

"Hey, what are friends for if not lending a hand when needed?" Cole wrapped her arm around her shoulder and side-hugged her. "Looks like the storm has just about passed. Let's load your tools. By the time we're done your clothes should be dry."

All she could do was nod. The more time she spent with Cole, the more she wanted to be around her. The idea of complicating their growing friendship worried her. She'd never slept with a woman she considered her friend. If she slept with Cole, what would happen to their fledgling friendship?

❖

Cole handed the last of the items to Lee. "That's it." For the first time since meeting her, Lee shyly looked away. Perhaps now was the time to ask Lee for a favor in return. It might help her feel less self-conscious. "Actually, I'm glad you stopped by. I wanted to ask you if you'd run by the house and look at the roof."

Lee's eyes narrowed with suspicion. "Is that your way of providing charity?"

"Of course not."

"Look, I know I might seem like a loser right now, but I don't need—"

She held her hand up to stop the rant. Lee's defensiveness was likely a direct result of her current situation and she wouldn't hold it against her. "I was going to call you, but I don't have Dan's number, or yours. There's a spot on the ceiling in the den at the back of the house. I think the roof might be leaking." Cole flicked her gaze up at the pale blue sky. "This is probably a good time for you to check it out. If you don't do that sort of thing, I'll try to find someone else."

The tension left Lee's face. "I'm being an asshole. I can definitely check it out. Let me go change and I'll go with you whenever you're done here."

"I won't be done for a while today. Just head over and let yourself in."

Lee shook her head. "You'd let a total stranger into your house? Alone?"

Cole shrugged, grinning. "We've had a beer together and you're Dan's niece. You're not a stranger anymore."

Lee laughed. "If you say so. I'll go change." A few minutes later, Lee came back smiling. "All set."

Cole was going to ask if she wanted to stay for dinner before realizing it might be a mistake. Lee might need a little space. She'd been upset, then relieved, then suspicious. All those run-on emotions had to have taken a toll on her. Even though she enjoyed Lee's company and she could do with some herself, it would have been a selfish move on her part. "Great. Give me your phone and I'll enter my contact info in case you have any questions." After a quick entry, she handed it back. "I hope you don't mind I sent a text to myself, so I'd have yours, too."

"I'm glad you did." Lee's voice was laced with a smoky edge. "There's no GPS in the truck, but if you—"

"I have my phone." Lee cupped the back of her neck and ran her fingers through her hair in a surprisingly sensual gesture. "Thanks for everything."

She waved her off, but she wanted to say much more. "Gas her up before you go."

"Haven't you done enough already?"

"We're not going to start this again, are we?"

"Is this your butch side coming out?" Lee asked, laughing.

"You haven't seen my butch side yet. You actually haven't seen any of my sides."

Lee's eyes fluttered. "I'll gas up the truck."

God, she's infuriating and so damn sexy at the same time. Cole wanted to smile, but she faltered. Confusion pulled her back. As much as her body wanted release, the idea of having unattached sex was losing its appeal, which was obvious since she still hadn't made that road trip for another woman's company. And Lee would be a temporary fix. Cole wouldn't take advantage of her when she was clearly an emotional wreck, even while she imagined doing things to Lee she'd only fantasized about.

CHAPTER EIGHT

Lee followed the map on her phone to Cole's place. Cole told her to say hi to Dixie, her old beagle, when she arrived and not to worry because Dixie would likely pay her no mind. She couldn't get over Cole sending her over without coming with her. She would have never thought of doing that in New Jersey. She jumped out and glanced over at a trail that led to the edge of a small pond. Maybe she'd ask if she could take a swim sometime. Something safe that friends did. Then she thought about what might be lurking in the murky water. Maybe there was a pool.

The property was beautiful, and massive sunflowers stood along the side of the house like sentries standing guard, but against who or what she didn't know. Walking around the perimeter, Lee was amazed at how big the house was. From the ground, she couldn't see any obvious signs of damage, but that was more common than not. A lot of the time the more extensive damage appeared on the inside long before there was exterior evidence. An uneasy feeling curled around her as she opened the front door. It was kind of creepy to be inside Cole's home when she wasn't there, though she'd done the same thing plenty of times when she was working, but somehow that was different. Anonymity was far more comfortable. Being in Cole's home felt intimate. *God, I need to get laid.* Lee rolled her neck and shoulders. She did a slow turn to get her bearings.

The home was a mix of classic farmhouse meets modern functionality. She made a mental note to ask Cole when the updates had been done. The workmanship was clean and appeared seamless, and she wondered if she could have done as well. She ran her hand over the walls in the hallway leading to the back. Based on the smooth texture, they'd been redone in the last five years. Lee ducked her head into the kitchen. It didn't take long to locate the old dog lying on a thick bed.

"Hey, Dixie. I'm a friend of Cole's." Dixie raised her head, yawned, and flopped back down. *So much for being a watch dog.* After passing a formal dining room on the left and a half bath on the right, she entered the den and stood in awe. The room spanned the width of the first floor and had to be at least twenty feet deep. The entire wall on either side of the double doors held floor to ceiling oak bookshelves with sliding library ladders. Directly opposite stood a massive fireplace with matching easy chairs fronted by ottomans with floor lamps behind each and a deeply polished birdseye maple stand between them. It was the perfect place to curl up with a book on a cold winter night. Three thick carpets were evenly spaced in the middle of the refinished hardwood floors. A large desk with painted motifs sat on the far right and held a laptop computer, printer, and an array of framed pictures. To the left was an L-shaped sectional with a long coffee table that faced the largest television screen she'd ever seen.

"Wow."

Cole was a paradox at every turn. This room—hell, this house— spoke of old money, and Lee couldn't help wondering what she was doing out here in the middle of nowhere when she could easily afford to be anywhere. Her imagination got the better of her as she pictured some shady reason for Cole's wealth, then she berated herself. Why did she think everyone she came in contact with had a devious nature with ulterior motives? Just because her former boss had taken advantage of her didn't mean everyone else was out to get her.

She strolled to the desk and picked up a photo with a young version of Cole in jean overalls leaning against a tall man. Both had the same smile and shared eye color. Father and daughter. Another one displayed Cole as an adult, kneeling with a beagle pup and grinning for the camera. One additional photo showed a woman with salt-and-pepper hair, also slender, clad in jeans and a flannel shirt. Her arms were wrapped around Cole from behind, the man standing beside her, his arm around her shoulder. Again, everyone was smiling.

Lee's gut twisted. She had no photos of her own parents. Couldn't even remember having any taken, and if there were any, no one would be smiling. Envy stabbed her like a hot poker and reminded her of one more thing she'd missed out on. Shaking off the melancholy, she moved away in an effort to dispel any lingering turmoil for feeling sorry for herself, especially regarding things that couldn't be changed.

Time to get on with the reason she was there. She used her Maglite to inspect the ceiling as she walked from one end to the other. A dark patch about the size of a basketball marred the upper right corner. It looked damp, but she couldn't really tell without inspecting it further. To do that she needed a ladder. A really tall ladder. She tapped the icon for Cole's cell and hoped she didn't mind her calling.

"Hi."

"Hey. I'm in need of a ladder that can reach the ceiling."

"Uh-oh. That sounds ominous."

"I don't want to alarm you, but I won't know what's going on until I can get up there and take a closer look." Lee dropped onto the leather sofa. "Great room, by the way."

"Thanks. I spend so much time in grime I wanted someplace vastly different to come home to."

"Mission accomplished."

Cole laughed.

She loved hearing her laugh. She cleared her throat, unwilling to go there as she repeated her mantra. *Friends.*

"I do have one. A ladder, I mean. But it's a beast to maneuver with one person."

Silence followed, making her look to see if she'd lost the connection.

"Care to have dinner with me? Then we can carry it in together and you can do whatever it is you do to figure out what's wrong while I cook."

"I should probably have dinner with Dan. He's probably already planning on something."

"You're welcome to bring him."

She cringed at the idea of sharing Cole, though that was nonsense. Her whole living situation still felt a little odd, through no fault of her uncle. "I'm not sure that would work."

"I've known Dan for years. You're not comfortable around him?"

"It's not that." A vision of Cole on the dining room table with her legs spread made Lee's breath hitch.

"There's still the little matter of getting his car back to him."

"Shit."

Cole laughed heartily, the sound light and warm. "Did you leave the keys? I could bring it to him and walk back."

"Walk? It's like two miles."

"That would take me all of thirty minutes. Tops."

"Show off," Lee said. "Besides, the keys are in my pocket, so that won't work." The earlier crackle of attraction flared. She wanted to spend time alone with Cole. It was more than sexual, though the concept of feeling Cole's smaller, firm body under her wasn't totally lost on her. There was another component to Cole she couldn't figure out, and she wanted to. When they talked, it had mostly been about Lee and her circumstances. Cole hadn't revealed anything of consequence about herself. Lee bit her lip. It wasn't like she'd have to drive a hundred miles to fix the situation, but she'd need a ride back to the garage either way. "Okay. I'll come back to the garage and take Dan's car home, then whenever you're ready, you can pick me up there. Then swing back to the garage so I can grab the truck."

"Her name is Jessie."

Damn. Cole was involved with someone. "Who's Jessie?"

Cole chuckled. "The truck."

"Oh." Relief flooded in. Lee wasn't sure why it bothered her that Cole might be taken, but it did. What she really needed to do was concentrate on being the kind of friend Cole deserved, and hoped they continue to be so, even when distance separated them. She hadn't let anyone in since leaving her childhood home because it hurt too much. But she was an adult now, not a teenager, and Cole was nothing like her parents. Lee punched a speed number.

"Hey, Uncle Dan."

"Hi. Are you okay? That was a hell of a storm."

Heat washed over her as she pictured herself standing naked in front of Cole while her gaze branded her skin.

"Lee?"

"Yeah, I'm fine. Cole's lending me a truck to use until mine is fixed. Do you mind if I have dinner with her tonight? She has a roof leak that I want to check out."

"Of course not. Cole's good people. So was her dad. It was a shame he died so young."

"I didn't know." Even if she had, what would she say? Asking for details felt like an invasion. Like being in Cole's home did. "I'll bring your car back in a little while."

"No hurry. See you then."

She stood for a minute to do a quick best-case/worst-case scenario estimate. She mumbled to herself as she often did when she worked, but a sound from the front of the house made her pause. After not hearing anything else, and unable to do more without a ladder, she turned to leave when she heard someone talking.

"Why are you driving your old truck?" a female voice called out. "Did something happen to your shiny red one?"

Lee froze. Whoever it was she didn't want to scare them. "Hello?"

"Who's there?"

"Uh, my name is Lee. I'm a friend of Cole's." She walked slowly toward the front, hands out to show she didn't have any weapons, a posture she'd learned living in the city. When she reached the end of hall the woman from the picture on the desk, though older now and about Cole's height, stood with her hands on her hips, her watchful eyes sizing her up. After a minute, the woman waved her hand.

"Nobody's gonna shoot you, unless you stole my granddaughter's truck, but I reckon you'd be sporting a bruise or two if that was the case."

Lee slowly lowered her hands. "Cole let me borrow her truck because mine needs repairs."

"And you're in the back because?"

"Oh, she has a leak in the roof and wanted me to take a look."

"You show me where, then I'll decide if I go for my pistol."

She felt the blood drain from her face. The old woman laughed, then attempted to look chagrined, but failed. "Sorry. Cole always said my sense of humor is warped. I don't have a pistol. Well, I do, but not with me. I came by to drop off a blueberry pie. You like blueberry pie?"

"Yes, ma'am. It's one of my favorites."

"I'm Betty, Cole's grandmother," she said and stuck out her hand. "Anyone who likes blueberry pie is okay in my book."

"Glad I don't have to worry about picking buckshot out of my ass." Lee was mortified she'd said that out loud. "No disrespect."

Betty laughed. "I'm heading out. Tell Cole about the pie."

"I'll be sure to mention it when I see her. I'm leaving, too." Once outside, she looked around. "Where's your car?"

"Too old to drive. I walked. About a mile in that direction." Betty pointed west.

"I'll take you home."

"That's all right, dear. I don't mind."

"Please? I can't in good conscience drive off and leave you to walk."

Betty stared at her. "Okay. I'll get in the truck with you." Betty let her help her in, though she didn't really need it, then Lee jumped in the driver's seat. "Don't try any funny business. I leave that stuff to you youngsters." Betty smiled.

"I wouldn't think of it." Cole was definitely cut from the same cloth.

❖

Cole shook her head. "She said no funny business?"

Lee laughed. "And with a straight face. At least she didn't shoot me."

Cole pulled apart a piece of fried chicken and nibbled on the crunchy skin. She had helped Lee with the ladder when they first arrived and left her to do what she needed to while Cole headed to the kitchen to make potato salad to go with the chicken. Dixie had meandered outside at a snail's pace only to return a few minutes later to her bed after slurping some water. She only ate sporadically now, and Cole tried to prepare her heart for the inevitable. She glanced over and was happy to see she was still breathing.

"Oh my God, will you cook for me every day? This chicken is outrageous." Lee took a big bite and made satisfied sounds.

Cole stopped chewing and imagined her moaning during sex. For weeks she'd longed for physical contact with a human, a woman who could embrace her need not only for sexual satisfaction, but for accepting her in a different presentation than the one she'd worn since high school. But Lee would leave, probably sooner rather than later, and Cole didn't want to reveal things she'd fantasized about with someone who already had enough going on between moving and not having income. Besides, she'd promised friendship and that came first. "Is there someone special in Atlantic City?" she asked, throwing all rational reasoning right out the window.

Lee placed her partially eaten thigh on her plate and slowly licked her fingers. "No. Women I sometimes slept with, but no one special." Lee took a swig of beer, then wiped her mouth. "What about you?"

"No."

"Because no one interests you?"

"I…" What could she say? The women she met outside of Inlet were there to serve her body, not her mind? Even thought it was true, saying it out loud would make her feel like a player, which she wasn't. "I haven't found anyone who's my type, really."

"What is your type?"

That was a question she was still trying to answer. She'd never quite felt comfortable in her own skin and finding someone who didn't have expectations based solely on her looks had never happened. Not that she minded being viewed as masculine of center, but there was more to her than that. She'd never been able to broach the topic out loud. Lee must have taken her silence as not wanting to tell her.

"You don't have to answer if you don't want to. I was just curious." Lee sat back, watching her.

Cole shook her head. "It's not that. It's confusing." That was an understatement.

"What is?"

She let out a breath. Maybe Lee was someone who could understand her anxiety over presentation. Younger lesbians were so much more aware of who they were…and weren't. "I don't think I've ever quite fit into the label I grew up with." There. She'd said it to someone other than the face in the mirror.

"What label?"

"Butch, basically. The options were either that or femme when I came out." She pushed her plate away and picked up her beer.

Lee's smile was sultry. "There's a lot more than two, but I'm sure you know that."

Cole considered if she should delve deeper. "How do you identify?"

"Good question." Lee chuckled, not seeming put off at all by the conversation. "I guess most women I've been with would peg me for masculine of center, MOC, which is fine. I'm just not one to identify myself or others in terms of gender or sexuality. People are who they are, makes no difference to me. If I'm attracted to someone, that's all that matters."

"Have you been with women who were…" She stumbled over the correct term. "Non-traditional?"

"The community uses non-binary now, among other terms, and yes. Physical pleasure is as much a mental experience as it is a physical one. As long as both people are enjoying what's happening the rest is just setting a scene."

Cole thought about that. She'd never been comfortable having this kind of open conversation before. Who would she have had it with, anyway? Lee made talking about the subject easy. Maybe she'd have to go to a bigger town to scratch that itch she'd thought about soothing.

"Were your parents open to your sexuality?" The minute the words left her mouth she knew she'd gone too far. Lee's walls visibly snapped into place as though it were a gate meant to keep intruders out, and now she was the intruder. "Don't answer that. I can see my question bothers you." She went to pick up their plates, her appetite suddenly gone, when Lee's hand stopped her.

"Don't." Lee took a visible breath.

Cole hesitated. "Only if you're sure."

Lee slid her hand away. "I haven't talked about them in years. Not to anyone other than Uncle Dan, anyway."

Cole settled in her chair, understanding what Lee was about to share was big. If Lee could trust her enough to share her pain, maybe Cole could reveal more about herself and let go of reservations she carried concerning how others interpreted her presentation in the world. Not everything was black-and-white, and Lee sounded open to the gray areas.

"I haven't seen my parents in more than a decade, except for a brief visit when my mother was at my uncle's," Lee said. "I'd never seen my father as angry as the day I came out to them. His eyes were so full of rage, and he told me I'd never known my place." Lee frowned.

Cole touched her trembling hand. "I'm so sorry. Did he hit you?" She couldn't imagine anyone directing anger toward Lee as she remembered how touched she'd been at the offer of her truck.

"No, but I think he wanted to, and even though my mother didn't say anything to stop him, I think that's why he didn't. Then he told me to get out."

Cole couldn't imagine a parent would send away their child just because of their sexual orientation, though as a teenager she always suspected her mother's leaving had more to do with her shame of Cole's refusal to fit into her idea of how a little girl should dress and act than how unhappy she was. She'd only come to realize how illogical that idea was after she was an adult, yet never understood how her mother could totally abandon her when she was still a child still hurt at times, and she could understand Lee's obvious pain. "How old were you?"

Lee reached for her beer, but it was empty. She took their bottles and went for more, sensing Lee needed the break. When she came back, Lee looked so lost she pulled her to her feet and held her. The feel of Lee's hard body against hers crystalized her desire for a physical connection, but she ignored the pulse that jumped between her thighs. Cole rubbed her back a minute longer before stepping away.

"Thanks." Lee took a shuddery breath and sat, tipped the bottle toward her, then took a drink. "I was seventeen, just getting ready to start my senior year."

"What did you do? Where did you go?" What would she have done if her family had reacted the same way? She couldn't envision it happening.

"I didn't know what to do. I called my best friend, Jackie. She couldn't believe it. A few minutes later, she called me back. She'd pleaded my case to her parents and told me to pack up and come stay at her house until I graduated." Lee smiled. "She was my savior. Funny thing was Jackie's parents made me feel more comfortable and at home with them than my own parents ever had."

Cole couldn't miss the threat of tears in Lee's eyes. "I'm glad you had somewhere safe to go."

"Me, too."

The revelation of Lee's history churned her stomach. She was still getting to know Lee and hearing how much her parents' rejection hurt made her angry. But Lee didn't need her anger, or her sympathy. She seemed to want acceptance and understanding, her furrowed brow an indication she was still seeking it, and Cole recognized a change of subject might be welcome. "Do you want more?" She gestured to the food.

Lee patted her stomach and pushed away the plate that had a small pile of bones and two chunks of potato left on it. "I'd love to, but I'm already stuffed. It was delicious. Do you cook often?"

"Whenever I have a reason to. I love to cook, just like my grandmother. When I made plans to remodel, I insisted on having a modern kitchen."

"I love the mix of old and new. The kitchen is great, but the den is beautiful. Do you spend a lot of time there?"

"Mostly in the winter. I like reading in front of the fireplace. It's a big space for one person." She heard the loneliness in her voice and hadn't realized until then how much being alone bothered her.

"Your desk is gorgeous."

She smiled. "I think so, too. It's a vintage teak and burl Dutch Colonial style. My grandfather found it in a shop somewhere in New York City and had it shipped here." Cole was young when he died, but when her grandmother spoke of him she saw the love they'd shared in her eyes. The older she got, the more she wanted that kind of love.

"Whoever you hired to do the renovations did meticulous work."

"My cousin Michael did most of it. He has a small crew and does historical restorations, so he's gone a lot. He comes home every now and then between jobs. If you hadn't been here to take a look at the ceiling, I probably would have left it until he came back to town."

"You have a close family." Lee looked down. Her forehead creased.

"We've lived here for generations, first in the lumber industry, then helping with building sections of the railway system. My cousin's side became interested in historical preservation, and Michael loved learning about a building's past." Cole rarely talked about family, mainly because the locals all knew her family's history and sharing any more was futile. Lee wasn't interested in roots, evidenced by saying she was only in town temporarily. She stood and began clearing the table.

Lee brought the leftovers to the kitchen. "Can I put this chicken in something?"

There were five pieces left and a nice portion of potato salad that she planned on sending home to Dan. "There are glass dishes with covers in that cabinet." She pointed to one of the slide-out drawers. She hated plastic for storing food, and glass was easier to reheat in. Once the leftovers were stored, she set the containers in a cooler and Lee took it out to the truck. When the kitchen was tidy, she handed Lee another beer. "You want to show me what the verdict is?" Cole let Lee go first, giving her a chance to admire her tight ass.

"So, I cut out a section of the dry wall," Lee said.

"Oh." She was taken aback to see a four-foot square hole in the ceiling.

"It looks worse than it is. I cut it so I can easily put in a replacement sheet. Once it's patched, you'll never be able to tell."

"I trust you." If she could only trust Lee would be around for a while she'd be happy, but she'd made a promise to herself to enjoy Lee's company for however long it lasted and to let their friendship build at its own pace.

"Thank you. It means a lot to hear you say that." Lee's gaze held hers.

The shadow of someone who'd been deeply wounded remained, and Cole now understood why she'd glimpsed Lee's protective walls. Trust was probably a huge issue for her, and Cole never wanted to give Lee a reason not to trust her. She had to keep telling herself that wanting to sleep with Lee wasn't good for either of them, even if her body continued to send signals otherwise. The last thing Lee needed was someone else hurting her or wanting more than she might be able to give.

"So," Lee clapped her hands together, obviously excited about the opportunity to use what she knew and talk about what she enjoyed. "Here's the plan. I'll go on the roof," she said, and then looked quickly at Cole. "Please tell me you have an extension ladder, too."

"I do. Several, in fact."

Relief was quickly followed by a frown. "I hate not having my own equipment."

Cole disliked seeing people suffer. "Hey, you'll be working with another company soon. Until then, whatever I have is yours." She moved her fingertips along Lee's cheek. A whisper of a touch that Lee leaned into. She shouldn't be touching her, and she knew it. But something about Lee called to her, and she couldn't help herself.

"Cole." Lee pulled her closer, hands on her waist. "I not sure about much these days." Lee stared into her eyes. "Why do you keep offering things?"

Cole closed her eyes as their mouths met. Soft, yielding lips moved beneath hers. Lee's tongue slipped inside exploring and tender beyond belief. For the briefest instant she let herself believe Lee would stay and be in her life for the long term, but she knew better. Lee was younger. Wilder. A free spirit without roots. She didn't want to clip her wings by keeping her in Cole's sleepy little town and the quiet life she'd accepted for herself long ago. "Lee…" It would be selfish to encourage her when Cole was beginning to see what *she* wanted, and it wasn't something temporary.

"Sorry. You make me feel things I never knew I could feel." Lee backed away and took a breath. "Uh, where was I? I tend to forget everything when I'm near you."

"Is that a bad thing? Are you sorry?"

After a long beat, Lee answered. "I'm not sure."

She swallowed the hurt. Lee's response was honest. Whether she wanted to hear it or not, speaking the truth would be the only way to build Lee's trust. Cole had a truth of her own, but she wasn't willing to share it. Not now. Maybe not ever. "Why don't you tell me about the repairs, then we can go outside where it's cooler."

"All right."

Lee seemed to sense there was more she wasn't saying, but she wasn't all that anxious to delve into feelings that might be better left unspoken.

CHAPTER NINE

Lee stared at her empty plate. She was tempted to lick the last bits of blueberry clean, but that would be rather uncouth even for her.

"Do you want more?"

She glanced up, smiling. "Hell yes, but I can't. It was delicious. Please tell your grandmother for me."

"Will do." Cole drank from her coffee cup and stared at the color-streaked sky.

Earlier, they'd been sitting in porch rockers talking about all manner of things. How Cole had fallen in love with tinkering with small motors her father let her play with, then as a young teen moving on to work side by side with her father. Lee talked of her love for roller blading and how it was her only mode of transportation until her second year in college. She didn't revisit her leaving home, or her first time with a girl "that way," certain it would come up sooner or later. Lee breathed in the clean scent of the fields surrounding the house. A variety of old growth trees stood in groups not far from Cole's home and diffused the quickly fading light.

"I can't remember spring being this hot in a long time," Cole said.

"Anything less than ninety is bearable compared to the city." The only saving grace had been the nonstop ocean breezes, though they provided little relief when she was working in a building without electricity or perched on a roof in the blazing sun.

Cole glanced at her, the shadows obscuring her features, leaving her profile in stark relief. "I can't conceive what it was like to be boxed in by buildings and concrete every day. I don't think I'd survive it after living here."

"It's one thing I don't miss." What she did miss was the warmth of female encounters, when sex meant a few hours of distraction from an otherwise cruel world.

"Want to go for a swim?"

"Now?" She glanced out over the shadowed landscape. "It's almost dark."

"Aww. I'll protect you."

Lee bit her bottom lip. She was being ridiculous about something Cole had probably done a thousand times. This was just another insecurity she needed to get over. "Sure. Why not." Her voice was stronger than her conviction.

Cole took their mugs inside then stopped at a hallway closet and pulled out a blanket, towels, and a flashlight.

"I don't have a bathing suit."

"That's okay, neither do I." Cole began to strip. "Besides, I've already seen you naked. Remember?"

Lee flushed. She marveled at Cole's lean, muscular body. Her breasts were small, firm mounds tipped with dark centers. Her hips flared in proportion to her shoulders and led to a vee of fine dark curls. Lee looked away and dropped her clothes in a pile near the door. "This is private property, right?" She might not be shy with the people she slept with, but that didn't mean she wanted to be on display. Not to mention, she hadn't slept with Cole. Did friends hang out naked in pools together? Maybe she'd been missing out on the friend thing after all. Platonic friendships were possible, she'd just never had one.

"You don't have to do this if you don't want to."

"It's fine. I just…it's so weird being able to be naked and outside." She couldn't believe she was heading to a pond in the middle of a field where anyone might see her, though that was against the odds. Crickets chirped from every direction, and the thought of stepping on one in her bare feet sent a shiver through her. Cole must have noticed her hesitation.

"Here," she said, handing her the flashlight. "If you keep it pointed down in front of you, the litter buggers will probably take off." Her struggle not to laugh was obvious. "Most of them, anyway."

Lee was all for walking barefoot in the house, or on a deck, or patio. This wasn't something she was used to at all. "Fine." She stuck her chin forward in a show of defiance as she stepped into the ankle high grass. Cole's laughter followed her.

"You know, living in the country might toughen you up a bit." Cole tossed her stuff on the ground and ran for the water's edge.

On a fast sprint, she made it in first. Cole had only taken one step into the water when she caught her, lifting her off her feet and making her laugh and yell. Cole fought back, but Lee was a little taller and more muscular, and they ended up tumbling into the water together. All thought of what might be lurking in it left her mind as she held on, enjoying the flex of Cole's muscles against her body. Cole finally broke free and came up sputtering but still laughing. So was she.

"You can't get rid of me that easily." Cole grinned. She walked through the thigh high water toward her, then brushed something off her face.

"I'm glad."

Cole splashed her and she laughed again. "God, it feels good to laugh," she said.

Her expression grew serious. "You haven't been laughing much?"

Lee hadn't meant to share her internal thoughts. It seemed her filter was pretty much in the off position when she and Cole were together. "No."

Cole went behind her, rested her chin on her shoulder, and wrapped her arms around her waist. "You don't have to hide from me. Whatever you're feeling it's okay to feel."

For the first time in her life, she hoped Cole's words were the truth and not a way to placate her. Dan was the only other person to validate her feelings. When she'd first arrived, she had no great plans aside from avoiding living on the street. Cole's friendship felt genuine. She seemed to live simply, but that didn't mean it wasn't fulfilling. The solid warmth of being held, feeling cared for, was a nice change. Maybe sticking around a little longer wasn't a bad idea.

❖

When they'd gone swimming, the twilight revealed a patterned tattoo that covered Lee's back, but that wasn't the time to mention it. Hopefully, she could examine it more fully another time. For now, she held Lee against the front of her body as Lee shook in her embrace. Knowing there was nothing she could do to stop the flow of tears tore at Cole's heart, but maybe this was exactly what Lee needed. To cry for the unexpected upset of her life and having to pull up stakes, and for whatever other pain hid inside her. Maybe she could provide the cathartic healing Lee needed. Being forced to leave home was vastly different than Cole considering going somewhere else over the last few years. But Inlet was everything a home should be, and she intended to stay for the duration. She couldn't imagine not having roots and wondered if that was part of Lee's pain, too.

Lee covered her face with her hands. When the sobs slowed, she wiped at the tears but didn't turn around. "I don't know why I'm crying. Again. I seem to be doing it a lot."

She guided her around. "All people cry. We carry so much of the world's pain and suffering, I don't think there's room for our own sometimes." She pressed her lips to Lee's cheek and then put some distance between them. Being naked and touching was too much to take, and she wasn't about to misinterpret an important moment based on her body's reaction. "Maybe you should give yourself a break."

Lee took a shaky breath and Cole led her into deeper water. They paddled around a little while and when Lee looked more settled, she took her hand and headed for the shore. She shook out the blanket, and they toweled off in the sultry night air. Lee lay down and closed her eyes and Cole lay beside her. As much as she wanted to have a physical connection, Cole didn't want *just* physical—with Lee or anyone else. Her father hadn't had a partner to share his life with after her mother left, and she'd always wondered if the shadowed gaze in his eyes was from a loneliness he'd never filled. She was coming to understand she didn't want to follow in his footsteps anymore. At least the being alone part. If she and Lee touched, Lee would have to initiate it. After several minutes, Lee sought out her hand.

"Touch me."

"Are you sure?" She'd never been someone to take advantage of another person's vulnerability, and although Lee was sexy as hell, warning bells clanged in her head even as her body surged with desire like a distress flare from a stranded boat.

"Please?" Lee's eyes remained closed.

Cole let Lee guide her hand between her legs, and she opened to her probing fingertips. Lee's center was soft and warm and wet, and she luxuriated in the feel of her, in the feel of being connected to another woman in an unexpectedly intimate way. Slowly and gently, guided by Lee's soft moans, she brought Lee to the edge before moving away, unsure if she should continue.

Lee groaned and raised her hips. "Don't stop."

Cole wanted to kiss her, knowing if she did she'd want so much more. Lee's hand guided her again, and she moved inside, slowly filling her. Lee trembled. Her chest heaved. She wanted to give Lee what she needed, but she also wanted to take her pleasure for her own selfish reasons. It had been far too long since she'd enjoyed a woman this way, and she meant for it to last as long as it could. And if it turned out to be a mistake, and the only time it happened, then she wanted to imprint the feel and sounds and scent of Lee in her memory.

"Please, please."

"Just let go, baby," she said, as she moved faster, deeper while her other hand played her clit. Lee tumbled over the edge and into her climax, thrashing beneath her touch, and the pure nakedness of her climax made Cole ache for more.

CHAPTER TEN

Lee's climax ripped through her. It centered and grounded her. Cole had a way of getting her to open up and the tears had come easily. But she had no intention of letting her any closer than a random moment of sex. She wasn't worthy of anyone's love, that much had been made clear by her parents. And no one since had given any indication they were interested in more than a casual fuck. She tried to shake off the melancholy stealing away the high of the orgasm, but instead the all too familiar sadness washed over her. Even after phenomenal sex, Lee was always left knowing there was nothing beyond the physical. She couldn't breathe. Nothing made sense. Not the bad luck that found her, not her life, and definitely not her attraction to Cole that felt dangerously close to a connection of some sort. She had nothing left to give and felt hollow, drained, and spent. Whatever reserves she'd had floated away in the calm waters a few feet away.

Cole had settled beside her. She didn't demand attention. Didn't ask for anything in return. She was just there, strong and steady. Lee's heart ached. She would never be able to return Cole's kindness. If she took after her father, she wouldn't know how, and she didn't know how to respond now. She sat up, inwardly flinching when Cole tenderly stroked her back. She couldn't look at her.

"I have to go." She took a breath. Let it out. "I'm sorry."

Cole removed her hand and she immediately missed its warmth. "Okay."

She wanted to scream. To tell her nothing she did was okay. It was selfish and single-minded. It was how she survived, without connection or commitment, and she didn't know any other way. Cole deserved so much more. Someone who wouldn't run away and make excuses—or keep parts of her psyche to herself. That's who *she* was, and she hated herself for it. She'd known that sex with Cole would be a mistake, that they should keep it on friendly terms. But lying there in the grass with the warm air caressing her body and her mind a jumbled mess of emotions, she'd given in and asked for what she wanted. Now that she'd gotten it, she knew she'd fucked up. Just like she always did.

Cole sat on the blanket, hugging her knees to her chest as Lee got up and went into the house, leaving Cole to figure out what had just happened. She hadn't said anything when Lee got up. What would she have said? *Please stay. I don't want you to leave like this. If you stick around maybe there could be something between us.* She wasn't desperate. Yes, she was lonely, and she had a feeling Lee could more than fill the gap, but that wasn't what Lee wanted. Maybe she wasn't attracted to her for more than a quick fix following an emotional breakdown. It appeared though, this might be the end of the line for anything romantic between her and Lee, and she'd have to be okay with that. Cole would do whatever necessary to keep their friendship alive. Touching Lee and bringing her to orgasm had warmed her more than sexually. The experience had been cathartic, along with opening her eyes to not limiting herself when it came to attraction. She hoped she'd provided something beneficial to Lee, too.

She heard the house door open then the truck start, and a battle raged inside her as she debated whether or not to run after her. Naked, she raced up the incline only to catch a glimpse of Lee staring ahead, her face streaked with tears as she drove away. Cole gathered her things and slowly climbed the stairs and went in. Numb, she pulled on her discarded clothes then got the coffee ready for morning. She took a long hot shower on autopilot, and robotically got ready for bed. Sleep refused to come and the day's events replayed in her head.

She'd known better, and she wouldn't regret what had happened between them, although she couldn't help but feel a little used and sad. It was a memory she would keep close when she was lonely.

A fitful night of tossing and turning had done little to help Cole come up with a new perspective. She dressed for work and stalked through the house. The gaping hole in the den was another reminder of how easily a situation went from good to...she wasn't sure what. *So be it.* Lee would move on and she'd be left behind. Again. Forcing herself to calm down, she remembered her own promise to not slide back into reactionary mode. She'd survived this long on her own, and she damn well wasn't going to settle for less than what she wanted anymore. Ginny hadn't been "the one." She'd been an interlude. A pause to give Cole a chance to figure out who she was and who she wanted to be. Ginny hadn't much liked the end result, but her departure hadn't shaken Cole's world, and she'd gotten over it quickly.

She leaned down and patted Dixie's head. Her time was limited, too. She barely moved anymore, drinking sporadically, and eating even less. Since she wasn't in obvious pain, Cole had accepted the inevitable and decided to let her be, not wanting her last days spent in the cold, sterile environment of the veterinary clinic with barking dogs, rather than her peaceful home. The only one she'd known, much like herself. The bigger question remained. Was she doing right by Dixie? Or was she just not ready to let her go?

"Hey, girl. Hang in there. Okay?" A feeble wag of her tail was the only evidence Dixie heard her.

She threw herself into her work as soon as she got to the garage, not bothering to wait for coffee to finish brewing. A few hours later, a delivery truck pulled up.

"Steve, how's the family?" she asked. Twenty years of parts shipments and the same driver behind the wheel had cemented their familiarity with each other's lives.

"Cole," he said, nodding as he pulled up information on his hand-held. "They're good. Determined to keep me working till I drop with one in college and another considering a career as a doctor." He laughed.

She signed the small screen, and he hefted heavy packages from his truck. The crankshaft and other parts for Lee's truck. After a careful examination, she'd determined the rest of the engine was in decent shape, and she'd ordered what was needed the day after Lee had shown up looking like she'd lost her best friend. As soon as she finished the tune-up on McGregor's Mustang, she'd start the repair. The sooner the better. She didn't want to use the truck as an excuse to keep Lee around. She'd gone from confused to sad to mad and back around again. Cole could have told Lee no, that the timing was wrong, but she'd chosen to touch her anyway. Lee showing up and catching Cole's attention had been a coincidence, and Lee had made it clear she wasn't into relationships. She had no one to blame for her tangled feelings but herself.

Lee stood at the front door moving nervously from foot to foot even though Cole's truck was gone. The house was unlocked just like before, so she had no excuse not to go inside...except she did. Guilt over running out on Cole had tormented her since she drove off. Lee had used her for sex to chase away her demons after Cole had gotten her to open up. The only person who came close to knowing all her secrets was Jackie.

Thinking back, she realized it was the expression of total understanding on Cole's face that had driven her away. That kind of empathy was foreign to her, and there was no way she could let someone like that in. No matter what, she'd promised to do the repair, and she owed Cole that much for her friendship, not to mention loaning her a truck. She'd gotten a few calls for basic repairs and would schedule them later. Lee took a deep breath and stepped inside. Cole's scent wrapped around her like a dense fog, making her heart heavy. *I've really fucked up this time.* She refused to pay attention to the voice inside her head.

"Hello?" Cole wasn't home, but if Betty was around, she didn't want to surprise her. She still wasn't sure if she had a gun.

The first thing she did was spread a tarp below the opening she'd cut in the ceiling. On her way back to the truck, she stuck her head into the kitchen. Dixie lay on her bed, opened one eye, then closed it again. She imagined the unenthusiastic greeting would be the same from Cole the next time Lee saw her.

She set up the ladder at the corner of the house, climbed to the roof, and removed a section of shingles. There was a bundle of replacements in the barn where she'd done some extensive searching when Cole told her to use whatever she wanted. After locating an exterior outlet, Lee cut away a damp section of plywood, certain she'd found the leak. The day quickly turned hot and she peeled down to her sports bra and cargo shorts.

Once the roof was repaired and the shingles replaced, she moved inside. It was warm even without the sun beating down on her. She opened one of the big multi-paned, floor to ceiling windows and let the breeze cool the sweat on her skin. Two hours later, she started to clean up the debris beneath the new Sheetrock patch. The tape and mud she'd applied around the seams would take a day to dry. She'd need to come back tomorrow, sand the surface, and apply another layer of the compound. It was a tedious process, but she wanted it to be perfect when she was done.

Her mouth was so dry she had a hard time swallowing. She hoped Cole wouldn't mind if she took a bottle of water. She grabbed a paper towel and wiped the sweat from her face, then drank the entire contents. Feeling better, she turned her attention to Dixie. The beagle didn't acknowledge her when she approached, and she bent down to pet her. Lee's heart sank in her chest. Dixie was barely breathing. She pulled out her cell.

"Hello." Cole's tone was cool.

"Hey. I think you should come home. It's Dixie. She's…" Lee wasn't good at giving bad news under the best of circumstances, and this was anything but.

"I'll be there in five."

Not knowing what else to do, Lee sat on the floor next to Dixie and lightly stroked her head. Lee wasn't her human, but it was the best she could offer until Cole arrived. A few minutes later, she heard the roar of an engine, then a vehicle door slamming shut. Cole appeared in the doorway and took in the scene. Lee scooted away to make room for Cole to take her rightful place.

❖

Cole gently placed her hand on Dixie's chest. "It won't be long, girl," she said before touching her silky ear and rubbing between her eyes, a spot Dixie particularly enjoyed being petted when she was a pup. She glanced at Lee as she leaned against the wall with her knees to her chest, much the same way Cole had done the night before when Lee left.

"Thank you for calling me."

Lee nodded. Sadness marred her beautiful face.

"What are you doing here?"

"I should have called first, I know. I fixed the roof and patched the ceiling. I looked in on her first thing, to let her know it was me. I didn't get much of a reaction." Lee's forehead creased.

"Don't feel bad," Cole said. "I haven't been getting much of one myself."

"I came in for a bottle of water. Again, I'm sorry for acting like I had a right." Lee's head dropped, her face coloring. "That's when I found her like this."

As much as she'd been upset at the way things had ended last night, Lee had checked on Dixie and hadn't hesitated to call her. Cole touched Lee's hand. "It's okay. I told you to take whatever you needed."

"Even after I treated you like shit?" Lee asked, emotion coloring her words.

Cole looked away and shrugged. "Things happen. We were in the moment, even if we both knew it was probably a mistake."

"God dammit, Cole. You deserve better. For once will you just tell me to fuck off? That you won't put up with my bullshit."

She studied Lee's reddened face. "No, I won't. Friendship isn't conditional, at least not to me."

"Unlike mine, you mean?"

Cole continued to stroke Dixie, her chest moving in less frequent intervals. "Can we talk about us later?"

"Jesus, I'm an ass. I'm going to go." Lee moved to stand, but Cole stopped her.

Lee had reached out to her last night for comfort and now, with more of her world crumbling, Cole needed it. "Please stay. I'd prefer not to be alone." Everything she'd done in the last twelve years she'd done virtually alone, including being alone in the garage with her father when he'd collapsed. This was one time she was grateful to have someone there. Lee silently dropped beside her, held her other hand and rubbed along her thumb.

Twenty minutes later, Dixie was gone. She was truly alone now. Cole stroked the silken ear one more time. "I'll bury you in your favorite field, girl." She took a shuddery breath and stood, her world surreal and hollow.

Lee stepped in front of her. "Let me help."

Cole hesitated, unsure if she wanted to share more with Lee than she already had over the last week.

"Please let me do this for you."

She nodded. "There's tools in the barn. I'm not sure where."

"I'll find them."

She looked down at her long-time companion again. "I'm going to wrap her in her favorite blanket."

"I'll be outside whenever you're ready."

Cole took a few minutes to say good-bye before gently placing Dixie in the blanket that was more like a worn-out rag after years of washing. She didn't think Dixie would mind. They'd lived simply for sixteen years.

Lee stood on the edge of the driveway with a couple of shovels and a pickaxe. Cole held Dixie's still warm body against her. They had been good for each other. In her mind's eye, Dixie was a tumbling pup, tripping over her long ears. Riding in the truck with her on the way to the garage, those same ears flapped in the breeze as she hung her head out the window. Her breath hitched and her vision blurred. Cole stumbled on a divot, and Lee's strong hand steadied her. She kept going while dreading every step. She didn't want to think about Dixie lying in the ground or not being in the house when she returned.

Lee walked beside her in silence, and Cole refused to give space to the lingering disappointment. People made decisions that affected others every day. Who was she to say what was right or wrong for Lee? They were just getting to know each other, maybe already as well as they ever would. She was here now and that was all that mattered.

Cole passed the path for the pond and kept going. Another hundred yards and she stopped in front of a lone box elder in an otherwise treeless field. Wildflowers of calendula and cornflower, along with wild lupine and echinacea were spread out among the tall, untamed grasses.

"Here," Cole said. "Whenever she was missing as a puppy, this was where I'd find her."

Lee looked around as though trying to find the perfect spot. She stopped moving and looked up. "Is this okay?"

She nodded, then sat crossed-legged a short distance away and laid Dixie in front of her. It took Lee less than thirty minutes to excavate a space large enough and deep enough to hold Dixie's remains. When she was done, Lee met her gaze and nodded.

Cole gathered Dixie to her for the last time. She'd grown cold and Cole tried not to think about it as she knelt to place her in the earth-lined grave. "You can chase rabbits again. I'll miss you, girl." She choked on the words. Together, she and Lee shoveled the dirt back in before pressing it firm to keep the critters from digging her up.

She should have said something, but she couldn't. She'd buried her father before his time, and now her dog was gone. The only one she had left was her grandmother, and she too, would be gone before long. Loving others came at such a high cost, and as she fought the desire to become numb or to scream in frustration, she wondered how much more she could lose before losing herself altogether. She'd already lost herself to expectations. Cole didn't know if she had anything more to give.

Chapter Eleven

Lee's heart sank in her chest as Cole walked away, her shoulders slumped, her hands shoved in her pockets. She gathered the tools into a pile before pulling out her pocketknife. Lee prayed nothing was poisonous as she cut stems of various colorful flowers. At least she thought they were all flowers. Once she had enough, she took the tools back to the barn. The house was quiet, and she found Cole at the kitchen table drinking brown liquid from a mason jar. Cole's sharp gaze met hers.

"Care to join me?" Cole gestured to the other jar.

She would have comforted her if Cole's eyes showed any sign she'd be welcome. Instead, she went to the kitchen and found a pitcher, filled it with water, and brought the flowers to the table. "I don't know if I should. I'm driving someone else's vehicle."

Cole shrugged. "You can always spend the night. I'd find something for you to wear." Emotions raged in her eyes as she poured a healthy amount of bourbon into the jar, then added more to her own.

Lee had never met anyone as strong as Cole. On the outside, she seemed to take disappointment and heartache in stride, and Lee wondered how much it cost her to hold her feelings in check. Or maybe she was just as strong on the inside. Lee wondered if she'd ever have that kind of strength.

"I'm sorry Dixie's gone." She swallowed and embraced the burning heat that spread through her. *Cleansed by fire.*

"I'm glad she wasn't alone." Cole glanced at the flowers and rubbed a petal between her fingertips without leaving a mark. For someone who worked on metal, Cole had an incredibly light touch.

Lee drank more. Her head swam a bit. She should get out of there. She was probably the last person Cole wanted around. "I'll finish cleaning up in the den before I go." As she stood, Cole grabbed her wrist. There was nothing gentle or tentative in the touch.

"Leave it. I don't want you to go."

She caught the plea in her eyes along with so much more. Sorrow, of course, and the flare of desire. God help her, Lee's body responded. "Why would you want me to stay?"

Cole finished off her drink. "Because despite what's happened between us..." Cole said, then stood. "I want you." Cole wrapped her arm around her and cupped the nape of her neck. Their lips met with renewed urgency, as though they'd been apart for months instead of hours.

I shouldn't stay. Even as the thought played through her head, she knew she couldn't go after abandoning Cole once. She'd given Lee what she needed. Now, Cole was hurting and needed something in return. Whatever the consequence, she would act selflessly for Cole's sake.

Lee forced Cole against the wall and buried her tongue in her mouth. She opened Cole's pants and shoved her hand inside, her fingers instantly coated with the slick juices that flowed there. If this was what Cole wanted, then that's what she would give her. "Do you want me to fuck you?"

"Yes." Cole clawed at Lee's clothes.

A primordial drive overtook her. She was an untamed beast intent on mating. Lee pressed her fingers into Cole's tight opening and bit Cole's lower lip. Took her harder, deeper. "So fucking wet and ready for me." She pushed in again. Lee moved her other hand to the top button of Cole's shirt, but when it proved to be more than a little uncooperative, she gave a sharp yank and the buttons flew across the room, the pings a musical prelude to the next act. Everything stopped when Cole's black silk camisole was revealed. *Fuck*. Nothing was hotter than a woman unafraid to embrace every side of herself. She pushed the fabric out of her way and palmed Cole's breast to take as much as she could into her mouth. Cole bit her neck, sending shock waves of pure electricity through her.

"Take me, and I'll come in your mouth."

Lee groaned. It took her less time to strip her than she would have thought possible before picking her up and laying her on the table. Lee's vision blurred. She shoved her own pants down as she buried her face in Cole's crotch and fingered her clit in tight circles.

Cole held her head in place. "There, right there."

Cole's legs shook, her head arched back, and the moment she climaxed, Lee's body exploded, too. She grabbed the edge of the table, her legs buckling as she continued to lick the flow from Cole's center. Cole pushed her head away and slammed her legs closed.

"No more. I can't," she said, her voice a strangled mixture of relief and sadness.

Cole's eyes glistened with unshed tears. How many times had she chased away her own sadness with sex? Cole pushed up and took her face in her hands, then kissed her like she'd never been kissed before. She swayed for a minute before Cole took her hand and tugged her toward the stairs. Lee started to protest. Cole turned her stormy, red-rimmed eyes on her.

"Not a word. I don't want to hear your reasons or excuses. This is what I need. Nothing more." They climbed the stairs in silence. Standing next to the bed, Cole lifted the edge of her camisole.

"Wait."

Cole pursed her lips.

Lee fingered the material. "This, on you, is one of the hottest fucking things I've ever seen." She was breathless.

Cole's face softened. "I forgive you for talking. Now get in bed."

Lee scooted to the middle and Cole slid in next to her.

"Hold me."

She gathered Cole against her, tucking her along her side, and pressing her head to her chest.

"Promise you'll be here in the morning."

"I promise." This was one time she had no intention of disappointing Cole.

CHAPTER TWELVE

True to her word, Lee was lying beside her in the morning. She stroked her fingertips along the edge of her jaw. Lee's eyes fluttered.

"Hey. How are you feeling?"

She took a minute to weigh her sorrow against her pleasure at waking with Lee in her bed. "Okay. Better than last night." The memory of asking Lee to service her and then sleep with her left her feeling adrift. "Lee, I don't normally—"

Lee held her hand up. "Ask for what you need?" Lee took her hand, held it to her chest. "If you think for a minute that I regret last night, you're right. I regret that you lost your dog. I can't imagine how much that hurt."

"Thank you."

Lee ran her fingertip over the tiny mole on her upper lip. The touch was tender, soft, caring. "You don't have to thank me. Just let me do what I can for you."

She took a minute to think about what that might be and went with her gut. "Shower with me?"

Cole got out of bed, and when Lee rolled away to get out on the other side, she remembered their swim, wincing at how it ended before she banished the hurt. Lee's entire back was covered with a tattoo of a phoenix rising through flames of blue, orange, and red. She met Lee at the end of the bed. "I meant to ask you about this." She trailed her finger along the wings that hugged Lee's shoulders. Lee shivered under her touch.

"I don't think about it as much as I used to." Lee looked over her shoulder when she turned her back to the full-length mirror.

Their eyes met in the reflection. "When did you get it?" The outline was crisp, but it wasn't new.

"After I graduated high school. I'm not sure if I did it for punishment or as a badge of survival." She shrugged. "I needed something to prove I was tough enough to go on. To be the real me instead of what my parents wanted me to be."

The real me. Had Cole ever fully embraced the real her? Her authentic self? She tried once, a long time ago. The embarrassment of that night had lost its sharp edge over the years, but the hurt had remained for a while. She'd knee-jerked and abandoned any further pursuit. Since then she presented herself how others expected her to be, the way they'd always seen her, and that was okay with her. She accepted the expectation and made peace with it. Mostly. But there was another part of Cole that longed to break free of the stereotype, to embrace the sides of herself that had been hidden away except on rare occasions when she'd gone to towns so far away no one knew her or didn't care to. Like the black camisole she'd worn the day before, just because she liked the way it felt against her skin. She'd had a flash of panic when Lee had opened her shirt and saw it, but her reaction had been perfect, and she'd relaxed under Lee's hot gaze, warmed by her acceptance.

"It's beautiful. Like you." She fanned her hand on Lee's lower back, her fingers following the flames.

Lee took a step away, breaking the connection. "You have to stop touching me."

"Why?"

"Because I already want you, and if you keep doing that, I may not be able to stop myself." Lee's chest rose and fell rapidly.

Cole ached to take a stiff peak in her mouth, roll her tongue around the tip, pull with her teeth. "And you don't want to touch me?"

"That's the problem. I do."

She wasn't sure she wanted to know the reason Lee fought against her desires. It was enough to know she was confused, and her unwillingness to continue meant it wasn't a good idea. Instead of saying anything, Cole slid her hand into Lee's and tugged her along. She needed a shower, and she was determined not to be alone.

❖

Coffee and a bagel served as breakfast and gave Cole time to reflect. She'd carefully washed Lee, and Lee had done the same for her. How she managed to keep her mouth off of her glistening, tanned skin was a miracle unto itself.

Lee insisted on finishing the ceiling, and there was no denying the awkward tension between them remained as Cole got ready for work before leaving for the day. Lee didn't want a relationship, was used to a faster pace, and Cole had a hard time seeing her settling in a small town. Cole wouldn't...couldn.t...leave, and she needed a partner who wanted to stay and keep to the simple life. They couldn't want more opposing things, and as exceptional as the sex was, and as attracted as she was to Lee, there didn't seem to be any common ground. She'd always felt some type of connection when she shared a bed, but not the sense of wanting permanency, like there was now. She called out to say bye as she left Lee to finish the work and sighed deeply. Life didn't used to be so damn complicated.

Cole had every intention of paying her, even though she refused to tell her how much the materials cost. She knew everyone in the home repair store, and a phone call would provide what she needed to know. How many spikey-haired blonds with a muscular body could have shopped there in the last few days? Not to mention, Cole had her own agenda. Lee's truck engine lay in pieces in her shop. She planned on surprising her with a fully functional vehicle. She'd called Dan to find out if he had Lee's bank account number, so she could discreetly make a deposit for the house repairs. Lee wouldn't have to know who the money came from. He didn't have the information but stated the repaired truck would be a nice birthday present, and she had every intention of giving it to Lee as a gift.

It wasn't hard to see how much having to rely on Cole's generosity bothered Lee. It was one of the biggest differences in their sense of community. The people in her town relied on helping hands and repaid favors in kind when an opportunity arose. If it never came, no one cared. There wasn't a tally for good deeds. Cole wouldn't trade her upbringing for anything, and certainly not for city life where you didn't even know your neighbors, let alone depend on them.

She'd just opened the shop when her phone rang with the familiar tone. "Hi, Nana."

"Cole Anne, what's wrong?" Her grandmother's voice was still the strong one she remembered from childhood.

"What do you mean?" Cole fixed the coffee pot and turned it on.

"I have to hear from Miles that the station was closed yesterday afternoon, and I want to know why."

Oh. Calling her grandmother with the news about Dixie had never crossed her mind, since she'd been rather distracted by Lee's body on top of hers. She couldn't forsake the only family she had left because of her obsessive attraction. "Dixie passed yesterday while Lee was at the house."

"Ah, that explains it. I'm glad you weren't alone. Sorry to hear about your buddy."

She appreciated her grandmother's gentle tone, which was a rare thing. "Thanks. I'm glad I wasn't alone either."

"You're coming for dinner tonight."

"I'll be there." The idea of being with her grandmother when her heart was frayed gave her a different kind of comfort than Lee's and would serve to salve her emotional wounds.

"Have a better day, honey. I'll see you tonight."

At six o'clock sharp, Cole opened the screen door and greeted her grandmother with a kiss on the cheek before setting a bag of produce on the counter. "Glen had strawberries and rhubarb at the stand."

"Your subtle hint you want a pie?"

"Nope," she said. "I was going to beg for one."

Nana snapped a towel at her. "Ha. You don't have to beg." She cupped Cole's cheek. "You know I love cooking for you." A couple of minutes later, they settled at the table. "How's the ceiling repair going?"

"All done by now I imagine. Lee was going to put another coat of joint compound on today. She did a great job. I'm glad I got her to look at it before it got worse."

"Uh-huh." She dipped a piece of bread into the sauce before taking a bite. "She seems nice enough."

Cole almost missed the comment, lost in a flashback of the first time she'd seen her. "She is. She's had a hard time lately. Longer, really. Lee could use a friend."

Her grandmother was laser focused. "You know she's a lesbian," she said matter-of-factly.

"Yes, Nana. I know." She couldn't help smiling. Despite the rough moments, there was a lot to like about Lee. Cole looked up. Her grandmother chewed while studying her, a dead giveaway there would be more questions.

"You finally scratched that itch?"

Cole swallowed as warmth traveled up her neck. "Nana, please."

"Am I wrong?"

She could never lie to her grandmother, though sometimes she wished she could. "No, but we're just friends."

"Says you. I'm not convinced."

Cole sighed. "It shouldn't have happened."

"More than once?"

She ran her hand over her face. *Could this conversation be any more embarrassing?* "Yes."

"It's about time you brought her around. I want to see the two of you together." Her grandmother chuckled. "Besides, I don't want her to still think I'm going to shoot her."

She laughed. "I think she's gotten over the idea of you toting a gun." Cole remembered another conversation and her mood sobered.

"You all right?"

"Yes." She took a breath. "No?" God, she was pathetic. "I don't know. I can't believe Dixie is gone. And the situation with Lee is confusing, but I'll work it out." The more she thought of being alone, the more her mind wandered. "Nana?"

"Yes, dear?"

"What did you think of my mother?" Her grandmother sat back down.

"Why are you asking now?"

"I've been thinking about relationships." She sighed. "I looked for her once, after Dad died."

"Whatever for?" Her grandmother seemed pensive, something that never happened.

Cole shrugged. "I thought maybe she'd want to know how her other daughter turned out." She'd found her after searching the internet, though her mother was listed under her maiden name. She was living in a squalid little town in the Midwest. She'd almost been sad her life hadn't turned out the way her mom wanted.

"And?" Betty asked.

"I didn't try to contact her." She almost had, but to what end? Her mother knew how to reach her and hadn't bothered, so she'd decided to let it be. She was at an okay place and didn't need to get close to someone who valued money over people, especially their own flesh and blood. "I always thought she'd left because of the way I am. Because I was never the little girl she wanted, but I don't believe that anymore."

Her grandmother pursed her lips. "She left because your daddy had enough of her conniving to get his money. *Your* inheritance."

"He told me that too, but I always felt like there was more to her leaving than just money." The first year after her mother and baby sister had left, she'd lie awake at night imagining all sort of reasons.

"I swore I'd never tell anyone, but you need to know. Your mom had an affair not long before your sister was born. Your father found out somehow and he doubted he was Alice's father, but that wouldn't have stopped him from doing right by her. That's when your mother started harping and hounding him to sell it all so they could move away. Of course, he'd do no such thing. Jacksons have owned this land for nearly a century. I saw it, the growing distance between them. Then he found them in bed together when we came home early one day. That was the last straw. Your daddy was a loving man, but he told her to pack up and never come back."

Cole stared ahead, shocked by the revelation of what really happened between her parents. "Dad looked so sad after she left, and I was so worried he'd leave too. I'm not sure I gave him what he needed." She'd been so young then.

"You idolized the ground he walked on and loved him with all your heart. You always had. He knew it, girl. Trust me. And he loved you just as much."

She had a hard time processing the new information. "He looked so lonely."

"He was brokenhearted. Lori was his everything and she...well, she was a greedy soul from the start."

Cole thought about how her father had struggled to go on. She'd catch glimpses of him looking forlorn and lost, but as a teen she didn't know why. Lee looked that way sometimes. Maybe that was part of the draw. The part that didn't involve her body shooting into high gear when she was around. "Thanks for telling me, Nana."

"It was time." She gently tapped her hand. "It's the present that's important now."

"Yes, it is."

"Uh-huh. So you bring her over on Sunday for dinner and extend the invitation to Dan, too. Don't be late."

"I'm not sure that's a good idea."

"Glad it's settled then. I'll see you at two. I love you."

"I love you too, Nana." Maybe showing Lee a different side of her wasn't such a bad idea. She knew the mechanic side of her. The sexually hungry side of her. Why not let her see the family side of her?

An hour later, Cole sat on the porch with her coffee, grazing her fingers over the warm surface. She still couldn't grasp everything her grandmother had told her, but it all made sense now. She wished Lee could have met her father, seen them together and witnessed how much they'd loved each other. Even if Lee ended up being a fleeting interlude to something...someone...permanent, it wasn't a reason to not show her more of Cole's life. Her grandmother and the sense of family was an important part of who she was. Why she wished there was a chance Lee wasn't going to leave was confusing. True, Lee had made it clear about her situation and Cole would be hurt when she left, but she was here now. With or without sex, she enjoyed Lee's company, and Lee had opened up a bit, giving Cole a smidgen of hope Lee wasn't in such a hurry to go after all. If she had a chance at all, Lee should know about the things that meant the most to Cole, though learning the same from Lee would likely be harder. There was still the matter of that wall. Oh, she'd glimpsed over it a few times. But that's not how a heathy relationship worked.

CHAPTER THIRTEEN

The day promised to be another scorcher. If it weren't for the breeze that came across the lake at the edge of town, doing anything physical would be nearly impossible. By comparison, the weather in the Adirondacks was considerably more tolerable than being stuck between high-rises.

Lee checked the address in her notebook, then looked at the map on her phone though she didn't really need to. When the customer had said to turn left at the drug store and go to the blue house, that was likely all the information she needed. Yesterday she'd finished the work at Cole's and, after texting her, she'd returned this morning to pick up a few things from the shed. She hadn't seen her, but Cole asked her to come to the house and there'd been a note taped to the front door.

Thanks for doing such a great job. There are cold drinks in the fridge, and you might consider trying one of my banana nut muffins. They're to die for. Cole

She'd drawn a quirky little smiley face that made her laugh. A few minutes ago, she'd gotten a text message asking her to stop by the shop when she had time. They hadn't been together since the morning after Dixie died and she wondered how Cole was doing. She should have asked. At least sent her a text. But she wasn't sure she knew what to say.

Lee found the house without any problems, and the older gentleman who greeted her showed her the back door and the outer screen that needed replacing. While she worked her thoughts returned to Cole. She wasn't good with emotions that ran as deep as Cole's, and Cole had so many noble characteristics Lee couldn't begin to compare her to anyone she knew. Not that she let people close enough to know. Letting people in led to being hurt and she wasn't sure she'd know how to handle it if that happened. She'd done so well dealing with her parents' reactions.

She should have been prepared for her father's outrage and her mother's indifference. It wasn't like they'd ever been a warm, loving family, but as a teenager and living in an open community how could she have been? Most days her father barely acknowledged her, except when she was in her room and he came in unannounced to scowl at her for some transgression he'd fabricated so he could voice his displeasure. On the other hand, her mother hardly spoke, negative or otherwise. She wasn't mean, but she certainly wasn't coddling. A lump rose in her throat. There'd been no one at home to help her through those difficult adolescent years when she was questioning everything about herself and the world around her.

After she moved out, there'd been months of living in a drug and alcohol haze fueled by insecurity about her own worth. Jackie's parents had been patient through it all, and she'd somehow managed to graduate high school. They'd encouraged her to find her calling, and she applied to colleges with a surprisingly decent SAT score, but she'd never gotten over missing out on the moments her classmates had enjoyed. There'd been no one cheering for her at commencement. No one to hug her or tell her how proud she should be, and those scars ran deep. She'd vowed no one would ever see them or know her well enough to use them against her. She was right to keep Cole at a distance. Otherwise, she might have to drop the protective shell that had kept her from spiraling into despair, though her current situation had almost rocked her enough to send her into the vortex again. If it wasn't for her uncle's open arms, and Cole's friendship, she was convinced she'd already be there. Friendship was important. Sex she could find anywhere.

Once she finished the repair, the couple seemed pleased, and Lee was glad she'd been paid in cash so she could buy some groceries. She got into the truck and headed home. A shower was in order before she saw Cole.

"How did the repair go?" Dan asked while he put the finishing touches on their chicken salad sandwiches.

"Pretty easy. I'll go back when the weather cools and fix a couple of windows that were installed incorrectly. Even I had a hard time raising and lowering them." The poor wife had probably strained something in the process of trying to get them up, but there was little she could do in the heat to fix it.

"Does that mean you'll be staying?" He sat across from her.

Lee stared at her plate, unable to make eye contact. "For a while, anyway. No one's responded to my applications or my posted résumé." She finally looked up. "This place isn't so bad. It's just different from what I was used to. But I'm not sure about staying long-term. I don't really know where I want to be."

Dan daintily wiped his face with the corner of his napkin. "It's not just the location though, is it?"

She met his gaze, needing him to understand. "Cole's friendship is special, and if I stay too long, I might screw it up." Like she had other good things in her life. But she'd only told Dan a half-truth about her reasons for not wanting to stay longer. If she stayed, she'd have to let Cole see more of her scars. Though, if she stopped kidding herself, she didn't want to live with the secrets anymore. Midway to tackling the sandwich she stopped, then set it back down. "*Cole* is special."

He nodded. "That she is. So much like her father."

Lee took a bite, then crunched on a chip. "You said you knew him?"

Dan laughed. "It's kind of hard not to know everyone in a town this size. Will Jackson was a good man. Hardworking, honest. A good father, too. I remember Cole following him around the garage since she was big enough to pick up tools." He chuckled.

"And her mother left after Cole's sister was born?"

"Saddest thing. I don't know how hard Cole took it, but Will was devastated. I know the feeling." Dan ran his fingers over the condensation on his glass, seeming lost in thought.

"Uncle Dan?" When he looked up, she could see the unshed tears. "What happened?" She knew so little of her uncle's partner or what they shared, but that didn't mean he didn't want or need to talk about it, unlike her.

"Sometimes love isn't enough, no matter how hard you try." He picked up the glass of iced tea, his hand shaking, but he managed to take a drink. "Michael wanted a different life than the one we'd planned. He was convinced that the world was waiting for him and he was determined to find out what it had to offer. He packed up his apartment, rented a van, and headed west."

Lee didn't think if she found love like the kind Dan had obviously shared with Michael that she wouldn't do whatever she had to do to keep it, no matter how unlikely. At least, she hoped that's what she would do. "Did you not want to go with him?"

"I would have followed him anywhere, but that's not what he wanted. He said he needed to spread his wings. Go where the wind blew him. Alone." He picked up their plates and took them to the sink before gripping the edge with both hands. "I was young. An unsure, closeted man in a town I'd grown to love. It was a mistake not to beg to go with him, but I loved him enough to let him go." He took her hand and squeezed. "You never know when the love you're meant to be with will come along."

Lee understood his message. She just wasn't sure if she could follow his advice. The fear of having to trust another person enough to let them inside to see her faults and frailties was scary, and she wasn't prepared to face the consequences if things went sour with Cole, like she was convinced they would. But what if she was wrong, and this was an opportunity for something deeper than she'd ever known?

❖

The hot air moving lazily over the ground gave some relief to the relentless sun as Lee cut the grass and trimmed the bushes out front as a way to chase away the ghosts of the past and the uncertainty of the future. She sat on a lawn chair in the shade of maple trees and wiped sweat from her face and neck.

"I don't know why you insist on doing this in the heat of the day." Dan handed her a tall glass of iced tea.

She drank down half and smiled. "I'm used to working in it. Besides, I wouldn't want to lose this great tan." Lee laughed with him, then sobered. She'd been thinking about Cole since their talk earlier. "What happened to Cole's father?"

"She lost him about a decade ago. Heart attack, right in the shop. Cole found him." He shook his head. "I never saw Cole cry. Never saw her feel sorry for herself. She picked up the pieces and moved on. Did what she had to do and took care of her grandmother."

The information gave her a bit more insight as to where Cole's strength came from, but she couldn't help wondering what it had cost her. In a way, Cole had also been abandoned by her family, a common heartache they shared.

"I hope you're going to relax the rest of the day."

"Well," she began as she wiped at the sweat running down her face. "I definitely need a shower. Then I'll head over to the garage. Cole asked me to stop by. Said she has something to show me."

"I'm sure she does." Dan shared a quirky grin.

"If you need my help around here, I can tell her I can't see her today."

"Don't be crazy. Go have a good time. I'm sure you have a lot more in common than you might think." He gave her hand a squeeze. "Time is short, Lee. Don't leave this world with regrets. Enjoy what's offered."

Coming here had been the best decision she'd made in a long time. Dan's wisdom and understanding were two things that had been sorely lacking in her life. Meeting Cole had been a highlight of the whole debacle. Her friendship was unquestionable, and the ease with which they'd reached out to each other for comfort when suffering had been cathartic, along with the demanding, mind-blowing sex Lee had craved. Still craved. A tendril of dread began to form in her belly. Maybe Cole no longer wanted friendship with benefits. Maybe she'd misinterpreted Cole's offer, and now that the house repair was done, she wanted Lee to give the go-ahead to fix her truck so they could both get on with their lives. A tight knot formed in her gut. If that's what Cole wanted to tell her, of course she'd honor her request. It would be her own damn fault for going with what she always did to find comfort. Sex.

Chapter Fourteen

Cole lifted her head from under the hood of the convertible her neighbor had brought in for an oil change and inspection. She sprayed her hands with grease cutter, pulled a fresh shop rag from the industrial size box, and wiped her hands clean. She'd been chomping at the bit since she'd finished Lee's truck, and her heart rate picked up tempo as she watched Lee walk toward her.

"Hey," Lee said. Nervous energy wafted off her as she shoved her hands in her back pockets, forcing her chest forward. "You wanted to see me?"

Lee's nipples were pressed against the fabric of her fitted T-shirt, making Cole's mouth water. "I did." She reached behind her and produced an envelope. "This is for the materials and work you did at the house."

Lee took a step back. "I don't want that."

She closed the distance between them. "I insist. I asked you to take a look. You did the repair, which was spectacular by the way, and saved me from ignoring it until the problem became much bigger. Thank you." Cole shoved the envelope forward.

"And you lent me your truck. And tools."

"We're not doing this, Lee." Her resolve was firmly in place. "I refuse to play tit for tat. You either take this now or I find out your bank account number and make a deposit." She shrugged. "Your choice."

Lee glanced between the envelope and Cole. After several long minutes, she took it and roughly shoved the envelope into her pocket. "Fine."

"Good." She glanced over her shoulder to make sure Lee couldn't see her truck. She'd parked it in such a way that no matter which direction Lee arrived from, it remained out of view. "I have a surprise for you."

Lee rolled her eyes. "I'll bet. Now what?"

"Follow me." She made sure Lee was beside her as they went out the back door to the side of the building." Lee came to a dead stop when she saw her vehicle.

"What's this?"

"Unless you've forgotten what it looks like, it's your truck."

Lee's face paled. "Please tell me there's nothing else wrong with it."

"There isn't a thing wrong with it." Cole pulled the keys from her pocket. "She's good to go."

"What? That can't be. I didn't okay the repair yet."

"Happy early birthday." She finally smiled, hoping Lee wasn't angry at her for going ahead with the repairs.

Lee blinked several times. When she faced her, unshed tears pooled in her eyes.

"No, no." Cole moved closer. "Please don't cry." She brushed at the tears that cascaded over Lee's bottom lashes. "Are you upset with me?"

"Why?" Lee choked out.

"What do you mean 'why'? I heard you were having a birthday soon and decided on the perfect present." She held her hands out wide. "Ta-da!"

Lee crumpled against the wall and buried her face in her hands.

Cole wrapped her arms around Lee and helped her stand. "You have a strange way of showing you're happy." She rubbed up and down her back to soothe away whatever had Lee in despair. "You are happy, aren't you? Did I fuck up?"

Once she had her emotions under control, Lee met Cole's gaze. "No one has ever done anything like this for me." She brushed her lips over Cole's. "How did you manage to get the part so quickly?"

"I ordered it the day after you dropped it off."

"So, you were going to fix it whether I had the money or not."

"Of course." Cole was beaming.

"I've asked this before, but why?"

Cole ran her thumb over her lower lip, and the softness of it sent a shiver of desire through her. "I've told you, it's what small town folk do."

"Not all folk, Cole. You. It's what *you* do. Probably what you've always done." Lee held the sides of her face, brought her closer, and kissed her full-on.

There were promises behind the kiss, but they were promises Cole wasn't sure Lee could keep. Not now. Maybe not ever. Breathless, Cole broke away. "If that's the kind of thank you I get for doing what I enjoy, I'll have to do it more often." She touched her lips.

Lee took in a quick breath. "You strip away my defenses with a word, a look, a touch. I should run and never look back. I'll never be able to be the kind of friend you deserve." Lee whispered and went to the ground.

Cole knelt in front of Lee. "You make me out to be someone I'm not. I struggle with things, too. Christ, everyone does. All I want is your honesty. However much you want to share is up to you." As much as she worried she was giving Lee the means to leave sooner rather than later, Cole refused to be a clinging vine. Lee would have to make the decision to stay on her own, and now she could. She'd done the repair with altruistic intent, but as the weight of Lee's possible departure pressed down on her, a vise formed around Cole's heart and her breath caught.

"I'm a mess. You don't want to see what's inside." Lee stood.

"Don't be so sure," she said as she held Lee's jaw and kissed her tenderly. "Come to the house tonight. I'll make a special dinner for you." Lee hesitated and Cole saw the internal battle displayed in her eyes.

"Okay, but I want to pay you back."

Cole's eyebrow rose. "I could think of a few ways." She ran her fingertips over her collarbone. "If you liked the camisole, I've got another outfit you might enjoy."

Lee groaned. "I think," she said, then nipped at Cole's lip. "You would like nothing more than to have me die in your bed."

She closed the inches between them and brushed her hip against Lee's center. "I may want you to *think* you've died and gone to heaven, but death is a permanent thing, and I like having you around."

"So, when do I get to see this outfit?" Lee asked as she put space between them.

"Tonight. After dinner, I'll be dessert." Cole's clit twitched, her pulse racing like a thoroughbred. Mistake or not, she wanted Lee in ways she'd never wanted anyone before, and she'd be damned if she'd throw away an opportunity to be with her. She'd deal with the fallout later.

"What time?"

"Seven."

She sighed. "Seven. Christ, Cole. What the hell am I supposed to do until then?"

Cole leaned against her harder and licked the sensitive flesh beneath Lee's ear. "Anything you want, except play with yourself. That's all mine tonight."

Lee's mouth dropped open and Cole laughed.

"Come on. Bring Jesse around back and we'll load your stuff into your truck. Then you can enjoy having your number one girl back."

❖

Lee clenched her fist at her sides and tried to tamp down the onslaught of emotions swirling inside her. A customer showed up as she walked to Cole's truck giving her time to think, something she had a hard time doing around her. Cole's words replayed in her head. Could she trust that they were true? Surely someone like Cole would tire of her quickly. Every nerve in her body twitched. Her imagination was firing off in so many directions, she was lost. Would Cole be wearing leather? Lace? A combination? The idea of not taking what Cole offered before it faded away like the winter sun would be crazy.

But this wasn't how things were supposed to go. Relocating had started off simple enough by being in this little, uncomplicated town, with a loving relative and a nice place to live. But finding a friend who could be so much more hadn't been part of it. As wrong as it might be, the immediate future had taken on a life of its own, and Lee wanted to see where it led. After all, Cole returning her truck must mean she understood things between them were temporary. She could always run later if it all fell apart. She had lots of practice at that.

Once her tools were loaded, she waved to Cole who was still busy in the shop. She headed in the opposite direction from Dan's, needing to be in her own head for a bit.

She was having a hard time accepting everything Cole had done for her, especially since she wanted so little in return. Without even really knowing her, Cole hadn't thought twice about fixing her truck, and she soon discovered, the engine had only been part of what she'd done. Cole had also cleaned and detailed it, then filled it with gas. Tears threatened again. Cole was a wonderful person. Warm, caring, and kind. She was also sexy as fuck. Lee's clit swelled as she tried to imagine what Cole had in mind. She didn't know everything about Cole, but she was excited to see where tonight would lead. Funny that Cole hadn't asked if she had plans if she didn't find permanent work here. Cole didn't come off as a "one-night stand" woman, but Lord knew she'd read people wrong before.

The dashboard clock let her know she had three hours to kill, and although another shower and a change of clothes were definitely in order, it wouldn't take her that long to get ready. Then she remembered Cole was fond of bourbon. The only liquor store in town stocked a decent selection of wine and basic libations, but she wanted something special. She was glad to have the GPS back and located a store in Old Forge, the next town over. The trip would be a perfect way to kill time. Lee called her uncle to see if he wanted to join her, but he declined.

As she drove down the narrow country lanes, she reflected on the last couple of months. She might not be able to name it, but the thing with Cole could be real if she ever decided to see it through. She'd been so lost when she'd driven here, and definitely hadn't anticipated finding another lesbian so quickly who wanted to be friends, let alone someone with whom the heat of attraction had been instantaneous. That, along with Cole's personality and temperament, were influential in making her want to be someone different. Someone who could be loved, someone with roots. But then...what if she stayed and Cole decided she didn't want her? What if she overstayed her welcome or she did something stupid to cause her uncle shame? Then she'd be out on her own, alone again. The thought made her shudder. Was it better to leave as soon as possible, before it could all come crashing down? Or was she done being a coward who ran with her tail between her legs at the first hint of things turning intense? Before she knew it, her GPS announced she'd reached her destination.

The small parking lot was busy, and it took Lee a little maneuvering to fit into a space meant for a smaller vehicle, but she managed. The white envelope with her name printed on the front glared at her from the cubby where she'd set it. She slipped a finger under the flap and pulled out a small stack of bills beneath a handwritten note.

Lee, Thanks for your meticulous work. Fondly, Cole

She tucked the note back inside the envelope and fanned the bills. Five one-hundred-dollar bills trembled in her hands. She'd spent less than a hundred on materials. *Jesus.* Lee shoved a bill in her pocket and stowed the rest in her console.

Inside the shop, the array of bourbons was impressive. She wasn't a big bourbon drinker and asked the man behind the counter for guidance. Ten minutes later, she walked out with a seventy-dollar bottle of Caskers thirteen-year-old Tennessee whiskey in a silk drawstring gift bag. Mission accomplished. She'd never spent so much on a gift for someone, and it felt weirdly elating. It was time to consider her outfit. Dark jeans? Stonewashed with cuts? Black? Maybe she'd ask Dan. He had a good fashion sense. It wasn't like he didn't know she and Cole were more than just friends, though she wasn't quite sure what they were at this point. But then she thought of the way Cole kissed her, and the anticipation in her eyes when she'd talked about other clothing Lee might like, and she pushed the doubts away. She wanted it, whatever it was. She pressed the accelerator. She was going to need a bit longer to get ready.

CHAPTER FIFTEEN

Cole finished prepping dinner and climbed the stairs, tension snaking through her. She was nervous for the first time since meeting Lee. What she'd been thinking about doing didn't terrify her, but she was anxious to see Lee's reaction. Even though she'd ridden the edge of femininity a number of times over the years while experimenting to find herself, she hadn't been this far over the edge since her feeble attempt at junior prom, and it excited her. At nearly forty, Cole was still trying to figure out if the life she'd been living was her true life…her authentic self.

Maybe working as a grease monkey most of her life meant presenting as butch was second nature, but lately the urge to explore was more insistent, and she hadn't been sure what to do about it. The women she'd been with had expectations about her, and she'd gone along with it because she wanted to explore dating and have a good time. If that meant playing a certain part, so be it. But the reticence around being forced into a box was stronger with every passing year as she tried to figure out how she was most comfortable. Jeans and flannel, silk and lace, or somewhere in between. She'd tried them all. Maybe it hadn't been *her* attitude that bothered her as much as the women she'd been with. The looks of confusion, rejection, and unease had been just as responsible for backing her into that corner where she'd settled.

The hot shower helped wash away some of her anxiety. She heard Lee's voice in her head. *Sexy as fuck.* When she'd slid the camisole on that morning they'd had sex, she hadn't thought about anything but how it made her feel.

As she smoothed lotion over her heated skin, she thought about her recent purchases. Shopping wasn't her thing, but she tolerated online perusing as a necessary evil. When she found the lingerie site and flicked through the pages for the perfect look, she stopped dead on one of the last. Unbelievably, the model's shape closely mirrored hers. Cole wasn't curvy. She'd always had more of a lean shape. Before she could change her mind, she dropped the items into her cart and finished the transaction. The package arrived at the garage yesterday and her initial trepidation returned in full force until she remembered their recent night together. Lee had been surprised by the camisole, then the surprise turned to desire, and the smoldering gaze had quelled the question of whether Lee would be put off by the revelation of her clothing choice.

There were so many complexities to Lee that intrigued her. The look on her face when Cole presented the repaired truck had been one of disbelief, and she hadn't expected her tears. The depth of Lee's appreciation mixed with the idea she didn't deserve kindness weighed heavy. Cole had been raised with privileges Lee had never known and perhaps was one of the biggest reasons she felt compelled to show her how different her life could be despite the struggles she'd faced, and still faced now.

The night of Dixie's death and how steadfast Lee had been in wanting to ease Cole's pain had touched her heart, a place that hadn't been touched by anyone in a long time. She, too, had been lacking the type of connection she'd found with Lee, even if Lee couldn't see it… or didn't want to.

The clock numbers flashed at her from across room. She had to hurry if she wanted to be downstairs by the time Lee arrived. Cole bit her lip. What if this was all a mistake? What would happen if Lee showed up tonight, or another night, to tell her she was leaving? She hadn't thought this through. Lee was much younger, muscular, and sexy. She could have any woman she wanted. Did she really think Lee could be happy with her down the road? Was there even a road to consider? She stared at her reflection. The reason she'd invited Lee was clear. Cole craved feeling their bodies pressed together, banishing thoughts of the losses she'd suffered, and dreams left unrealized. When they made love nothing else mattered. But still. She shook her head. "Stop it," she said out loud. Taking a deep breath, determined to carry on, at least for tonight, Cole resumed getting ready.

Undergarments in place, Cole pulled her leather pants on, stuck her feet into her boots, and buttoned her shirt, then undid a few so that a small glimpse of her bra was revealed. She nodded at her reflection, took another breath, and prepared to wait.

❖

It was stupid really. Lee and Cole had been in each other's company enough times that nerves should no longer play a part, but the jittery flutters were real. She felt like a wild animal caught in a brush fire, not knowing which way to turn. Yet, deep down, she *wanted* more of what Cole was offering. Lee grabbed the bottle off the passenger seat and took the stairs two at a time. She chewed her lower lip. Should she go in? Knock, like this was a real date? The door wouldn't be locked, but did that give her the right to walk in like she lived there? She stretched her neck and rolled her shoulders, making tendons and joints pop, then she pushed the bell. A few seconds later, the door swung in and Lee forgot to breathe.

"Hi," Cole said. Her dark hair fell across one brow and her black shirt was open dangerously low. Black leather pants hugged her slender hips and ended at studded biker boots.

She cleared her throat and tried to swallow. Her mouth suddenly dry as desert sand. "Hi." Lee stepped in and brushed her lips over Cole's, afraid if she went for a full-on kiss, dinner would be seriously delayed. The smile she offered felt forced. "I brought you something."

Cole took the bottle. "Tonight is a celebration of you. You shouldn't have." She opened the bag. "Wow. I hope you plan on having a drink with me. This is much better than what I've shared with you."

Was that an innuendo? A glimpse of what was in store? "Okay. Sure." She shoved her hands in her front pockets to keep them from grasping Cole and dragging her to bed.

"Come to the kitchen. Dinner will be a little while. We can have a drink outside while we wait."

Cole set the bottle on the sideboard and strode with more confidence than Lee ever felt when they were together. *Fuck.* She was so out of her league with Cole. Cole had money. From what she could tell, old money. The kind that was passed from one generation to the next because it had been preserved and appreciated, though Cole never came across as privileged. Had never looked down at her as less-than or flaunted what she had. If anything, she was generous to a fault. Maybe growing up in a tight-knit community meant people didn't take things for granted, like she had when she was younger, thinking what she'd always had would always be. What was she getting herself into? It was way too late to ask. Lee had a thing for Cole and no matter if she thought otherwise, she couldn't seem to stay away.

Cole leaned on the island, and a shadow of dark material peeked through the gap of her shirt. "Red or white?"

Lee stared. Her vision swam. She could have sworn there'd been lace. Was there lace? Her gaze traveled up Cole's neck and the jut of her strong chin to her sparkling eyes. They held a hint of mischief that made her inhale sharply. She was caught in a vortex. Turmoil one second, and a desire that burned so hot she was suffocating in the heat of it the next.

"Lee?" Cole tipped her head, a smile on her lips, her voice deep and taunting.

"Sorry. You pick."

"Giving me the reins, are you?" One perfect eyebrow lifted.

She'd been lost many times in her life, but never had she yearned to lose herself in another person as she did right now. Cole handed her a glass of red wine and she gulped a good amount, unable to find the words she wanted to say. She'd felt off-kilter since the door opened. No. If she were honest, she'd been off kilter since she'd first met Cole, and there was no denying she liked it. A lot. Cole headed out the back door, her small, tight ass wrapped in leather. Lee caught up with her as she leaned against the railing. Cole glanced sideways at her, her lips slowly closing over the edge of the glass before sipping.

"Take a walk with me." Cole stepped off the porch and strolled to the edge of the clearing where she looked out over the vast open space that sprawled beyond the hills. "Beautiful, isn't it?"

Lee gazed at Cole's profile in the backdrop of the setting sun. In that instant, she wondered what being with Cole for more than a night, or a week, or a lifetime would feel like. She turned away, afraid to imagine more than tonight, and took in the breathtaking vista in front of her. "I like how open it is."

"It is that. My family has been on this land for generations. I can't imagine being anywhere else." She continued to sip her wine, appearing content with the evening silence.

When Lee took the time to listen, she heard the symphony of night life playing, and it settled her. Owls hooted in the distance and birds sang. Crickets chirped. She remembered her bare feet in the grass and smiled. She glanced at Cole again, unsure what to do. She wanted to pull Cole against her, kiss her in this serene setting, and forget what she thought should matter. She'd been seeking respect and accolades for her hard-won accomplishments all her life. From the parents who never praised her to the women she'd dated who didn't want more. Hell, even from the boss who took what she'd worked so hard for. But in this moment, all she needed...all she wanted... was Cole. She imagined those lips on her neck, or breast, or clit, and it swelled to life. Cole's hands weren't elegant, but her fingers were long and tapered. They'd brought her to orgasm once. How would they play her body again if given a chance?

Cole finished her wine and turned back toward the house, unhurried. "I love how the summer rains make everything lush and vibrant, and the way the air currents shimmer across the ground, like uncut wheat." Cole leaned her hip against the rail. "What about you?"

Lee shook her head to clear it. She hadn't been paying attention to anything but the timbre of Cole's voice. "I like heat."

Cole set her empty glass down and moved so close the warmth from her body hit Lee in full force. How could she wear leather in eighty-degree weather? Cole slipped her arm around Lee's back, putting the barest distance between them.

"I'm glad to hear that." Cole smiled. "Shall we?"

Lee was lost. "What?" All she could think about was burying herself inside Cole.

"Have dinner." Cole ran her fingers down her chest before catching a nipple between them and giving a sharp, quick tug.

She arched in response to the pain and release as the fire zipped from her breast to her already swollen center. Cole was playing with her, but not the way Lee wanted, or where she wanted her to be. Her concentration had slipped from her hands like water from a duck's back, but she wasn't going to let Cole have all the fun. As Cole turned away, she caught her hand, yanked her back, pushed her against the wall, and pulled her hair to expose her neck. Cole's chest rose and fell rapidly. Lee dragged her teeth along the column of her throat. She fought the urge to bite where it would be visible, and nudged open Cole's shirt to bite her shoulder, hard and fast. Cole whimpered, and she followed with a soothing swipe of her tongue before walking inside like she wasn't on fire.

❖

Cole took a bite of lasagna, her eyes never wavering from Lee. Lee had been quiet, her gaze intense since their interplay on the porch. The sexual tension between them was like a tidal wave that started far out at sea, building in strength beneath the surface, until it crashed upon the shore, obliterating everything in its wake. She wanted to be that shore. "How old are you?" she asked.

"Old enough."

Her body came alive with an explosion of nerve endings firing off at the same time. The feel of Lee's lips on her skin, licking and nipping, came roaring to the forefront of her mind. Her eyes closed and a scene of the two of them dancing the dance of giving and taking played in a loop. Cole squeezed her thighs against her surging clit and allowed herself a minute of indulgence before she pushed the scene away and responded to Lee's inviting smile. "Yes, you are, but not too old."

"What difference does it make?" Lee grinned and took a bite of food. "I don't think age matters in most instances."

Whether consciously or not, Lee's bicep flexed as she reached for a piece of bread, and Cole wanted that strength focused on her. A change of topic was in order, otherwise she was going to sweep the food from the table in a moment of uncontrolled desire and pull Lee on top of her. Or under her. She couldn't be sure what she wanted more. All she knew was the hunger gnawing at her, and it had been that way for a while. "How's your girl running?"

"Purring like a kitten. You did more than fix the engine, didn't you?" Lee wiped her mouth and pushed her plate away.

She shrugged. "A tune-up and a bath."

Lee reached for her. "Don't downplay what you did, Cole." She rubbed the flesh between Cole's thumb and index finger. "I'll never forget your kindness."

Cole's breath caught. Why did Lee's words sound ominous? "I..." She stammered, her thoughts and fears tangled together. "You're welcome." Her throat was tight with emotion. She didn't want to think about the day she'd leave. It didn't have a place in her plans for tonight, and she refused to be sad while they were together celebrating Lee's birthday. At least she hoped Lee viewed their evening together as a celebration. She picked up their plates to avoid any deep thinking. She didn't want to consider tomorrow. They moved around in the kitchen together as though they'd been doing so for years. Another dance. Another memory in the making.

"I think we should have a drink of that fine bourbon you brought."

"I'm up for that." Lee leaned against the counter, ankles crossed, her dark jeans tight along her thighs. "Why are you so nervous tonight?"

She ran her hand through her hair. Lee could already read her so well. She considered lying, but that wasn't who she was, and definitely wasn't who she wanted to be around Lee.

"That night you saw the camisole, did you really like it?" She averted her gaze and chewed the inside of her cheek.

"Absolutely." Lee leaned closer to make eye contact. "Why?"

She could do this. "Because I liked how you looked at me and I want you to want me...want you to fuck me, even though there's parts of my personality I don't show others."

Lee's eyes softened before she closed the distance, not letting her escape. "Hey. You can show me anything." She cupped her nape, pulled her closer. "Don't you already know how bad I want you?"

She laughed, as much from nerves as from insecurity, a rare occurrence. "Your eyes do give you away." She brushed Lee's long bangs off her forehead. "I want you, too, but there are some things you should know before we go any further."

Lee leaned her forehead on Cole's. "We're going to have 'the talk' first, aren't we?"

Cole swallowed hard, tried to smile. "We are, and I really do need that drink." She handed Lee two tumblers.

"Ice?" Lee asked.

"Not unless you want to ruin a good whiskey."

"No ice, then." Lee grabbed the bottle and headed out onto the side porch. She settled on the glider, broke the seal, and poured equal amounts before turning to face her. "Okay, you have my full attention."

Cole swirled the contents and peered at the legs that clung to the glass. She downed half and took a breath. "I grew up a tomboy. Dirt and grime followed me wherever I went. My father said I reminded him of himself at my age, always tinkering and fascinated by how things worked. When I was twelve, I realized even though I'd rather play with the boys, I was drawn to girls."

"That's when you knew you were a lesbian?" Lee asked, gently pushing the glider as they talked.

"I think so. I mean, kids I hung with seemed to know more than I did at the time, but we were all pretty close and no one said anything." The memory of her first kiss made her smile and long for a return to those simple days when nothing she did had serious consequences. "I'd been working with my dad in the garage by then, and the people in town were used to seeing me in overalls and grease, so when I became a teenager and dressed more like the boys than the girls, no one was surprised." She drew in a sharp breath. Her father's absence in her life had become second nature over the years except at times like these when her resilience waned and she wished he was still there, encouraging her to go on. *You've got this, Cole.* That's what he'd say, and she let the words buoy her.

"Junior year was tough. I...I don't know. I guess I was trying to figure out if the person on the outside matched the person on the inside. I decided to go to the prom and my cousin, Michael, agreed to take me. I went shopping thinking I'd find a nice tux or suit to wear. Instead, I found a dress. Not super frilly or feminine, but when I tried it on it felt good on my body and I got it." She was so excited the night of the dance; she was all thumbs, and her father helped her with the clasps and buttons. "I was a bit anxious of course. I'd never let on there was a softer side to me, but Michael was the perfect escort." She finished her drink. Lee must have seen something in her face because she lifted the bottle and poured more into her glass.

"I take it things didn't go as you thought they would?" Lee sipped her bourbon.

Understanding had replaced the earlier fire in her gaze, and Cole wished the fire would return. "It started out fine. At seventeen and naive about a lot of the way the world worked, I didn't yet know anything about how cruel it could be. Then the pointing and snide remarks started. I ignored them as long as I could. Michael and I danced for a bit, until one of the jocks asked him why he'd brought a dyke to the dance. He would have defended me, and I loved him for that, but it wasn't his fight. It was mine." She swallowed her pain. "But my courage vanished, and I ran."

Lee set her glass down and took Cole's, then pulled her back against her hard body. "I know all about running."

She nestled against her, glad Lee couldn't see her face as her lips touched her neck, kissed the pulse point pounding there.

"That one event solidified the woman you are today, Cole. The strong, kind, giving woman I know. If you're still looking for that young girl, I'll try to help you find her."

It was a nice thought. Not that she doubted Lee would help, but that she'd be around for the long haul. But that was on her and not Lee. She smiled, though it felt forced. "I got over that night pretty quick. I figured girly stuff wasn't for me, and I let myself get boxed into an identity, in being what people expected. But I don't want to be in that box anymore. I just want to be...me. I want to be hard and soft, and greasy and sweet, and sometimes I want to wear boots and sometimes I want to wear sandals. But when I've tried to break out of that cage with other women, they've shot me down." She was touched by what Lee was offering because she'd never had the opportunity to explore with anyone in an intimate, sexy way. She had to be sure Lee understood there were times when the two became blurred and she may present herself in unexpected ways. Lee's nimble fingers began to unbutton her shirt and she stiffened.

"It's okay," Lee said, as she traced the shell of her ear with her tongue and nipped at her neck. "I want to see what you've hidden from others."

Cole shivered against the mix of heat and cold on her skin. Lee's warm hands smoothed over her ribs before cupping her breasts. Her thumbs rubbed her nipples through the lace, and she moaned.

"So fucking sexy." Lee moved to the corded muscle on the side of her neck, skimmed her teeth along it, then smothered her in a searing kiss. "I want you so much. I want to touch you. Can I?" Lee's breath was hot on her skin and her breathing labored.

Her pulse raced. "God, yes."

Lee lowered her zipper and slowly worked her leather pants off before she leaned against her again. Lee's nipples were diamond points against her back. Knowing Lee was turned on as much as she was brought a wave of lightheadedness, and Cole closed her eyes.

"You should wear lace whenever you want. You're beautiful."

She sucked in a breath. Had anyone ever called her beautiful? Some women said she was handsome, but that wasn't the same. She wanted to be both. Cole turned her head and Lee's mouth found hers again. The kiss quickly turned smoldering and her tongue sought Lee's. When Lee's fingers traced the edge of her thong, then slipped beneath the fabric, her body surged.

"I want to make you come, baby."

She whimpered as Lee's fingertip traced her swollen clit. Cole was so close to climaxing already, she tried to back away from the touch.

"Let me, Cole. Let me." Lee lifted her breast from the cup and teased the tender point into an even harder knot.

She hooked her arm around Lee's neck and brought her down for a passionate kiss as Lee continued to stroke her slow and steady, with just enough pressure to make her crazy. "Harder," she gasped, her body chasing release. She moved onto Lee's lap for greater access, and Lee sank her long, strong fingers inside, filling the emptiness in her heart. Realizing she was lonely took her by surprise.

Lee cupped the back of her head. "I want to watch you come." She alternated between circling her tight bundle of nerves and entering her deeper and harder with each stroke. "Keep your eyes open, love. Let me see all of you."

Cole's body went rigid before she tumbled over the edge of the precipice, soaring so high on the current of her climax she feared she'd die when she landed. She need not have worried. Lee continued to murmur to her, telling her how magnificent she was and how grateful she was to be trusted with such a precious gift. As her body calmed, Lee turned her, kissed her softly, then carried her inside.

CHAPTER SIXTEEN

Lee took Cole into the den. She was lured by the solidness of her body and lost in the softness of her surrender. She cradled her close as she wrapped one of the quilts around her. Cole had come so hard the beauty of the moment moved her to tears, but she hadn't let Cole see her cry. She hadn't wanted to spoil whatever affirmation she'd found in the moment they shared.

As Cole dozed with her head nestled on her shoulder, Lee again questioned what she was doing. It had been plain from the start of the night that Cole had opened herself to more than sex. She was honored that Colt trusted her enough to show herself without being judged. Lee had to admit that whatever Cole did for her own comfort and pleasure, she wanted to be there for it. She inwardly sighed. She shouldn't have told her as much when she had no idea what next week or next month would bring, let alone tomorrow. Certainly, if she had a job prospect, she'd take it without thinking twice, wouldn't she? Cole mumbled something unintelligible before lifting her head.

"Wow," Cole whispered. She slowly sat up, her bra and thong still on, albeit a little askew.

She smiled as she brushed a few strands of hair out of Cole's eyes. "I think so, too."

Cole managed to straddle her lap, then held her face and kissed her hard. "Did you slip me a Mickey?"

Laughing, Lee rubbed her hands along Cole's sides and around to squeeze her firm ass. "One thing I'd never do. I like you aware of what's going on when we're together." She nipped at Cole's mouth.

"I was doing pretty well until I exploded in your hand." Cole glanced down and her face colored. Her hands moved to cover herself.

"Don't, baby. Why do you want to hide?"

Cole shook her head. "I don't know if I want to be in lingerie anymore. Sometimes it doesn't feel quite right. I guess it's an in the moment kind of thing."

"Simple enough," she said as she removed Cole's bra, peeled off her own outer shirt and took her tank top off, then slid it over Cole's head. "It's a little big, but how's that?"

Cole's shoulders visibly relaxed. "Better." Cole bent to suck one nipple, then the other. Lee moaned. "Much better."

Lee shivered at the intense pleasure. Her body was primed, and it wouldn't take much to set her off. "Good." She slid her hands down Cole's bare arms.

"Can we move to my bedroom?" Cole traced her lips with her tongue.

Her mind and body were in conflict. She wanted Cole again, understanding Cole might be more comfortable directing what happened next, and how. She'd help her find her fulcrum however she could. Lee stood and set Cole gently on her feet, then took her hand and waited.

"There's so many things I want to do *to* you and for you," Cole said, tracing her cheekbone. "I crave your muscles moving against mine. I want to feel your full, soft breasts and the weight of them." Cole kissed her fleetingly. "I want to please you in a way I've never needed to with anyone else."

She smiled and covered her inner turmoil with a breath-steeling kiss. This thing between them was terrifying, and she should put a stop to it. But with Cole's body pressed to hers, she couldn't fathom stepping away. But what was it going to cost in the long run? Who was going to pay the ultimate price?

As Cole stared into Lee's eyes it hit her. Lee was quickly becoming so much more to her than someone satisfying the need that had been hammering at her insides for the past few months.

She wouldn't—couldn't—deny the sexual attraction that continued to grow since that first day, the first touch, and even more so while getting to know Lee's character.

This connection between them brought the word caring to a whole different level. For her, it was intense and consuming. As amazing as it was to finally be able to enjoy letting go to reveal all of herself, she worried about the end result. The more she let Lee learn about her life, her fears, and her dreams, the more she was left questioning what effect Lee's leaving, if or when it happened, would have on her.

Cole understood what she had to do. Tonight was her chance to show Lee what being on the receiving end of caring meant. Because like it or not, she cared about Lee. She didn't think Lee had many people in her life who cared about her or for her, and she deserved feeling like she mattered. That *she* was special.

She pulled Lee along, making a quick detour to the kitchen for drinks, then up the wide well-worn staircase. Once through the door, she closed it and backed Lee against the solid surface of the bed, stepped into her space, and pressed her thigh between her legs. Lee inhaled sharply and groaned.

"Being in lace worked for a while, but this…" Cole gestured to the tank top she wore. "Is me most of the time," she said, her lips close to Lee's ear as she pressed harder, driving her muscle against Lee's center.

"Okay by me." Lee moaned as she tugged at her lobe with her teeth. "God, I hope you're going to touch me soon. I've been hard all day thinking about you."

Cole moved her lips over Lee's jaw and down her throat to one of her nipples. She blew across the surface before running her tongue over the point and pulled with her teeth. Lee grabbed her hips.

"A little mercy would be good, babe."

Lee's pelvis surged forward when she bit down, and Lee countered by biting her shoulder hard enough for her excitement to coat her thighs through the flimsy thong. She'd never met a woman whose passion and desire matched hers.

"What are you doing to me?" Lee asked with a shaky voice as she leaned back on her hands.

"I'm giving you the rest of your birthday present," she said as she sucked the tender flesh at the hollow of her throat.

Lee groaned and Cole felt the muscles of her belly tightened. She lifted her knee higher and pressed the seam of Lee's jeans against her clit, swearing she could feel it grow, then leaned away. "Unless you don't want it."

"Fuck, yes, I want it." Lee roughly kissed her. "You have me so turned on."

"That's good." She pressed her tongue inside Lee's mouth, exploring. Her nipples became painful points. They were both gasping when she broke away. She dropped to her knees and removed Lee's shoes. "Get all the way on the bed." Lee's breasts were heavy in Cole's hands, and when she thumbed her prominent peaks, Lee's hips jerked in response.

"I need to feel all of you against me." Lee's voice was tight.

Cole moved lower and placed her lips to Lee's trembling stomach, before pressing her thumbs on either side of her zipper.

"Christ. I'm not going to last."

"Do you like that?" She manipulated the metal grommet, pulled the zipper down, and slipped her fingers inside.

"Yes. No. Cole…" Lee's clit surged. "I'm going to come."

Cole wanted Lee to surrender to her. Not just her body, but to the possibilities of more than sex. That's what she really wanted. Somehow Cole needed to convey her dreams and desires of a life with Lee by her side. Her breath hitched. She couldn't go there right now. She slid her hand under the edge of Lee's boi shorts and pressed hard on her abdomen. "Wait for my touch. Can you do that for me?" Cole watched Lee's eyes darken as she fought for control. "Just a little longer. I want to enjoy you being so turned on and ready to explode." She had been playing with her own comfort zone, but she knew exactly how she wanted to play Lee's body. Cole peeled away the rest of her clothes and settled between Lee's thighs. "I want you." Her voice was deep with desire. Lee's face contorted, evidence of her losing battle, and when Cole kissed the inside of her thigh, Lee cried out.

"Please, please."

She held Lee's thighs open and made first contact by cradling her throbbing clit between her lips, Lee pressed into her and she imagined hot summer days and heated nights spent in the throes of passion in the months ahead. If only she had the power to help Lee realize how good they were together. Not just in bed, but in all the ways that mattered. Cole knew Lee was afraid she'd lose something of herself in the process. How could she blame her? Hadn't she lost a part of herself based on the actions of another? There was nothing to be done but to give Lee what she needed right now. The rest could wait until the time was right.

Cole slowly circled the shaft with her tongue, and Lee shuttered beneath her, writhing and rising up with the force of her orgasm, calling her name over and over again. Her heart swelled every time Lee dropped her walls and let her in. Maybe the next time Lee would willingly let them fall.

CHAPTER SEVENTEEN

Lee blinked several times. Bright sunshine fell across the foot of the bed, and she rubbed her eyes to dispel the last vestiges of sleep. Cole wasn't beside her as she replayed flashes of their night together.

God. She'd come so hard, like she'd shattered into a million shards of sharp glass, each one adding to the pain/pleasure threshold she tumbled over again and again. Cole's strong hands had held her hips as she drank her essence, milking her until she was empty before her world faded away. Funny, she hadn't even cared. All she'd wanted was the bliss to go on forever.

She ran her hand over her chest and down her center, not wanting to touch herself and be robbed of the lingering image of Cole between her legs and looking along her body with lust-filled eyes. Then Cole over her, thrusting against her and into her, taking every drop she had to give. None of her previous lovers had driven her so high for so long and, if they had, they wouldn't have been there to catch her when she tumbled into the abyss of pure pleasure.

Between mind-blowing orgasms, Lee managed to give pleasure to Cole too. Cole had the upper hand in directing what happened, and she'd enjoyed every minute. Where had this small-town gal learned her skills? Cole had definitely turned her upside down in the process. Still, even now, when her center was sore and she wasn't able to move, Lee wanted her. It was a craving she wasn't sure how to handle since she'd always been able to walk away before and keep sex casual. This thing with Cole definitely wasn't that.

"Look who's finally showing signs of life," Cole said as she pushed open the door and carried in a large tray, setting it on the end of the bed. "Hungry?" She held out a steaming cup of coffee.

Somehow, she managed to sit up. "Starved." Lee took a tentative sip and made a sound of pure pleasure. Cole's coffee was dark, rich, and smooth. "You're a lifesaver."

Cole tossed her silk robe onto the side chair, giving her a glimpse of the athletic boxer briefs she wore before climbing in beside her and pulling the tray closer.

"Thanks, but you're not drowning, are you?" Cole smiled.

She almost said she was drowning in attraction, or something else entirely, but it was too early for true confessions and something she didn't care to engage in. "Nope. Right as rain."

Handing her a cloth napkin and a fork, Cole placed the tray between them. "Coffee and food, then."

"Looks like you've had practice doing this," she said. The idea of Cole taking care of another woman the way she was taking care of her right now rubbed a sore spot.

Cole rearranged the plates. "Not really." She eventually looked up. "You're the first woman I've had in my bedroom." She tried to sound casual about it, but Lee could tell there wasn't anything casual behind its meaning.

Lee took a bite of toast and chewed. She didn't want to pry. She knew what being on the receiving end felt like, so she went in a safer direction. "I kinda like that I'm the first, but I'm not sure what you want in return."

"Your friendship, definitely." Cole sat back and ran her hand through her hair, looking deep in thought as she sipped. "For what seems like forever, I've tried to please others. Do what I thought was the right thing…the expected thing."

She turned to fully face her. "And now?" she asked, not sure if she wanted to hear the answer.

Cole's face grew serious. "I'm not getting any younger, and soon I'll be without close family. I don't want to be alone for the rest of my life."

Thinking about the choices she'd made, Lee wondered if she should have tried to salvage her relationship with her parents. It was way too late for that, wasn't it? Cole had never mentioned her mother. What little she'd learned had come from Dan. "What about your mother? Do you talk to her?"

Cole set her mug down. "I asked my father about her a couple of years after she left with my sister." She glanced away. "We'd never been close. Not like other mothers and daughters I knew. At first, I thought she'd left because of me. I wasn't ever a well-behaved little girl in frilly dresses she could parade around town and be proud of." Cole's smile didn't reach her eyes. "I think she was disappointed I was rough-and-tumble from the start."

In the silence that followed, she fought the urge to reach for Cole, her pain clearly raw, but she wasn't sure her touch would be welcome.

"He didn't say much except they wanted different things. Nana told me what happened in that no-nonsense way she has." Cole shared a genuine, if tentative, smile then. "Anyway, it's water under the bridge, as they say."

"I'm sorry." Whatever the Jacksons had or didn't have, she understood how important family was to Cole and the legacy she wanted to pass on.

"I was mostly okay with her leaving. My father though…I think his heart was in pieces. I was never sure if it was because he loved her so much or because he discovered the real reason she'd married him, or something else entirely. I never heard from her, but I did sometimes think about her, and my sister."

She moved the tray out of the way, wrapped her arms around Cole, and pulled her close. "I really am sorry." Lee might not know what a real family looked like, but she understood loss.

Cole rested her head on her shoulder. "Family has always meant everything to my dad and my grandparents. I'm the same way." Cole took her hand and pressed her lips to her palm.

Lee swallowed around the lump in her throat. Her whole life, she'd felt like a disappointment to the people around her, especially the ones wanting to get close. Cole was going to be another person on that list. Though tears threatened, she had to be honest with Cole. "That's where we're different. I don't know what family feels like." She'd tried to imagine it since meeting Cole, but she just didn't know how.

Cole put some space between them. "There are no more Jacksons after me. I want—need—family. I want more in my life than grease and coming home to an empty house."

Sadness washed over her, drowning Lee in a need she couldn't get on board with. "We're not on the same page. I have no idea about tomorrow, let alone the future."

The wry grin on Cole's face couldn't have been clearer. "I know. I just wanted to tell you where my head is because I like you, and…" Cole shrugged.

"I like you, too. We're friends. No matter what happens, I hope we stay friends." She brushed her fingers over Cole's cheek.

Cole looked lost in thought, a small smile appeared. "Shower with me?"

Lee took a breath. "You know how dangerous that is, right?"

"Why? Are you going to go psycho on me?" Cole laughed, the sound breaking the tension that hung between them.

"Not like that." She rolled her eyes.

Cole scooted off the bed, dropped her boxers, and waited. "I promise not to hold anything against you."

It might not have been the smartest move, but nothing she did with Cole made sense. Cole's body was a beacon in the darkness that surrounded her. As long as they both understood that their relationship wouldn't go any further, what was the harm in a little slip and slide before she left?

Cole walked Lee to her truck. "Thanks for indulging me last night." She ran her fingertips through Lee's damp strands and continued down her arm, liking the way the muscle twitched under her touch. "And for this morning."

Lee held her hand. "It wasn't a hardship," she said, gently squeezing. "Thank you for a great birthday." Her lower lip trembled. "I'm sorry I—"

"No. Don't be sorry for being honest. I'd rather that than the alternative."

"You mean getting your hopes up?" Lee leaned against her truck, seemingly in no hurry to leave.

She moved beside her, their shoulders touching, fingers entwined. "Expectation leads to disappointment. I'd never push what I want onto anyone else. Especially not my friend." Cole gently shoved her shoulder and smiled before facing Lee again. She kissed her with slow, deliberate care. "Have a good day."

"You, too." Lee got in her truck. "I'll call you tonight." She swung the truck around and crept down the road while waving out the window.

Cole stood with her hands shoved in her pockets for a long time after. What was she doing? She'd known from the beginning Lee was skittish, but she'd been unable to heed the inner voice and had gone with her gut instead. It had never let her down before. Then again, she'd never encountered anyone like Lee before. Beautiful, independent, intelligent, and sexier than any woman she'd had the pleasure to bed.

Shaking her head, Cole went into the house and climbed the stairs. In her bedroom, Lee's familiar scent conjured up snippets of their time together while Cole pulled off the rumpled sheets. As she put fresh ones on, a rush of emotion brought her to her knees. She had to hang on to a tiny bit of hope that Lee might reconsider and stay. *Foolish.* That's what she was, and she knew it, but still…

CHAPTER EIGHTEEN

"What are you doing?" Cole asked.

Lee could hear an engine running in the background. "I'm heading up to Eagle Bay to do a small job. What's up?" She'd gotten a few hits from her ad, as well as by word of mouth. She suspected Cole had been one of those mouths. Thinking about Cole's mouth sent a shiver of pleasure through her and made her fingers tingle.

"I forgot to tell you Nana wants you to join us for dinner Sunday. She said to make sure you extend the invitation to Dan."

"Uh...I'm not sure." That was a pathetic response. "Why would she invite us?" All she could remember was the conversation of a gun, especially since Cole didn't refute her grandmother had one.

"Lee," Cole said softly. "It's the way we are. Neighborly, with a genuine interest in getting to know someone."

"Sorry. I don't know what's wrong with me."

"No strings, if that's what you're afraid of."

God, she was fucking this up. Whatever *this* was. She still wasn't sure. "No. Damnit, Cole. That's not what I meant." She heard Cole take a breath.

"It's okay. Come to dinner. Otherwise, I'll never hear the end of it from Nana."

She could picture it now. The petite spunky woman wagging her finger at Cole and not taking no for an answer. "I imagine so." Lee ran her hand down her face. There wasn't a good reason to say no. "Okay, and I'll ask Uncle Dan. What time?"

She and Cole talked a few more minutes before hanging up. The morning hadn't been as awkward as she'd thought it might be following their chat. In fact, when she'd left Cole standing there, the absence of remorse had reassured her how important it was they understood each other. The good-bye kiss had curled her toes and she'd almost stayed, but she couldn't continue to give mixed messages or make promises she couldn't keep.

Lee was oddly pleased by the invitation. *A family meal.* Lee slammed on the brakes and quickly checked her rearview mirror. Christ. She took a minute to argue with herself. No need to panic. It was just a gathering of friends. She and Cole were friends, and Dan knew both Cole and Betty on a long-term basis. Yes, friends. She could use that argument for the time being.

"Okay, okay. I've got this," she said to the otherwise empty cab. Lee turned the radio up and concentrated on the road ahead of her. She wouldn't let a sudden case of nerves ruin what she and Cole clearly understood.

The next day, Lee rubbed her hands along her thighs. "Do you think this is okay for a Sunday dinner?" She'd changed four times until Dan had insisted they had to go or be late. She had a feeling being late to Betty's wouldn't be viewed kindly and she'd hustled out the door after a spitz of cologne.

"She's not as tough as you think." Dan eyed her while they waited for the light to change.

"Cole?"

Dan chuckled. "No, Betty."

She laughed. "Cole told me her bark was fierce and so was her heart." Lee shrugged. Hearts were funny things and hard to read. She was used to dealing with barks.

"That's for sure." Dan tapped his knuckle on the steering wheel.

"What?"

He cleared his throat. "Nothing. Just…should I take this as a good thing between you two?"

How could she share what was going on? Hell, no matter what they'd talked about by agreeing to say their friendship was special, all she did was think of Cole. If she wasn't careful, she'd walk away from one more person she was connected to. Deep connections always led to pain. Keeping it light was her survival plan. "We're friends. More really, but we've agreed that's all we can be. Once I find permanent work I'll be leaving, and I don't want either of us to be hurt by the inevitable." Even as she said the words out loud the picture of life with Cole played in her head. Did a few sexual encounters define a relationship? She'd had repeat partners before. They were casual and fun. Nothing more. It could be nothing more this time, too.

Dan pulled onto the dirt road and maneuvered the car slowly until they were parked alongside Cole's truck. Before getting out, he turned to her. "At some point you might want more. Just don't analyze it so much you don't enjoy it, okay?"

"Yeah."

"Good."

He got out and retrieved jars of homemade relish from the back seat while Lee grabbed the bottles of wine. She wished she had some of that bourbon Cole liked.

Betty's house was a much smaller version of Cole's, but the wraparound porch was the same. Dan knocked on the door and she took a breath. *Just dinner.*

The door opened and Cole's bright smile greeted them. Her dark, boot-cut jeans hugged her slender figure, and the crisp checkered shirt brought out flecks of gold in her eyes Lee hadn't noticed before. She was beautiful, and handsome, and sexy, and...*fuck.*

"Hi." Cole stepped back and waved them in. "Nana's in the kitchen. Go on in and say hello."

Lee followed Dan in. Cole closed the door and leaned closer. "It's good to see you."

The warmth of Cole's breath sent gooseflesh over her chest and down her arms. She spun and held out the bottles. "Wine."

Cole shared a lopsided grin. "I see that. Would you like a glass, or should I just open it and stick a straw in it?"

It took her a minute to get with the program, but when she did her shoulders lowered and she returned the smile. "A glass with a straw would be good." She leaned in and brushed her lips over Cole's cheek, unsure if she should do more, considering where they stood.

"You better go say hello or Nana will think we disappeared to have sex."

Mortified, she quickly remembered not all families were against their children, or grandchildren, being gay. "Funny." She followed the voices and when she turned into the kitchen, it was as if she'd stepped back in time.

A six-burner white Tappan stove with side-by-side ovens served as the centerpiece of the wall facing her. The pristine farmhouse sink was below a multipaned window that looked out on rolling hills dotted with elm and maple trees. Open shelves flanked the window and held an array of mismatched serving plates, dishes, pitchers, and bowls. The kitchen table was chrome and Formica, the wingback chairs thickly padded and covered in blue checks and tiny red flowers. Betty leaned against a counter wearing a faded bib apron, and Lee wondered how many family meals had been prepared while she wore it. Dan sat at the table, the scent of strong coffee wafting between him and where she stood. Betty uncrossed her arms and moved toward her.

"Lee, glad you could grace us with your presence."

Heat traveled up her neck and landed squarely in her cheeks.

"Nana." Cole's warning tone was clearly in jest.

Betty launched at Lee so quickly she had just enough time to brace herself for one of the best hugs she'd ever received. She gently pulled back and Betty winked at her. "She knows I'm kidding. I didn't threaten to shoot her, so we're good."

Cole handed her a glass of wine. One she desperately needed. She mouthed her thanks, and after a swallow, she turned to Betty. "I love your kitchen." Authentic anything was hard to find in the city IKEA built.

"Thanks, but the design is all Cole's doing."

She glanced at Cole who shrugged and sipped from her own glass. She shouldn't be surprised after seeing Cole's home. The mix of eclectic and retro suited Cole's personality, and she imagined Cole had tapped into her grandmother's sense of tradition for the kitchen.

"There was a small fire in here a few years back, and Nana was so upset her beloved kitchen was ruined. I sketched the design and Michael did the work. It's almost a perfect replica of the original."

"Better," Betty said, beaming at Cole.

The love for her granddaughter was obvious, and Lee pushed away the stab of envy for what she's never had and would never know.

Cole kissed her grandmother's cheek. "That's enough bragging, Nana."

Betty harrumphed. "Just like your father, never wanting praise," she said as she stirred something on the stove. "You two set the table while Dan and I look over the garden."

Once they disappeared out the back door, Lee grabbed Cole's arm. "I don't know how to be."

Cole lifted a stack of dinner plates from a built-in hutch. "What do you mean?" She handed the stack to her. "Just be yourself."

"I never know when she's kidding."

A smile spread across Cole's face. "Trust me, you'll know when she isn't."

They set the table together. Everything was fine until Cole's hip brushed her thigh and the need for Cole's touch, and tongue, and body, came back in vivid relief. If it had all been film clips of sexual instances, she'd chalk it up to her libido and ongoing need for release. Instead, there were also many of her and Cole talking, laughing. Of being quiet together and saying things without words. More than her body was involved when it came to Cole and she pushed the notion of a much deeper meaning away, afraid she'd have to acknowledge what her heart was telling her.

Cole's hands rested on her hips. "Are you okay?"

She didn't want to lie. No matter how terrified she was of the indications she refused to face, she would be honest with her. "I'm nervous." She hadn't meant to offer a half-truth but hoped it would be enough, at least for now.

"No need. She already knows we've slept together."

"Oh, God." Lee covered her face with her hands. "Not helping," she mumbled.

Cole laughed, pulling her hands away. "Come on. Let's call them to the table. Food will give you something else to think about."

"Like I'm going to be able to eat knowing your grandmother knows we've…" She didn't even want to consider how much Betty knew, or guessed, and she wasn't sure which was worse.

"If you don't want an inquisition, you'd do well to show up at the table with a hearty appetite. We can always go back to my place after dinner for a stiff one."

Great. Now all she'd be thinking about was fucking Cole. Not a horrible thought at all, but she couldn't get lost in fantasies while sitting across from Betty. Dan followed Betty inside, winked at her, and then they all helped move massive amounts of food to the table. Once dishes were passed and the room grew quiet, Betty watched her from the head of the table, reminding her of a matriarch among her people.

"Cole tells me you came from Atlantic City."

Lee chewed and swallowed. "Yes, ma'am." She wasn't sure where the conversation was going, and she glanced at Cole nervously. Cole's warm hand slid to her knee and squeezed.

"Bet you're bored stiff in our little town."

"It's definitely a change, but I'm not bored. I've found ways to keep busy."

Cole cleared her throat and smiled.

"I like a go-getter. Cole's the same way, but she takes time to slow down and appreciate things, too. I hope you do the same."

Betty's words were plain enough, but she had the feeling there was a whole underlying network of meaning, and she desperately wanted to figure it out. Dan was quietly taking in the exchange with the corner of his mouth twitching as though he wanted to smile but didn't dare. She hadn't really slowed down since she'd moved out of her parents' house. She'd never felt the need. Before Inlet, that is.

"I'll try to remember that, ma'am."

"I hear there's going to be a bumper crop of apples this year, Betty. What's in store for your kitchen?" Dan asked.

She took a breath, thankful the spotlight was no longer on her. Cole's hand moved higher on her leg and the heat of it spread to between her thighs. Lee glanced at her and Cole's warm smile calmed her nerves and heighted her desire.

With dinner leftovers stored away, she and Cole did the dishes together. Hot glances between them stoked the fire already burning in her belly. Cole hadn't said anything about coming home with her when they'd talked, but she'd packed a bag just in case. As she watched Cole lift heavy dishes onto shelves and put plates into cupboards, the corded muscles that flexed under her smooth skin made her yearn for those muscles to be flexing over her. More than that, there was a feeling of comfortable cohabitation about the way they moved together that made her smile. Was this what a real relationship, one that included more than just getting off, could be like? So different from the one her parents had? They'd existed in the same location, but they were hardly together. Could passion coexist with day-to-day life? She'd never wanted anything like that before, but in this moment—

"Lee?"

Jarred out of her fantasy, she looked at Cole and caught the knowing shimmer of mischief in her eyes. "Sorry. What were you saying?"

"Can you carry this in for me?" A large tray laden with a service of coffee and fixings was ready to go.

"Sure." She tossed her towel on the counter and picked up the tray. How long had she been lost in the idea of things she'd never dared to dream of? Lee set the tray down near the center of the table.

"Ah, here we go," Betty said as she rubbed her hands together. "Nothing like a cup of coffee to finish off a meal."

"And a wonderful meal it was, Betty. I'd forgotten about your kitchen talents. I try, but I'll never master your finesse with comfort food."

Betty smiled and laughed as Lee poured. "Thanks, Dan. I love to cook. Sometimes my hands don't cooperate like they used to, but I manage."

Cole swept in and placed a double layered cake on the table near Lee, then kissed her grandmother's cheek. "You've still got it, Nana."

Sunday dinner with Lee's family had never been this relaxed. She'd always felt buffeted by tension and was basically ignored by both her parents, though her mother would occasionally glance at her and smile tightly. How had her father managed to instill such stifling obedience in her mother? What had he done to keep her from defending her own daughter when he had berated her at every turn? Clearly, Betty's love for Cole would lead to her stepping in if Cole was ever threatened, emotionally or otherwise. Where was that kind of love in Lee's life? Tears began to swell, and she rapidly blinked them away.

Cole produced a single candle and lit it with a taper. Everyone was smiling at her and when they began to sing the Happy Birthday song, she was overcome by the caring that embraced her. The last birthday cake she'd had was as a ten-year-old girl. This celebration meant more to her than any other. When the small group clapped and told her to make a wish, Lee struggled. What did she want more than anything else? When she looked at Cole, she dared to wish for a lifetime of feeling cared for. Lee took a breath and held it while she let the silent words form in her head, and as she blew out her candle, she sent them into the universe.

"Thank you." She smiled. "You do know I'm older than one, though." Everyone laughed at her joke. As the candle was removed, Cole handed her a knife and a stack of plates.

"It's just a number, Lee. It's how your heart feels that matters." Cole took the plate containing the first piece and put it in front of her place at the table. "I hope your heart stays young forever."

The tears clouded her vision, and she blindly set the knife down before escaping outside. On her way, she heard Dan telling Betty and Cole she'd had a rough time of late. The voices faded as she made it out the screen door and stumbled to the end of the porch. She didn't want to cry. Not again, and not in front of Betty. How could something that made her feel so good, make her so sad?

Cole focused on the empty chair. Lee's abrupt departure tore at her heart.

"She's had a rough time for years, actually." Dan said, pursing his lips. "She's been on her own since she was a teenager. Her parents... well, let's just say they never should have had a baby if they weren't going to love her."

Her grandmother took her hand and squeezed. "Go check on her."

Lee must have heard her footsteps and she stiffened. Cole put her hand on Lee's shoulder, and she shuddered at the touch. "You don't have to say anything."

She rubbed Lee's back in a soothing motion, and Lee leaned into it, allowing the comfort she clearly needed, and then finally turned into her embrace. She tried to imagine what it would feel like to think you were an unwanted nuisance to your parents. Even though her mother had been somewhat cross with her, she'd never been cruel or indifferent. Lee cried on her shoulder, and all Cole wanted to do was shelter her and take away her pain. She held her tight, not knowing what else to do. "I've got you."

After a few minutes, Lee stepped away and swiped her tears roughly away. "Why, Cole? Why do you care?"

She thumbed away the last of Lee's tears. "Because you're special and you deserve to know that." Cole took her hand pulled her down onto the love seat.

"You make me want too much." Lee wrapped her arms around herself like she was trying to keep from flying apart.

Cole rubbed her thumb over Lee's bottom lip. "There's no such thing as too much." Her gaze flicked from Lee's eyes to her mouth and back again. With her chin in her hand, Cole guided her forward until their lips met. She teased them apart with her tongue and soaked in the soft, wet heat of Lee's mouth. Lee moaned before breaking away. God. The feeling of something real was so close to the surface, she could feel it under her skin. As much as her insides ached every time Lee walked away, her heart beat just as hard the next time they were together, maybe more so. There was no reason to hold on to hope. No reason to pursue what fate had already determined wasn't going to happen. Try as she might, this thing with Lee wouldn't go away, and Cole wasn't ready to give up.

"We have to stop. We have elders inside." Lee's chest heaved.

Laughing, Cole reluctantly let her hand fall away. "You're sweet. Come home with me tonight?"

Lee made a face. "Oh, great. Not like they won't figure out what's going on there."

She stood and pulled Lee to her. She couldn't resist sliding her thigh between Lee's. "Does it matter?"

"Cole—"

Cole pressed her fingers to Lee's lips, guessing she was going to protest against the wisdom of chasing a fantasy. Lee wasn't a fantasy. She was a living, breathing, sensual soul and she wouldn't walk away. She'd given up enough of her desires and dreams already.

"You make saying no impossible." Lee grinned.

"Let's go have cake." *Sometimes you* can *have your cake and eat it, too.*

CHAPTER NINETEEN

When they'd finally made it back to Cole's place, the frenzy of lust had propelled them straight to the bedroom, and they'd hardly come up for air between deep, breath-stealing kisses and frantic touches, then coming in a torrent of shouts and moans without even being fully undressed yet. Lee nuzzled Cole's neck, rubbing her face over her smooth skin. "You're amazing." She slipped her finger inside the edge of Cole's boi shorts. "I want you again." Her lips met Cole's and moved over them until she couldn't hold back. "I want to taste you. Be inside you. Please tell me that's okay." Her blood ran like molten lava.

"Do whatever you want. If I don't like it, I'll be sure to let you know." Cole dug her fingers into the flesh of her ass, driving her against her center.

She rolled them over, kissed Cole's neck, and pressed her knee to the vee between her thighs, making her arch into her. "I like you this way, too. Your passion comes through every time we're together, no matter what you're wearing. Everything about you drives me crazy." Tonight, Cole wore undergarments similar to her own. The sports bra had to go. Lee discarded her own, and Cole sat up to do the same, revealing her small, high breasts and deep rosy nipples. "I love your body."

Cole laughed. "I always thought mine was too wiry and muscled, but yours puts mine to shame."

"I think your body is perfect for you and you should love it as much as I do."

Cole had a runner's body, lithe and lean in all the right places. Lee clamped down on her throat, then sucked along the pulse point and pulled the flesh between her teeth until Cole shivered beneath her. She needed to touch her more than she could remember needing with any other bed partner. Once Cole's underwear was gone, she slicked her thumbs along the sides of Cole's extended clit.

"Oh, God." Cole's hips surged "Wait," Cole gasped, hands circling Lee's wrists.

"Why?"

"I'm so close already it's not going to take much to make me come."

"What's wrong with that?" Lee asked.

"I don't want the night to end before it's begun."

She kissed Cole gently. "Babe, we're nowhere near being done." Lee could sympathize. Ever since Cole had asked her to spend the night, she'd been high strung and ready to explode. Cole had that effect on her, too. "I love watching you come. Can I see it now?" Cole groaned and she moved toward Cole's center, the heat reaching her face. She inhaled her scent. God, she loved how each woman had a distinct musk when excited. A gush trickled down the inside of her thigh. She closed her lips around her clit and Cole gasped above her.

"I'm going to come in your mouth."

She stroked her tongue over the tip. On the third pass, Cole's legs shook before she stilled, then roared as her climax overtook her. Lee wanted to possess her. Not for one orgasm. Or one night. It was wrong to want so much knowing it was all a dream she'd soon wake from. Cole in the throes of passion sent her over the edge. Her mouth closed over Cole's wet, pulsing center, and she drank all of her as she squeezed her thighs, milking her own climax.

"God, you shatter me." Cole grabbed at her, wanting her closer.

Lee weakly laughed. "I'm a little boneless myself. Give me a minute." She lay with her head on Cole's abdomen. The tremor still vibrating deep inside made her smile. Cole sifted her hair through her fingers.

"Can I ask you about tonight?" When she nodded, Cole went on. "What upset you earlier?"

Oddly, the question didn't make her uncomfortable, and Cole sounded genuine in her desire to know. "It's been forever since I had a cake for my birthday. Even longer since the day actually felt like a celebration. I partied in college. But that's not the same." Doing for herself rather than someone taking the time and effort for her made her feel special. She couldn't explain the feeling of family, of acceptance that had come over her, then the overwhelming sense of loss she'd never regain. Her parents didn't care about her. "It all kinda hit me at once."

"I'm sorry your life hasn't been as loving as it should have been. No matter how much the past haunts you, being in the here and now is what matters. You're a beautiful person, Lee. You deserve to feel loved."

She wished she could open herself to what she thought Cole was offering, but she'd gone without for so long, she couldn't trust herself to be able to return it. Affection, that she could give, and she hoped Cole would understand there just wasn't more inside her. Maybe that was the reason she'd never found love because she didn't know how. She could express gratitude though. "Thank you for everything. The surprise of the truck, and so many other things. Thank you for letting me be around even though I can't give you more." Gathering what little strength she could, she crawled up Cole's body and dropped beside her after they kissed. Cole always made her feel appreciated, cared for. "Hold me?"

"With all that I am." Cole kissed the top of her head.

Something in her words should have made her panic, but she was too sated and tired from the emotional day to try to figure it out. All she knew was the warmth of Cole beside her and the steady beat of her heart.

❖

Cole slowly came up from the depths of a deep sleep. It took a bit longer to recognize the heat of Lee's body pressed against hers. Face down, Lee's tattoo was illuminated by the morning light. She hadn't been able to study all the detail before now. The entire bird was outlined in a fine white line, making the colors pop. She gently traced the flames licking at the great bird's claws, its mouth open and the expression fierce, as though daring the fire to try to touch her. Lee was like that. She was forward and brave and enticing, yet when the possibility of actually being touched in her soul became too real, she showed her claws and spread her wings in a war cry of "keep away." Cole wondered if it was all posturing or if she really did want to keep everyone outside of her emotional barrier. Perhaps she was embarrassed by circumstances clearly out of her control, but that was a natural defense mechanism for most people. More likely Lee would do anything to guard herself from becoming emotionally engaged.

She let out a long, silent sigh. She had no control over anyone but herself and she was who she was, no matter if she wore denim or silk, leather or lace, inside, she was a person who cared about others. She could live with that, though she'd still like to explore her own interests more. Lee was the perfect partner to willingly engage in those explorations, but Cole wanted more—the whole package. Not someone just sexually compatible, but who also enjoyed the small-town atmosphere. Lee wasn't that person, or so she said, and Cole had to accept her at her word. Regardless, they'd come to an understanding of sorts, and their friendship was solid while enjoying hot sex and she refused to analyze why.

Lee stretched beside her, muscles flexing as she flipped onto her back and smiled up at her.

"Good morning." Lee reached for her and placed her hand lightly between her breasts.

"Hi. How did you sleep?" Cole asked. They'd fallen asleep wrapped in each other's arms, their legs entwined.

"Really good. You?"

"Like I'd been fucked senseless." She grinned and kissed the soft rise of Lee's breast. "Let's shower and I'll fix breakfast. At some point I have to open the shop, and if we stay here much longer, that's not going to happen."

Lee got out of bed with a groan, then laughed. "How are you on your feet?"

"I'm sorry?"

"Balance-wise, how are you on your feet?" Lee rummaged in her backpack and produced clean underwear and a tank top.

"Average, I guess. Why?"

A mischievous smile accompanied the sparkle in Lee's eyes. "Can I take you on a little adventure after work?"

She reached into the shower and turned on the hot water. "Okay, but I'll need to shower first."

"Don't bother. You'll probably be working up a sweat." Lee's gaze slid over the length of her and she shivered at the raw desire reflected at her. "You should change into a pair of jeans and a T-shirt though."

Cole stepped into the steam-filled space and adjusted the temperature before grabbing the sponge and rubbing lilac-scented soap over it. "Dare I ask what we'll be doing?"

"You could," Lee said as she took the sponge and began washing her shoulders. "But that would ruin the surprise." Lee moved down her arms and along the sides of her breasts before continuing down her stomach. "Spread."

She sucked in a lungful of warm air. Lee went to one knee, smoothed the sponge along her thighs and over her mound, then slipped her fingers along her folds and gently spread soft suds around. They were gone too soon, and she moaned at the loss.

"You're the one who has to go to work. Maybe after our outing I can take care of any lingering issues."

Cole grabbed Lee's hips and spun her against the wall, pressing her thigh between Lee's and making her drop the sponge. "You forget I'm the owner and sole employee. If I want to be late, I don't have to worry about being fired." She stepped back. "Pick up the sponge." When Lee bent over, she pressed inside her, finding her slick and hard.

"Cole..."

"Do you want me to stop?"

Lee's body shuddered. "No."

"Good, because you're more than ready for me." She pulled Lee up and pushed her against the wall, her fingers still buried inside as she reached around with her other hand and found Lee's swollen clit. "I love your body." She nipped at her shoulder while she fucked her.

"Coming. Oh God." Lee's thighs were steel columns against her.

Her center throbbed with unanswered longing. Strangely, she didn't want to climax. She craved gratification of the emotional type, not just the physical, and she couldn't shake regretting that Lee wasn't able to be that person. Cole ignored the wash of melancholy. They were together now, and she vowed to enjoy it. Cole slowly withdrew and kissed her back. She could get used to more mornings like this, and that was the problem.

Lee smiled at the tentative look on Cole's face. She sat in the open door of Lee's truck and glanced around at the deserted parking lot of the high school. "I'm not sure this is a good idea."

"You'll be fine." She held a skate open and gestured for Cole to slide her foot in. "Tap your heel." Satisfied, she snugged and tied the laces. "This is called the power strap," she said as she fed the strap through the loop and secured it. "And this is the buckle." Lee snapped it in place on her lower calf and checked the tension. "How does that feel?"

"Okay, I guess. I don't know how it's supposed to feel. With all the gear I'm wearing I don't know if I can stand, let alone skate." Cole looked her over. "Where're your pads?"

The only protection she wore was a helmet. "I've been doing this a long time, and I rarely fall." She grinned in hopes of putting Cole at ease.

Cole groaned. "Great. I'll be sure to watch the pro in action as I land on my ass."

Lee went through some basics, like relaxing her knees and keeping her weight evenly distributed. She demonstrated different moves a few times, then helped Cole to her feet.

"Why did I let you talk me into this?" Cole asked.

Lee loosely wrapped her arm around her back. "Because I promised you a reward later." She wiggled her eyebrows. Cole laughed and flailed her arms when her concentration slipped. Lee steadied her. "Ready?"

"Do I have a choice?" Cole asked, a small grin playing on her lips.

Lee wondered if there had been times in Cole's life when she hadn't had a choice. The death of her father hadn't been her choice, but that was different. When Cole had been tentative in revealing herself in silk and lace, Lee had felt a pang of empathy. Since moving out on her own, she'd made decisions based on what she wanted, or at least what she *thought* she wanted, and never due to obligation or a sense of duty to someone else. There'd been no one else to think about. Cole's life had been vastly different from hers, where family and community were taken into consideration.

For a brief minute, Lee wondered what that would feel like. Not so much to be obligated, but to have another's feelings at stake. To be emotionally invested in another person and to want to do anything and everything to make them smile. That first night when she'd asked Cole to give her respite from her raging emotions by touching her and then she'd left, she hadn't considered how her abrupt departure might affect Cole. All she'd thought about was *her* need and how to insulate herself from all things that touched her. But Cole had touched her more than physically, and she continued to. So where did that leave her?

"You always have a choice." She touched Cole's face, losing herself in the depths of her warm, inviting eyes. Cole's hand covered hers.

"Then we need to get this adventure started."

For her, the adventure had started the minute she'd arrived in Inlet. The question was, where would it lead her?

Chapter Twenty

Cole swayed after she took the skates off. Despite sweating profusely, she'd done okay. Only once had she taken a tumble and it had been her own fault for panicking and not listening to Lee as she told her what to do. She'd been too busy watching Lee's ass and the powerful flex of her thighs.

"Congratulations on your first rollerblade lesson." Lee beamed at her.

"I had a great teacher." She did some stretching and shook out her legs. "How long have you been skating?" She was going to be sore tomorrow after using muscles in ways she wasn't used to.

Lee looked up, her mind clearly working to figure it out. "Since I was about thirteen. I loved lacing up after school and just letting go. There was a skate park not too far from the house. I spent a lot of time there."

Lee grew somber and Cole imagined whatever memories she was lost in weren't good ones. "Now I know how your legs got so muscular. It's definitely a workout." She rubbed her palms along her thighs to distract herself. She wanted Lee in the best possible way.

"We need to get more water and then some food."

They'd been on the blacktop lot for more than an hour. Lee had produced water from her backpack half-way through, but she could still use about a gallon of the stuff. Cole held the skate bag out. "I definitely need a shower now."

Lee took a step back. "Those are yours. I bought them for you."

She had no idea how much the equipment cost, but it had to have been an expense Lee couldn't afford. She was touched, but she wasn't about to let her pay for them, though Lee would likely fight her on it, just like the ceiling repair and the truck, so she let it drop. "You're convinced I'll try it again, are you?"

"Well, I was hoping we could work it in to your busy schedule." Lee shared a heart-stopping smile.

While she thought about how much fun she had, Cole also thought about how different they were regarding childhood memories. "Only if I can introduce you to one of my pastimes."

"Sure. What are we going to do?" Lee jumped up like she was ready to tackle anything Cole suggested.

Cole stepped closer, their lips nearly touching. "It's a secret." She flicked her gaze between Lee's expressive eyes and her pale red lips. She cupped Lee's nape, turned her till her back pressed against the side of her truck, and bit her exposed neck hard and quick. Lee gasped.

"We can't do this here!"

"Why not? Everyone knows I like women." She glanced over her shoulder. "Nana's nowhere in sight, so you don't have to worry about being shot." Her lips twitched.

Lee groaned. "Don't even kid about that. I'm still not sure about the whole gun thing." Lee's hands trailed over her breasts and her nipples sprang to life. "Water, food, then we'll see how much energy you have left."

Suddenly, she didn't feel tired at all.

Cole held Lee to her and listened to her soft, steady breathing. Their lovemaking had been sweet, gentle. Her center was still heavy, her clit still swollen with need, but for now she was content to hold Lee and enjoy the moment. Inhaling her scent reminded her of the ocean air from her trip to Provincetown, the LGBTQ mecca of the East Coast, years ago. The breeze always blew there, coating her lips with the salt that dried on them. As they snuggled together in the sheets, there was a hit of a childhood memory of warm linens hanging on the clothesline in summer.

She had hundreds of similar memories. Her gut tightened. Lee had shared some bad memories. Did she have any nurturing memories to share? Would she ever allow herself to be loved in order to form new ones? Cole couldn't erase the bad memories, but given the chance she was sure there'd be many moments of love and laughter and peace. Something she had struggled with over the years. Not that she hadn't been loved. Her family's love had never been in question. What occasionally nagged at her was the fact that aside from the brief interlude with Ginny, she hadn't had the love of another woman, and in the end, she hadn't been sure Ginny ever loved her.

She need not compare Lee to her ex, if she could even call the on-again, off-again relationship with Ginny as her ex. Especially when she hadn't even let her in her bed. They were nothing alike. Where Ginny depended on her roguish nature and take-charge attitude to maintain clear lines of comfort, Lee wasn't bothered by the details of who did what in the bedroom, or anywhere else for that matter. Cole had always felt like she was expected to perform and act in a specific way. Had she and Ginny ever made love? It felt more like she was providing a service and, if Ginny was in the mood, she'd get her off.

No. Lee was nothing like Ginny. In fact, Lee seemed to like not knowing which presentation she'd get on any occasion, and Cole welcomed being able to follow a whim and be whomever she felt like in the moment, without the restraint of expectation.

Cole moved her hand over Lee's stomach and stopped on her breast, gently squeezing. Her nipple instantly tightened, and her hips thrust forward.

"Mmm...good morning." Lee kissed her neck. She wiped sleep from her eyes and studied her, her brow knit. "How long have you been awake?"

"A little while."

"Why do you look worried?"

She skimmed her fingertips along the ridge of Lee's abdomen, smiling when the muscles contracted. "Not worried. Thinking."

"Care to share?"

Cole didn't normally skirt what was on her mind. "Random stuff. Nothing important." She knew the deal between them, and more words wouldn't change the situation. "How did you sleep?"

Lee was silent for a bit longer, watching, before stretching again. "Like a rock. Your touch had me undone. You?"

Lee continued to move beneath her fingers. She considered telling her fine, but the lie would sit like bitters on her tongue and she couldn't do it. "Not so well."

Lee pushed up. "Why not?"

A sigh escaped. "I was restless." Not a lie, but not the reason either. "I wasn't quite done."

"Sorry I fell asleep. You didn't take care of yourself?" Lee moved over her with a thigh between her legs and slid along her slick center. "Obviously not," she said before capturing her mouth. The kiss started slow, in that just from sleep way and built-in intensity until she was breathless.

She pressed forward when Lee's mouth moved to her nipple and began sucking with just the right pressure that the sensation traveled straight to her clit. She whimpered. "Please, please."

"Tell me what you want." Lee gazed into her eyes. "Not what you need, what you want."

What did she want? She knew, but she wasn't sure if Lee would want it, too. "I want to fuck you."

"Oh yeah?" Lee smiled and desire flashed in her eyes.

"With my cock." Cole flipped them, catching Lee off guard in a move she imagined Lee capable of in much the same way.

"Shit, babe. You've got me all worked up now, too."

Cole trembled as a visual of being buried deep inside of Lee surfaced. "Is that a yes?" Lee took her hand and pressed it between her thighs. Moisture covered her palm.

"Do you have to ask? That's a definite yes."

"Don't go anywhere." She left the bed, opened the nightstand, and produced a harness with a purple dildo attached. Cole stepped into the openings, then got back in bed with her favorite bottle of lube. Lee was waiting with her thighs spread. Lust colored her eyes a deeper hue of aquamarine, the vivid greenish blue of foreign waters she'd only seen on TV. She smoothed her hands over the apex of Lee's pelvis and leaned in for a kiss. Lee's tongue swept over hers and her excitement grew. She didn't think trust was something Lee gave easily, and she would do everything she could to keep it. Cole trailed her fingers down Lee's cheek, and she pressed into the touch.

"I want you inside me," Lee said as she captured her mouth again and snaked her tongue inside.

Cole was so turned on her vision was blurry, and it was hard to breathe.

"Please, babe. Take me."

She grasped her cock. Looking along Lee's body, she pressed forward, the pressure against her throbbing clit riding the fine line of pain and pleasure, and she wanted more. Wanted to bury herself inside so deep, Lee would never need another woman to fill her. She pushed the thought away and turned her focus on Lee.

"Can you take all of me?"

Lee held her hips and pulled her forward until Cole was buried to the base of the dildo. "You feel so good."

Cole lowered over the length of her and pumped in steady, measured strokes. It wasn't long before the threads of her impending orgasm tingled along her arms and legs. "Come with me?"

Lee's eyes darkened and she reached between them, her fingertips poised above her distended clit. "I have to touch myself."

Cole locked her elbows and rocked back and forth several times. "Now. Do it now." Cole watched Lee play with herself before she locked Cole inside. The sudden jarring brought her to a roaring climax as she continued to thrust against Lee while they moaned in concert. Spent and shaking, she withdrew, then settled on top of Lee and kissed her passionately.

Lee rolled them onto their sides. "You're a wonderful lover. You never cease to amaze me."

"You're the one who's amazing. You're so willing to please, no matter what I want, you always say yes."

"It's not a hard decision," Lee said, laughing. "I'd be a fool not to want your passion." She kissed her lightly but there was a shadow in her eyes.

Cole backed away enough to take in her tentative expression. "What's bothering you?" She pressed her hand to her chest, needing another point of connection. Lee's eyes flicked away.

"I've thought about doing the same to you. I mean, asking…if I could, you know…fuck you?"

The idea was foreign. Cole had never let another woman take her that way—though she'd ridden her own toy many times. Even now, Lee was cautious about asking for something she may not want. But when her body reacted, when her clit swelled beneath the harness she still wore, the idea of her and Lee switching places made her wonder if that, too, was a side of her previously left unexplored. Lee must have taken her silence as reluctance.

"I'm sorry. You don't have to say anything. It doesn't matter to me one way or the other."

"You're sweet. It's not that I don't want to. I just haven't let anyone before, and I don't think I'm ready just yet."

Lee held her face, kissed her gently. "It's not a deal breaker. You taking me was really hot." Lee slid the straps off her hips. "I'm happy holding you against me and feeling your strength. Not just your body, but your inner strength." Lee rubbed her cheek over her, like a content feline needing to mark her territory. "I like how safe I feel with you."

Lee's eyes spoke of adoration, and Cole couldn't help thinking Lee hadn't felt safe before. She rubbed her back, pressed her lips to her shoulder. As much as she would have enjoyed staying in bed cuddling for hours, she glanced at the clock. She had a customer scheduled to meet her at the shop in an hour. She needed to get moving.

"I have to get ready for work. You're welcome to stay as long as you want." She brushed Lee's silky strands from her eyes and wondered not for the first time how the long bangs falling in her eyes didn't bother her.

"No reason to stay if you're not here." Lee tossed the covers and picked up the discarded dildo. "I'll give this a wash while I brush my teeth. Do you want to shower first?"

What she really wanted was for Lee to join her, but time was pressing up against her practical side. If Lee joined her, she'd definitely be late. "I'll be quick. I've got blueberry muffins for breakfast."

Lee stopped moving. "I think you missed your calling. You should have been a chef."

Cole cast her gaze downward. Over the years, the idea of doing something different with her life had struck her in moments of longing to change her profession. Be someone else. The years had slipped through her fingers without her ever trying. She was done not trying. Lee had offered to help her find her inner self. Her authentic self, as Lee put it, and she had every intention of finding all of her before it was too late. Before she lived with one more regret.

CHAPTER TWENTY-ONE

"Hello." Lee cradled the phone between her shoulder and ear as she followed the GPS up a winding mountainside to a house that needed a room painted and a new window installed. She'd been getting a few jobs a week, and even if it wouldn't pay for living expenses, they provided a sense of purpose and she'd gotten to know some of the residents. Everyone was welcoming.

"Hey, stranger. How's life treating you?" Sam's booming voice came through loud and clear.

"Hi, Sam. It's good." She and Cole together were more than good. "Better than I thought it would be, that's for sure."

"I'm almost sorry to hear that. Listen, I've decided that dick R.J. is never going to pay up, and I need to be more proactive. I'm going to start my own business with a select few from the crew, and you were at the top of the list."

Lee pulled into the nondescript driveway and turned off her truck. "Seriously?"

"Absolutely. Unless you have a gig where you are, I want you on my team."

The last thing she'd expected was an offer to return to her former life. She'd sent the occasional text to Sam, checking in on him and the family, but he'd never hinted he was interested in having his own business, and she wondered what had changed to move him in this direction. She glanced at the passenger seat and remembered the last time Cole had been there, sunlight reflecting in her eyes and the easy smile that played on her enticing lips. Her heart seized. If she accepted, she'd be leaving Cole behind. "I appreciate you thinking of me, and the offer."

Sam laughed. "I know it's out of the blue. Take some time to think about it. I'd really like to have you join me on this adventure. What have you got to lose?"

Based on her restlessness when she first arrived, the obvious answer would have been to accept. But now…now there was a sense of belonging she'd never really had. Not in her first home in Lancaster, PA, or in college. Definitely not in Atlantic City where she was just one more blue collar in a sea of them, eking out a living and having meaningless sex. And then there was Cole. Even after discussing their vastly different outlooks on life, losing Cole after finding someone who understood her and didn't ask her to explain if she wasn't ready to, kept her from accepting an offer that a couple of months ago she would have jumped on. And that was the problem. Lately, she'd begun to feel a tighter bond. A need to be with Cole more often than not. This was one of those need versus want moments. What did she want? Whatever it was, she owed it to herself to not cut and run because it was the easy or simpler thing to do. It was time she not act on impulse without thinking about the consequences of her actions. For once, she needed to slow down.

"How much time do I have?"

Sam laughed. "You can take whatever you need, but I've got a job lined up for October first, so I'd like you on site a few weeks before so we can go over details and give you time to settle in."

"I'll get back to you as soon as I can." She rubbed her hand over her face. "And, Sam, thanks for the vote of confidence." Lee sat in her truck chewing on her lip. She should have been excited by the news, but excitement wasn't what she was feeling. Trepidation. Confusion. Angst. They were all spot-on descriptors banging around in her head.

The unemployment she'd finally started to collect had helped her feel less like a freeloader and more like a contributor, and she insisted on paying for half the groceries and the Wi-Fi bill. The jobs she was picking up also had perks. Aside from being paid in cash, her customers gave her a variety of items including homemade baked goods, jars of soup, and she'd even gotten a carved wooden sign that said, "Home is Where My Heart is, Not Geography," a sentiment she was beginning to believe. The longer she stayed in Inlet, the more she liked it. The slower pace, open spaces, and friendly people were easy to acclimate to. And Cole…what could she say about the woman who had welcomed her with a smile and a kind word when nothing had felt right in her world?

Lee didn't think Cole would be happy to find out she was considering leaving, but it would be foolish on her part to dismiss the chance to join an employer she could depend on. One who wouldn't screw her over just because he could. She had time. A couple of weeks to put the idea into perspective and weigh the pros and cons. Her head was telling her to say yes and get back to doing what she loved—earning a decent living and giving herself stability so she never had to depend on anyone else. Her heart, however, argued that she enjoyed where she was, what she was doing, and who she was doing it with. She froze. She was *happy* here.

"Fuck." Lee pounded the steering wheel. Her life had turned in a much different direction than she'd have thought possible, and the notion of returning to the fast-paced rat race that was Atlantic City had lost its appeal. She got out, put on her tool belt, and picked up her clipboard. With any luck the job would take her all day. If she worked, she wouldn't think, and thinking was the last thing she wanted to do.

❖

A couple of days later, she and Cole stood on the bank of Fifth Lake, but to her it was more of a large pond than an actual lake. "That's disgusting," Lee said, crinkling her nose.

"It might be a little cruel, but I don't think it's intended to be pleasant," Cole said as she slipped a worm onto the hook, then checked the pole, tightening the nut holding the reel. She pointed out various items like the correct position of the hook and sinker before picking up her baited line and moving a few feet away. "Timing is important. You press the spool control button, and just before you reach the top arc of your cast, you'll release it, and the line will sail out. If you release too late, it lands in front of you. Too early, and it will fall behind you." She demonstrated without actually casting.

Lee watched, unsure she'd understood. "I'm going to mess up your equipment." She bit her bottom lip.

"It's called fishing gear, and don't worry about that. You'll get the hang of it. Take a couple of test swings. You can either cast overhead or sideways."

"You go overhead?"

"Yes. My timing is better overhead, and I can cast farther that way, but you do what's comfortable for you."

After a couple of practice casts, she appeared to have the hang of it, and made an actual cast, landing about thirty feet away. "Now what?"

"We wait for a nibble." Cole showed her how to rest the line over her index finger. "When you feel a tug on the line, or the end of your rod dips a bit, you know a fish is at your bait. Patience pays off here. If you yank too soon, the fish might steal your bait and you'll miss hooking it. Too late, it'll likely swallow the bait and hook."

"I'm not sure I'm going to like this," she said as she tried to concentrate. Sam's call had her in a constant state of turmoil. She'd been avoiding Cole, unsure what she should do. Cole was intuitive when it came to her moods, and she'd been afraid she'd know something was bothering her.

"I wasn't sure I was going to like risking bodily harm by having wheels on my feet, but I gave it a try and actually liked it."

Lee growled. "Oh, so now you're using guilt tactics?" She studied the end of the pole.

Cole took Lee's unoccupied hand and made eye contact. "I would never use guilt to make you do something you didn't want to do." Cole studied her, tipping her head in that way Lee had come to recognize as Cole trying to decipher the silent communication between them. "Something's going on with you. You're usually up for anything and rarely complain."

This was why she'd kept her distance, and she glanced away.

"What's going on? Tell me." Cole trailed her fingertip along her jawline, and she shivered at the touch.

"Nothing." She shrugged, took a breath. "I have cramps." She stared out over the water, anywhere but into Cole's eyes. "I'm just in a shitty mood." Her gut was churning, along with her mind. She'd been on an emotional roller coaster as she went from a euphoric high at the prospect of full-time employment to deep depression at the thought of leaving Inlet. She'd become comfortable with the easy rhythm of everyday life and the people who knew her by name. No one stole your stuff. No one seemed to have a hidden agenda. The change was refreshing. But the part that bothered her the most was the thought of leaving Cole. That one factor caused her more angst than any of the other recent upheavals in her life, and she couldn't shake the feeling that if she left, the decision would haunt her forever.

"I'm sorry, babe." Cole kissed her. "You should have told me. We can go."

"I'm being a jerk." The least she could do was enjoy their time together, no matter what she decided about the job offer. "I'm fine. Really."

"I'll tell you what. How about we do this for a little while and then you come to the house and I'll massage your back and stomach." Cole licked her upper lip where a light sheen of sweat had formed. "I have a special remedy for cramps that might help."

Lee smiled. Cole took every bump in life in stride. If—and that was still a big if—she decided to head back to the city, Cole would be fine. She had to believe the rationale, even if the pain of leaving told her otherwise. "That sounds like an activity I'd like."

"We don't have to wait." Cole turned and began gathering items.

Lee's pole dipped. "Look, I think there's a nibble."

"I think you're right." After another dip, Cole took a step behind her. "The next time that happens, jerk your pole back hard and quick and start reeling in the line."

Lee waited, standing stock-still. The next little dip, she yanked hard and started reeling in like a madwoman. When the water parted, a small fish flopped at the end of the line. "I got one!" A tingle of excitement shot through her as she kept winding until Cole gestured for her to stop.

"That's a whopper." Cole grinned at her.

"Funny. Now what?"

"You remove the hook and toss it back in."

She tried to figure out where the hook was, but the fish was flopping so much she couldn't see a thing. "How?"

"There's two methods. You can hold it and gently remove the hook, or you can lay it on the ground and keep it still with your foot on the fish until you work it free."

Looking between the still moving fish and Cole, she shook her head. "I'm not doing that. What if it bites me?"

Cole belly laughed. "Babe, most fish don't have teeth. You do have to be careful of the barbs on its back fin though."

"I think I'm gonna just drop the string in the water and let him figure his own way off." The fish looked slimy and not something she wanted to touch at all. Cole shook her head and grabbed the line with one hand, then slid her other hand along the fish's body until she had a hold of it. With the fish opening and closing its mouth in slow motion, it took her just a few seconds to work the hook out.

"Say good-bye to your little buddy." Cole held it up much too close, and she backed away.

"Bye-bye, fishy."

Cole bent over and dropped the fish into the water. "Okay, time to bait your hook again."

"Nope, not doing it. How about I just sit and watch you fish."

"We can leave. I thought you might find it relaxing." Cole shrugged. "It's not for everyone."

She looked dejected and Lee couldn't stand to see her like that and hoped she wouldn't give Cole another reason to react that way. She brought her pole over to Cole. "If you put a worm on for me, I'll give it another try."

"You don't have to do that," Cole said without looking up.

"I want to. Really."

Cole's smile assured her she'd said the right things, but when she came in for a hug, she drew the line.

"Do NOT touch me until you wash your hands."

Cole chased her in a circle with outstretched arms until they were both laughing so hard they were out of breath. Lee leaned over, hands on her knees, panting.

"Are you done threatening me with your nasty fish-slime hands?"

"Oh, all right." Cole rolled her eyes and snagged a worm from the bait carton. "First one to catch a fish, wins."

The odds were stacked against her, but she was willing to play along. "Deal. What do I win?"

"The loser has to free the catch and return it to the water."

She pursed her lips. "Fine." If that's what it took to convince Cole she was okay and not worried out of her mind that she was a hair's breadth away from fucking up her life, so be it.

❖

Lee had held up her end of the bet, though from the look on her face, touching the fish had grossed her out in a way that made Cole's heart swell. At the last second, she'd taken pity on her and given her a rag to hold the fish with. Lee had been so gentle with the creature, all the while talking to it as she worked the hook loose, and her true tender nature had shone through.

As she stood outside the shower, she studied the athletic outline of Lee's body behind the glass. Lee's back, arms, and legs were an anatomy lesson in well-developed muscles and flexing tendons as she moved and stretched. She'd never tire of the sight and did her best to commit every detail to memory.

"Hey. You going to stop playing voyeur and come in?"

She stepped into the steam and into Lee's arms. "I can't help it. Your body fascinates me. You're different from anyone I've ever been attracted to."

Lee leaned against the wall and held her waist. "Different good or different bad?" she asked, coming close enough to kiss.

Cole marveled, as she always did, at the softness of Lee's lips. Her kisses started gently and sometimes stayed that way, but often the intensity grew, and the beating of her heart increased in time to the rhythm. "Good, baby. Always good." She touched her stomach. "How's your cramps?" She had been one of the lucky ones. Menopause had come early, and she only occasionally suffered night sweats. Even they had diminished over the last year.

"Okay."

"So you don't need my remedy then." Cole watched Lee's face color and couldn't interpret what it meant. She didn't think anything could embarrass her when it came to her body or sex.

"I don't want to seem like a wimp." Lee ducked her head.

Cole smoothed her hands over Lee's chest. "Only when it comes to worms and fish." She laughed at Lee's wide-eyed response. "Kidding."

Lee pulled her against her solid frame. "Truth, but if you're still offering, I'd like you to take care of me." Her eyes shone bright, and Cole recognized the flare of desire.

"I'd like nothing better." She moved Lee under the spray, then rinsed away her suds. When they were done drying, she led her to the bedroom. "Lie down when you're ready and relax. I'll be right back." She went downstairs and rummaged in the linen closet until she found the clay heating pad. She warmed it in the microwave while she made a pot of tea and chose a small glass bottle from a collection in the pantry. When she returned, Lee was sitting against the pillows in a tank top, the sheet pulled over her hips.

"What do you have there?" Lee's curiosity was another adorable thing about her.

"Some good old-fashioned remedies." She poured the tea. "Honey?"

"Yes, please."

She handed over a mug. "This is ginger and cinnamon tea. Ginger is an anti-inflammatory, and cinnamon has anti-spasmodic qualities and relieves stress." She ducked out to grab a hand towel. When Lee was settled in and sipping from the warm mug in her hands, Cole produced a small dark brown bottle. "Can I move the sheet?" Lee nodded. She exposed her thighs and got on the bed. After shaking a few drops into her palm, she warmed the oil and began to massage, starting at her thighs and working downward. "Chamomile oil is good for sore muscles." She worked methodically, pressing deep into the muscles.

Lee sighed. "God, that feels good. Where did you learn all of this?"

"Nana was big into homeopathic remedies when I was growing up. I spent a lot of time with her and her knowledge rubbed off. For a while, she sold essential oils, made her own soaps, that kind of thing."

"What about the massaging?" Lee asked. She could tell from her movements Cole had experience and wondered how many women had been on the receiving end of her skillful hands.

Cole shrugged. "Videos. Some online courses. At one time I considered going to school for massage therapy. Can you scoot down so I oil your abdomen? I'll go easy."

"What happened?" She finished her tea and set her mug on the nightstand.

"Life happened." Cole continued her ministrations and finally made eye contact. "I'm going to wash my hands. Do you want more tea?"

"I'm good." She wanted to ask Cole more about why she hadn't pursued what she was obviously good at, but the subject was clearly closed. When she returned, she held up the sheet for her, and Cole slid in beside her. "Thank you for taking care of me." She cupped Cole's neck and brought her close, then kissed her slowly. Cole trembled against her.

"I'm not done yet," Cole said. "Lie flat." She reached for the towel-wrapped item she'd put on the bed earlier and moved the covers. She gently placed the package on her exposed abdomen, low on her belly.

The heat penetrated her skin and she sighed again. "I'm going to fall asleep with all this pampering." Content wasn't a word she often used to describe her mood, if ever, but that's exactly how she felt at the moment.

"Is that okay? It should be warm, but not hot."

"It's perfect." She touched Cole's face. "Like you."

Cole kissed her palm. "Close your eyes."

Lee felt her snuggle next to her before her fingers moved over her mound, massaging her flesh. Her hips rose to meet Cole, chasing the touch.

"Try to relax your body and enjoy what your feeling, but don't engage. Just feel." Cole's mouth was next to her ear. Her warm breath caressed her neck and cheek. Her lips pressed to her throat, then her shoulder, as her fingers slipped inside her folds and teased her clit as it surged.

"Cole," she whispered, her eyes still closed. "I want to touch you."

Cole kissed her chest. "Later. Let me do this for you."

As Cole's fingers stroked and circled and pulled, her orgasm built in slow increments. Her legs began to shake. "I'm going to come."

"I know, baby. I can feel you. Let go. I've got you."

And she did. Her climax washed over her like warm bath water, drawing out soft moans as her orgasm ebbed and flowed. She'd never experienced such calm and peace during sex. Never felt so cared for. For this one perfect moment in time, she pushed all her angst and doubts and fears out of her mind. She pulled Cole against her, kissed her forehead, and let the night claim her.

Chapter Twenty-two

A re you feeling okay?" Dan asked.

"I'm not sick." Lee answered too abruptly, her stomach churning at being short-tempered. "Sorry." She played with the food on her plate, her appetite gone. "One of the guys I used to work with called. He's starting a construction crew and offered me a job."

"I'll be sorry to see you go, but I'm happy for you." He studied her for a long time. "You don't seem all that excited about it."

She sighed and pushed her plate away. "I *should* be excited. It's what I'd been hoping for. It's just..." She shook her head.

Dan touched her hand. "You've grown fond of this sleepy little town, and a certain mechanic. Is that it?"

"Cole has been so good to me. For me." She couldn't deny her growing feelings, partly because they were great together in and out of bed. If she left, Lee doubted she'd ever find anyone like Cole in Atlantic City, or anywhere else for that matter. She just wasn't sure she was ready to make any kind of a commitment...to the town *or* to Cole. Lee had never had a reason to think anyone would be the type of partner she wanted. One who understood her. Understood that she didn't think anyone could love her or want her the way she'd dreamed of, until Cole. But even now, she doubted she could give back what a loving partner should. Unconditional love wasn't anything she had experience with. What did that say about her as a person? And what about her financial stability and independence? She was starting from zero again. "I don't know what to do."

"Making a decision about the future based on what you've always known is easy. It's when there's new information and new feelings that makes it hard. How do you feel about Cole?"

"That's just it. Obviously, I like her. More than like her, really. She's a great person and she deserves to be treated as special as she is. That's the problem, Uncle Dan. I can't trust myself to treat her like she's special. Everything about being with Cole is foreign. I've only done casual and unattached with lovers, but I care about Cole. I'm worried more about disappointing her than about myself." God, she was in much deeper than she'd ever been, and the quicksand was pulling her under fast. "I probably shouldn't be struggling so much against what I'm feeling, but it's not working so well."

"Why don't you talk to her?" Dan picked up their plates.

"Then she'll know I'm thinking of leaving." Her chest tightened.

Dan stared her down. "You'd rather lie to her?"

The words stopped her cold. Her uncle had put it simply and she'd needed to hear it. "No. Of course not, but I know me. If I stay too long, I'll screw it up." Like she had before. With her friend Jackie, and that woman who wanted more than casual, and probably countless other times that she'd been too high or drunk to even remember.

He held her by the shoulders. "You're a good person, Lee. You'll do the right thing."

It was proving harder than she thought. Dan had faith in her, she just had to have faith in herself while she figured out the kind of person she was and what she wanted from her life. Once they cleaned up, she excused herself and went to sit under the old oak tree.

She wasn't a coward, was she? She'd run from her parents, but that was different. She'd run from anything but casual relationships, but so did a lot of people. She wasn't an exception from the general population there. Then she'd run from her own home after her employer's abrupt closing, but that, too, had been born of necessity. Now, she was faced with another decision. Did she want to admit her growing feelings for Cole out loud or cut and run back to the safety of ambiguous sex and non-attachment? What did it say about her if she decided to leave the one person who'd put no demands on her, who hadn't asked her to act a certain way to make *them* feel better?

Cole was content to just let her be, and in return she hoped she'd shown Cole what mattered most was being comfortable in her own skin. If what she was thinking was true, why was she so conflicted? Why was she drowning in doubt? True, they weren't committed to each other, even if she was certain neither had sought out physical pleasure from anyone else since they'd begun whatever this dance was between them. Wasn't that a commitment? Outside, with the soft breeze that made the flowers sway like they were waving good-bye, Lee was restless. She leaned against the bumper and hung her head, refusing to cry. Life was fucked up. *Her* life was fucked up. The sad thing was that it wasn't anything new.

Cole hadn't seen Lee in several days and the loss stung. She said she had some jobs in neighboring towns and had claimed being tired, but Cole wasn't sure that was it. Their last time together, Lee hadn't been herself, and she'd tried to not read too much into it, all the while fighting an uneasy feeling that just wouldn't go away.

Tonight was a special night. She wanted to please Lee by giving her what she desired, and the outfit she'd chosen, while not overly feminine, made her sigh when she'd tried it on. She played with her hair and the wax sculpting product until she had what she hoped was a sexy, just out of bed look. Cole glanced at the clock. Lee would arrive soon. Downstairs, she brought the bottle of bourbon Lee had gifted her and two tumblers to the living room. The charcuterie board was already set out. She'd worked late, skipped dinner, and refused to drink on an empty stomach. Not that she planned to get loaded. Indulging in alcohol would leave her feeling disconnected, and she hadn't done that since her father's funeral. Would her father approve of how she was living her life? Encourage her to follow a different path? One that crossed her mind every now and again, especially when she was having a bout of loneliness. So why had she resisted till now? An oath made in hopes he wouldn't leave. A foolish teenage bargain at her father's death bed, and she wasn't even sure if he'd heard her. The years had slipped from her grasp, and she prayed it wasn't too late to reach for the brass ring. The one that would give her answers she'd been afraid to find.

She shook off the doubt. Lee was more than willing to let her experiment to find her own way, and she was uplifted by her encouragement.

The doorbell rang and Cole smiled. She'd been unable to convince Lee she didn't need to announce her arrival. When she opened the door, the air was sucked from the room. Lee stood there in black jeans that hugged her thick thighs and a light gray button-down open enough to reveal her naked chest.

"Hi," Lee said. "You look amazing." She leaned in for a quick kiss, then produced a single sunflower and a chocolate bar. "Flowers and candy."

Cole took the offered gifts, touched by their simplicity. "Does this mean I'm your gal?" Her stomach sank when Lee looked panic-stricken. She grasped her hand. "I'm teasing. Come in." She'd chosen silk lounging pajamas in a deep maroon and a matching robe that swirled around her legs as she walked. She was comfortable and felt sexy at the same time. Maybe she'd found her stride. Lee dropped her bag at the stairs and followed her to the parlor and she gestured to the couch. "I haven't eaten much today. I hope you don't mind a little delay."

Lee was pensive, tension radiating from her. Perhaps she was nervous about tonight. Cole had told her to bring her harness. Maybe Lee still had doubts if she really wanted her that way. Even the idea of Lee inside her had her swollen and wet. The more she thought about it, the more she wanted to be completely filled by her. It wasn't like she hadn't ridden her own dildo lots of times. Having a living, breathing person that you connected with on the other end was bound to be different. *Feel* different, and that's what she longed for.

"No hurry." Lee grinned tightly. "Unless you have somewhere else to be tonight."

Cole began pouring. "I do." She handed Lee the glass with one hand and caressed her face with the other, wanting to chase away the disappointment. "Upstairs with you."

Lee's eyes fluttered. "That's good, because I've been thinking about you all day."

"Then we better not have too much of this, since it's the good stuff."

"Don't worry. I can handle my liquor." Lee tipped her glass and drank half.

"I'm sure you can." She swallowed half of her own. "And I know you can handle me."

❖

While they snacked and drank, they talked of Dan's obsession with a new cable series and Lee's own growing interest in reading books from his impressive library. Through it all, Cole was attentive and engaging, but the turmoil Lee had been battling and the dread she'd tried to keep at bay nagged her nerves. With a jerk, she stood, pulling Cole with her. "I want you." Sex was what she'd used for ages to get over the rough times. Cole smiled and led her until they were standing next to the bed.

"Are you okay?" Cole dragged her fingers through her hair and lightly scratched her scalp. "You're preoccupied. Do you want to talk about whatever's on your mind?'

Lee averted her gaze, forced a calm tone. "Daydreaming." She pulled Cole to her, opened the buttons on her top, and was instantly aroused by Cole's soft, warm skin waiting for her.

"What are you daydreaming about?" Cole arched into her, her hips seeking more pressure.

"About doing this." Lee cupped her breast and squeezed the nipple. "And this." She helped Cole recline on the bed and lie next to her. She moved her lips downward, kissing along Cole's ribs, her abdomen, the ridge of her hip. Lee guided her hand beneath the waistband and brushed her fingers along the top of her downy soft hair. Cole trembled.

"Don't stop," Cole whispered.

Cole was so open to her, so accepting of her touch, Lee never wanted to stop. It was going to be an issue…for both of them. But not tonight. Tonight, she would do what she'd been wanting to do all along.

Once the discarded silk barrier was no longer in her way, Lee sank between Cole's strong, slender thighs. The first taste of her matched the flavor of her skin. Salty sweet and hot. Like homemade caramel just cool enough to eat. Cole's swollen knot slipped between her lips and beat against her tongue, making her moan. "Ever since the other night, I've wanted to do this again." The more she tasted Cole, the more she wanted to be inside her. It wasn't long before Cole's body began to tremble. "Let go, babe. Come for me."

"Almost there," Cole gasped as she ground against Lee's mouth, pressing her hard clit deeper.

Cole stiffened beneath her, and Lee sucked rhythmically until Cole cried out, her hips jerking and legs thrashing with the force of her contractions, ecstasy clearly written on her face. Lee couldn't help but enjoy being the one to put that look there. The telltale flush colored her otherwise fair complexion as it traveled from her chest to her cheeks. Her roguishly handsome features softened and filled Lee with awe.

"God, what you do to me." Cole traced her knuckles and fire shot up her arm, urging her up for a searing yet tender kiss.

"Babe?" She trembled in the semi-darkness. Her body was a live wire, and no matter her misgivings, she wanted to imprint herself in Cole, wanting her in a way she'd never wanted anyone.

"Hmmm?" Cole responded, her other hand playing over her back.

"Can I be inside you with my cock?" She trembled against Cole, her rising need so great she was close to climaxing.

"You know you can." Cole's mouth found hers, sealing the promise she'd made earlier on the phone when they'd made plans for tonight. "I'm ready for you."

Lee slid out of bed and returned once her harness was on. "You'll tell me to stop if you change your mind, right?" She touched Cole's face.

"I don't think that's going to happen. I promise if it does, you'll be the first to know."

Moisture trickled from her and settled beneath the dildo. She slid the shaft along Cole's slick folds and capture her lips in a slow, deep kiss. Reaching between them, she broke off and watched Cole's expression as she pressed inside. Cole shuddered, her pupils contracting, and she stopped moving. "Still okay?" Cole scored her sides with her blunt nails, producing an edge of pain/pleasure that forced her hips forward.

"More than okay." Cole's mouth sought hers.

She pulled back to slide in again and shook from the sensation. *So close.* "God, I'm going to come." Her voice was strained and low as she hung on for control. "I'm going to come inside you."

Cole dug her fingers into her ass, pulling her tight against her. "Now, baby," Cole said as her eyes darkened.

Head back, muscles straining, she pulled out just enough to slide deeper. The orgasm crashed over her, taking her breath with it. Cole held her, pressing upward, shaking and moaning. She rode out the all-consuming climax until she collapsed. Able to breathe again, she kissed Cole's neck. "Beautiful."

Cole touched her face. "You're so strong. So handsome." Cole held on and rolled. She worked off the harness, then pulled up the sheet. "Can I hold you?"

She was so tired suddenly. All the worry and doubt and indecision had weighed heavy on her mind for days. Now all she wanted to do was bask in the afterglow. She could go back to worrying tomorrow. "I'd like to hold you, too."

Cole guided her head to her chest, kissed her forehead. "Sleep, love. I'm not going anywhere."

❖

Cole blinked in the darkness of her room. The windows were open, and the night had cooled to a comfortable temperature, sheet draped over her, and warmth pressed against her side. She turned her head.

"Hi," Lee said, her fingers moving over her chest. "I think I fell asleep on you."

"You weren't the only one. Sorry about that."

Lee quietly laughed. "Babe, when a woman passes out after climaxing, it's a compliment." She bent to kiss her. "Unless you faked it, then we need to talk."

"I didn't fake anything tonight." She trailed her fingers down the center of her chest, Lee nipped at her.

"That's good. Is there something you *do* fake?" Lee drew ever smaller circles around each breast in turn.

"Not anymore. I'm glad you're here and like all the sides of me."

"It's not something you can rush." Lee nuzzled her neck. "Thanks for trusting me."

Cole ran her hands over Lee's muscular back and down her trim sides. She glanced at the clock. Sunrise was still more than an hour away. "You seem to be wide-awake."

"I woke up with a hard-on." Lee grinned mischievously then kissed her possessively.

She moved farther down along Lee's body. "I know how to fix that."

"Oh yeah?"

"Bring your center over my head." She adjusted the pillow after Lee sat up.

"Seriously?"

"Breakfast in bed sounds good to me." She cocked a brow.

Once in position, Lee looked down along her body and into her eyes. "I'm really going to enjoy this."

"So am I." Cole wrapped her arms around Lee's thighs. "Hold on to the headboard." She guided her closer and slipped her tongue inside. Lee jumped at the contact.

"Fuck. That feels good."

Cole played her tongue over Lee's clit until it was engorged and hard before she began to gently suck, occasionally flicking the tip with her tongue.

"Babe, just…" Lee tried to pull away. "I'm not going to last."

She felt the tremors in Lee's legs, her abdomen a hard plane above her. Cole changed the intensity, clamping tighter, sucking harder. Lee swore above her, a litany of moans and gasps as her clit became stone hard. When she entered Lee with her fingers, Lee's walls clamped down around her and she climaxed, calling out Cole's name. A gush of Lee's hot essence flowed over her chin as Lee trembled above her.

Lee dropped onto the bed, panting. "Oh my God," she said, laughing weakly. Cole grasped her hand, threading their fingers. The room grew quiet except for the sound of her breathing while she recovered. "Are you wet?" She rested her hand on Cole's belly.

"Why don't you see?"

Lee brushed her fingertips through her labia. She entered her with a firm thrust, and her thumb struck her stiff clit. "I want to make you feel good."

"You always do."

She tugged and circled Cole's swollen center between slow, deep strokes, and stealing kisses between Cole's breathy gasps. When she tried to withdraw, Cole grasped her wrist.

"Stay inside," Cole said, then played her fingers over her clit.

A few seconds later, Cole roared with a thrust of her hips. Lee pressed deeper until Cole had no more to give and snuggled into her shoulder, pressing her lips there. She stroked Cole's back as her eyes closed.

"I love you," Cole murmured as she drifted into sleep.

Lee's eyes snapped open. Her heart beat frantically against her ribs. *No, no.* Cole couldn't love her. She didn't *want* Cole to love her. Loving someone meant commitment and obligation and opening herself up to all the emotions and feelings she tried to keep her distance from. She hadn't let herself get close to anyone since she was seventeen, when her parents had withdrawn their albeit contentious attention and she found she couldn't rely on the people she trusted the most to accept and love her. That was her lesson in nothing lasts forever. She hadn't been worthy of their love then, and she certainly wasn't worthy of Cole's love now. She wanted to run again, but the soft, warm breath from Cole as she slept, calmed her enough to keep her from bolting. She'd enjoy this final moment, because she couldn't fathom how much she was going to hurt Cole.

CHAPTER TWENTY-THREE

Cole swallowed the lukewarm coffee, forcing it down around the lump in her throat. Lee had slipped from bed early, saying she had a job to do. She'd moved to get up with her, but Lee kissed her cheek and insisted she stay in bed. The strange thing was she didn't remember hearing the shower run, and Lee hadn't even bothered with coffee. Her gut told her something had happened to make Lee leave so abruptly, but she had no idea what.

There had to be a plausible reason for her sudden departure. Cole didn't know where the job was or what she had to do, and even though it was Sunday, it was probably the only time the customer had free. It happened that way sometimes. But still…it felt off.

With no plans and no idea if she'd see Lee later, Cole decided to catch up with her grandmother. She hadn't spent nearly enough time with her since Lee had come into her life and they'd been together a lot of nights, as well as quite a few days. Besides, Lee would probably want to be with her uncle for a change, and the time apart would do them both good. She didn't want to smother Lee, even if she did crave her company all the time.

Cole glanced at the spot where Dixie had always hung out. She missed her faithful companion. She'd already made her weekly stroll to check where she and Lee had buried her to make sure the wildlife had let her rest in peace. Someone had set a jar of wildflowers next to the mound and she suspected Lee had done some checking of her own. She held back a smile.

Keys in hand, Cole paused on the porch. The day offered a promise of warm sunshine and a steady breeze. What would it be like to share mornings like this with a partner by her side? Over the last few months, she'd allowed herself a glimpse of a different life. One full of laughter and passion and discovery. Cole sighed. There was only one person who came to mind when she looked ahead. Lee.

A quick drive later, Cole called out as she dropped her keys on the kitchen table. "Nana?"

"Out here," her grandmother called from the porch. "Grab a glass of tea and join me."

She added ice to her glass and poured the dark brew. Try as she might, Cole could never duplicate her grandmother's homemade iced tea.

"Where you been, girl?" He grandmother asked in her no-nonsense style.

"I've been spending time with Lee." There was no reason to make some inane excuse that her grandmother would see as a lie right off.

"I'm not too old to see you're smitten with her. About time you found someone, too."

"Nana, I—"

"You're not going to try to deny it, are you?" Her grandmother rocked, like she had for decades. Slow and steady, like her love.

Cole pinched the bridge of her nose. "Wouldn't think of it." She tried to conjure up images of a future with Lee beside her doing things like taking long walks and decorating for Christmas, but over the last week, the pictures that had been so clear once were now blurred and she wasn't sure it was Lee anymore. "It's complicated."

"Life is as complicated or as simple as you make it. The Jacksons have always opted for simple. If you want something different, you're going to have to change the course."

And that was the bigger problem. She wanted different. Wanted life to be more than the garage and her solitary existence, but she couldn't see herself living anywhere but Inlet or leave the land she'd always loved. "I'm not sure what to do."

Her grandmother reached for her and the familiar strength that was always there flowed between them. "I won't tell you what to do, Cole. I just want you to be happy, whatever it is."

Happy. She'd been happy once when life was simple and one day spilled into the next. Maybe if she stopped trying so hard, she'd find it again.

❖

"I just couldn't talk to her about leaving." She'd called Sam that morning to tell him she'd accepted his offer. Lee hung her head. "I'm not the person Cole thinks I am. She needs someone who isn't going to take off whenever emotions run high or things get tough."

Dan stared at her. "She doesn't know, does she?" Lee tilted her head, unsure what he meant, and he went on. "That you love her."

For a minute, she stopped breathing. Did she love Cole? She'd developed a deep friendship, but that didn't mean she loved her. Granted, they were amazing together in bed. Not to mention they had fun and laughed...a lot. They'd shown each other things neither had experienced before. But that didn't mean she *loved* Cole. And even though Cole had whispered the words on the edge of sleep, Lee was convinced she'd only meant it in a grateful sort of way. No. Cole couldn't love her because...well, because she couldn't. No one except her uncle loved her, but that was a different kind of love.

"I don't love her. I'm fond of her, and she's a great friend, but that's where it ends."

"Uh-huh. You keep telling yourself that."

She couldn't tell if Dan was pissed or disappointed by her behavior, or both. Not that it mattered. She'd been disappointed with her own actions so many times she'd lost track, and this would likely top the chart.

"Uncle Dan, please try to understand. I feel useless enough. I need to get back to work. I need to find purpose again and I need independence. Not someone who depends on *me* only to find out I'm not worth having around until death do us part." She waved her hand in frustration. She was a hot mess.

He held her shoulders. "I do understand. That doesn't change the fact that you're throwing out the baby with the bath water. Cole cares for you, and like it or not, you care for Cole. Don't you think she deserves to know how you feel before you disappear?"

Her vision blurred. Of course, he was right. Cole should know her plan, even if she hated having to do it. "I know. I'll tell her." She had to get herself together first. The day was slipping away. She didn't want to tell Cole at the station, and she definitely didn't want to be alone with her, afraid she'd break down and give in should the unlikely happen and Cole begged her to stay. She couldn't stay and be happy by living off someone else's generosity. She might be a lot of things, but she wasn't a freeloader. There wasn't enough work for her in Inlet to provide a living. Having a small job here and there had been okay in the interim, and she'd learned a few things she didn't already know by watching videos and putting the knowledge to use. But they weren't going to help her rebuild her nest egg. At thirty, it was past time to get that egg going again or she'd be working right up to the time she was dropped into the ground. Even though she was nowhere near ready to retire, the idea of not having to work at some point down the road was motivating.

Sooner or later, she'd feel trapped here, and she wouldn't make a promise to Cole that she might not be able to keep. Lee took a deep breath as she stared at her phone. She opted for a text instead of a call. She wrote and erased a dozen messages before she settled on asking her to join her for coffee at the only decent diner in town. Cole's response came a few minutes later.

Sure. I can be there in an hour.

Lee began to pace. An hour to get her head on straight and be honest with Cole about what she'd decided. She could do this. She had to do this. Once and for all she had to prove she wasn't a total loser and that she could make a life of her own choosing while doing the type of work she enjoyed.

Then why did the thought of leaving hurt so much?

Words couldn't describe how hard Cole's heart seized in her chest at the news.

"I know it's kind of sudden, but Sam took me under his wing when I started at R.J. He taught me a lot. He wants his crew together before the job gets started to go over the logistics ahead of time." Lee fiddled with the spoon, twirled an empty creamer cup.

She tried to pick up her mug, but her hand shook too much, and she left it. "I thought…" She shook her head and closed her eyes, refusing to give in to the tears that threatened. A one-sided relationship would never work, and it wasn't up to her to decide Lee's future. Only Lee could do that, just as Cole had chosen her own destiny. "When do you leave?"

"A couple of days." Lee reached for her but didn't touch her. "You're a wonderful person and a great lover, but I have to go." Lee broke eye contact, her lips pressed in a narrow line. "I can't give you what you want or deserve."

"So now you're clairvoyant?" she said sarcastically. The bitter tone was out of character, and she was unable to control the pain that came through. "You know me so well you can…" Lashing out wouldn't change Lee's mind, and, really, she didn't want to, but her ego was bruised. Damnit. It was her own fault. She was the one who'd assumed. She didn't want to be the kind of person who begged someone who didn't want to be with her to stay only to find out they were miserable. She could never be that selfish. Now that she'd found her comfort zone thanks to Lee's acceptance, she didn't have to be timid about what she wanted or how she lived her life. The bedroom was the place for her to play with her many sides. It was where she was comfortable being in the moment. She'd learned no matter what, at her core, she was always Cole, the woman she was destined to be. But God damn it, none of it changed how much she'd wanted to see where she and Lee might go together.

"I never meant to hurt you." Tears shimmered in Lee's eyes. "You've been a friend when I desperately needed one."

She had to know one thing. "The other morning when you left because you said you had a job to do. Was I wrong to think you were running from me? Again?"

Wincing, Lee ran her hand through her hair. "Cole…when you said those words and I couldn't say them back, I didn't know what else to do."

Cole sat back and tried to remember what she'd said. They'd given each other intense pleasure, several times, but she didn't remember anything specific. Anything that could have caused Lee to bolt. And what did she mean, she couldn't say them back? With the speed of a freight train, it hit her. *Oh my God.* In a post-climatic state, satiated and content, she'd mumbled the words she hadn't meant to say out loud. "Lee, you don't have to say anything. I didn't—"

Lee stood. "It's okay if you didn't mean them."

Though she was smiling, Cole understood the sadness that showed in her eyes. Her heart was breaking.

"I'm not easy to love. I never have been. Thank you for everything." Lee walked out the door without looking back.

She wasn't sure how long she'd been sitting there when the waitress appeared with a clean mug and a steaming pot. "I thought you could use a refresher." The woman stared at her. "You okay?"

Cole threw a twenty on the table. "No, I'm not, but I will be." How had things gone from so good to so horribly wrong? She held her head high and walked purposefully toward her truck. Once inside, she let her head fall back. Not since her father's death had she felt this empty. She hadn't meant to let Lee so far inside. She hadn't meant to tell Lee she loved her because she knew Lee ran from the things that scared her. Her fears had been validated. Could she blame her for returning to the safety of what she knew? Hell, Cole had done much the same when it came to personal relationships, choosing women who wouldn't be turned off by her quirkiness, especially since she rarely slept with the same woman twice. It had been her safety net. But Cole hadn't even considered having a net with Lee, which was irrational given their talk about where they were in their lives. Lee had been up front about what she wanted from life, and it wasn't her fault if Cole had dived headfirst into the shallow end.

And now Lee was leaving, and she'd be alone again, only this time the void was insurmountable. A chasm she had no means to cross. She thought about the more than half-full bottle of bourbon. Cole rarely indulged when she was alone, but if a broken heart wasn't reason enough, she didn't know what would be.

"I wish you weren't going." Dan hugged her tight.

She glanced at the remaining boxes still stacked in the garage and wondered when she'd come back for them. Sam had set the crew up in long-stay, temporary housing until the out-of-towners found a place of their own. She didn't want her stuff ransacked by the cleaning staff while she searched for an apartment, and there wasn't much room in the storage unit.

"It's for the best." She'd said the hollow words over and over the last couple of days in an attempt to convince herself the work she did gave her enough purpose. It made her happy. All along, she knew it was just a smoke screen. She couldn't admit that as much as she was going to miss her uncle, she was going to miss Cole more. But Cole wanted her love, and love wasn't something Lee could give her when she barely loved herself.

"If you change your mind, you've always got a home here."

Lee looked to the bright blue horizon. The mountain evergreens hung heavy with pinecones. Soon fall would come knocking and Dan told her there was nothing like it on earth. One thing was certain, the landscape was prettier here. She'd always thought nothing could compare to the ocean views, but she'd been wrong. She'd been wrong about a lot of things lately. She couldn't go back and fix them; all she could do was move forward. In time the pain would ease. The memories of Cole would always be there, but they would fade into the background, and her life would continue like it had before Inlet. Only this time she was the one doing the abandoning. Cole would pay the price, but she hoped that someday she'd forgive her. It was who Cole was, after all. Being the one to cause the pain tore at Lee's insides and made her physically sick. She had to go. Now.

"I'll call you when I get there. You take care of yourself, Uncle Dan. Thank you for welcoming me into your home, and for all you did for me. It was great to be with family."

"I hope you find what you're looking for." He hugged her again and kissed her cheek.

"So do I."

Chapter Twenty-four

Y ou two seemed good together." Her grandmother sat catty-corner at the kitchen table. "I thought Lee was the one."

Her breath caught in her chest. "I thought so, too. My mistake." Her eyes burned hot with unshed tears. "Her life isn't small town. She'd never be happy living here."

"I guess you'll never know. Her loss." Her grandmother studied her the way she had since she was a little girl. "What are you going to do?"

Cole went to the kitchen, picked up the coffee pot, and poured more of the strong brew. The hangover she was nursing reminded her why she didn't drink heavily. With the inch or so left in the bottle, she was lucky to be upright. Settling in her seat, Cole stared into the blackness while trying to see into the bottom. "I don't know. Lee..." Even mentioning her name brought a sharp, stabbing pain. "She showed me a different way of thinking." She held her grandmother's gaze. "I don't think I want to live alone...be alone...anymore. And I've been thinking about doing something other than the garage, but then I imagine Dad working on some junker, doing what he loved, and I'm not sure I can let it go."

Her grandmother reached for her and closed her wrinkled, heavily veined hands over hers. "Your father would not want you to stay stuck here if you weren't happy. We both know that. Take some time to figure it out."

"I can't leave you, Nana."

"Pshaw. I've lived on my own twice as long as you. I'll be fine."

She began to protest, but her grandmother wasn't having it. "Cole, I love you. Knowing you're happy is all that matters to me. Don't make your decision about anyone but you, you hear me?"

Cole let the warmth of being loved fill her. Her grandmother's love was a certainty she would always carry with her. "Yes, ma'am."

"Good. Now you go do whatever you have to and get rid of the alcohol in your head. You come back at six and we'll have dinner and see how far you've gotten."

She wasn't kidding anyone but herself if she thought her grandmother couldn't see what Cole had tried to do. She might have temporarily blunted the pain, but it was still there. Facing problems head-on was a characteristic her grandmother had instilled in her and one that had served her well throughout her life so far. There wasn't any reason to abandon it now.

"I'll see you later, Nana." Cole kissed her butter-soft cheek and turned to face the world that waited. No matter what she decided, her grandmother would be by her side, even if there was physical distance between them.

She went to the garage, where she could work on autopilot and think at the same time. But no matter where her thoughts led, she ended up at the same place. Lee knew how Cole felt about her, and she'd still left. She hadn't asked her to go with her, or even talked about trying the long-distance thing. It was just...over. And that meant she had to move on, without Lee.

"Cole."

She glanced around the open hood and smiled. "Hey, Michael." She quickly wiped her hands and gave him a long, hard hug. "To what do I owe the honor?"

"Can't a guy drop by for no special reason?"

"Sure, but that's not your normal MO, so what gives?"

Chagrinned, Michael stuffed his hands in his jean pockets. "I spoke with Aunt Betty."

"Oh." It had been more than three weeks since Lee left. Twenty-four days, fourteen hours, and...she glanced at her watch...thirty-two minutes. But she wasn't counting.

Michael threw his arm around her shoulders and walked her to the break room. He fixed two cups of steaming chicory coffee and handed her the one with a worn picture of a beagle on it.

"Thanks." The last thing she needed was more caffeine. She'd been surviving on coffee, some semblance of a meal here and there, and water. Somehow, she'd managed to stay away from heavy drinking. That was a victory, at least.

"What are you going to do?" Michael sat in the only other chair, their knees almost touching, like they'd done since they were kids while discussing problems they were dealing with.

She sipped, ignoring the burn of acid that exploded in her empty stomach. "I'm going to sell the garage."

Michael's eyes got big. "You sure? I thought you loved the garage."

Cole had done nothing but think about where she wanted her life to go, what she wanted to do, and who she wanted to do it with. "I loved it when I was here working with Dad. Right before he died, I promised to keep *his* dream alive. I'm not sure if it was ever my dream." She shrugged. "It was all I knew." She'd thought about doing something else, but then she'd remember the excitement in her father's eyes when he explained how a part worked, or how to fix a vehicle to "get it through another year" because the owner couldn't afford to really fix it. Staying in the garage originally kept her father close after he was gone. As time went on, staying had become habit more than desire. Now it held too many memories and her heart was no longer in it.

"And when you sell it?"

"I'm going to go to school for massage therapy."

Michael smiled. "I remember you talking about that years ago."

She nodded. "Once I'm certified, I can work anywhere in the state."

He groaned. "Please tell me you're not selling the farmhouse."

"I'm not sure if I could ever go that far, but it's a big house for one person. I could convert the front parlor into a massage room, work from home, or go to people who can't travel. I don't really need the money, I just want to do something I enjoy." Her overhead was minimal, and the rent on the land leases more than covered her living expenses. She worked because she loved being busy. There wasn't any reason she couldn't slow down a bit and enjoy more time with her grandmother. Make new friends. She and Lee had been friends. The pain sliced through her again like it did every time Cole thought of her, and she bled a little. Someday the bleeding would stop. "I would still be providing a service to the community. Maybe I'll get a dog, too."

"That's cool."

She slapped her thigh. "Hell, Michael, I'm shooting from the hip here. I've never been tied in knots over a woman before. All I think about is Lee, and I don't even know why. She obviously doesn't want to be with me." She'd sent a dozen text messages and left a couple of voice mails. To be honest, she was glad Lee hadn't picked up the phone. Hearing her voice would have probably sent her into another emotional tailspin. Lee returned most of the texts with short, neutral responses. Nothing to indicate she missed Cole or that she was sorry for the way things ended. She needed to move on for her sake.

"Maybe because you love her." He ducked when she shot him a glare. "Aunt Betty said it, so it must be true."

"I would caution you to not engage in unrequited love. It really sucks." She had refused to break down and cry over Lee's leaving. Michael had seen her at her best and her absolute worst, and her tears fell freely, staining her dark uniform top almost black. "I know I'll get through this, but it hurts like hell." He placed his hand on her knee, and the simple gesture grounded her. She'd taken for granted that the world—and Lee—would go the way she expected. It was her own fault.

"So, massage therapy, huh?" Michael adeptly changed the topic.

"Yeah."

"Guess that means you'll only be working on females."

She threw a spoon at him and he deflected it, chuckling the whole time.

"I got it. Only the pretty ones."

It had been weeks since she'd laughed, and it felt good. Michael's visit was just what she needed. "There's a thought." She put her cup in the small sink. "I need to finish the carburetor on Hank's baby, or he'll have my head. He's been without her for a week."

"You'll keep me posted?" Michael pulled her in for a tight tug.

"Promise." Cole hugged him back. "Thanks for coming by to check on me."

"I love you, Cole. If you weren't my cousin and gay, we'd be married by now."

She gave him a playful shove. "You're probably right." As Michael drove away, she took a deep breath, then another. They came easier than they had the last few weeks. Deciding to move forward felt good, even if it made her a little sad, too. She looked up. "Dad, I did my best." And she had, for him. For the garage. All she needed to do now was her best for herself.

❖

"Hi, Uncle Dan, how are you?" Lee had managed a few calls in the near month she'd been gone, but they hadn't *really* talked. That was all on her. Avoidance had always outweighed facing a situation head-on, reinforcing the notion she wasn't nearly as strong as Cole. *Cole.* Another person she'd run from but the only one whose absence had torn at her heart.

"Lee. How's the job going?"

"It's just getting started, but Sam's pulled together a great crew, so it should be fine. I managed to fenagle my way in on an apartment with two of the guys. I'm not sure if that was a good idea. Guys are such pigs, no offense."

Dan chuckled. "None taken. So, you're settled in, then?"

She would never be truly settled without Cole, and as much as she fought against admitting she'd made a mistake by running away, it was a truth she couldn't deny. "Some."

"Lee?"

"Yeah?"

"The garage is up for sale."

The stutter of her heart was real. "What? Cole's leaving Inlet?" She couldn't picture her being happy anyplace else. Was she selling the farmhouse, too? What about Betty? Surely, she wouldn't leave her grandmother behind. Her head began to spin with questions. She'd convinced herself the "I love you" had been meant in friendship because Cole hadn't tried to convince her to stay. There'd been no grand gesture to indicate she didn't want her to go. That wasn't Cole's style, and Lee knew it. She would never guilt someone into doing what *she* wanted for her own reasons. But soon after leaving she realized it's what Lee had hoped for. *God, I'm such a fool.* Her uncle's voice brought her back.

"I don't know. All I know is when I stopped for gas, there was a for sale sign out front."

"Why would she do that?" Lee ran her hand over her face. This was huge. Cole wasn't a knee-jerk type. She gave serious consideration to everything she did. "Did you talk to her?"

"She was inside the office with someone. I waved and took my time, but she never came out."

Fuck. She glanced around her stark room. The walls were naked and the furniture minimal. A straight back chair, a dresser, and a single bed that had been left by the last tenant. She hadn't even bothered to unpack her clothes. What did that say about how vested she was in her return to the city? "I miss her." Lee's hand shook as she doodled on a note pad. "I miss her a lot. God, what if I ruined her love for Inlet? What if that's why she's leaving?" Upset and saddened by the news, Lee's wheels kept turning. "I don't know what to do." She never knew what to do, she just reacted.

Dan let out a sigh. "Instead of your gut instinct, how about listening to your heart?"

Lee let his words sink in. Had she ever let her heart rule before? Had she ever had a reason to? Or felt the deep emotional and physical connection she'd experienced with Cole? When she stopped denying what was obvious and looked around a place she had no connection to at all, the answer was clear.

"Thanks, Uncle Dan." They talked a few more minutes before saying good-bye. She had a lot to do and the time to act had arrived. She opened her door to the sound of a baseball game blaring from the front room. It seemed the sports channels were the only ones her roommates ever watched. Just one more thing she wasn't going to miss.

Chapter Twenty-five

I think my truck is broken. Can you take a look?" Lee yelled into the cavernous space. She didn't see anyone around, but since the bay doors were open Cole had to be about somewhere. When a creeper appeared from under the last car, she couldn't help but smile. Cole sat up and intensely studied her. She deserved whatever came next, but she hoped she'd have a chance to say what she'd rehearsed a thousand times over the last four days.

"Hi." She finally got up but stayed several feet away. "If that's true, whoever repaired it did a shitty job."

"That can't be it. The mechanic who fixed it is extraordinary."

Cole tipped her head and took her in from head to toe. "What are you doing here?"

Lee moved closer but didn't try to touch her. Her heart pounded in her chest, and right or wrong, her clit had reacted the minute she looked into Cole's eyes. "We need to talk."

With her hand shaking, Cole reached for a rag, then wiped away the stains. She might have been trying to hide the trembling, but Lee saw it, nonetheless. Lee remembered every detail about Cole.

"I thought we did that before you left." Cole's voice was low but steady.

"No. I did most of the talking and none of the listening. I don't think I gave you much of a chance." Dark smudges under Cole's eyes were a clue she hadn't been sleeping well. "Can we? Talk."

"Lee, I don't know if there's anything to talk about. You've moved on, and I…" Cole took a breath without looking away, resolve clearly written on her face. "I'm going to do something different with my life. It's time. Past time, really."

"Please? I don't deserve it, but I'm asking for one more chance."

Cole's expression wavered. "Fine. My house at six. Bring some bourbon. I seem to have run out."

Lee was about to tell her she wouldn't regret it but that wasn't something she could say for certain. Cole likely already regretted having anything to do with her. She had one opportunity to get it right and she had every intention of doing just that.

❖

Cole stood on the back porch, her hands shoved deep in her pockets as she looked over the land. *Her land.* The farm had been in her family for at least five generations, probably more. Sadness engulfed her. She had worried about what would happen when she was gone. There had always been children to pass it on to, and since she could no longer have children of her own, she'd have to rely on a partner for that. One who wanted children, otherwise…she didn't want to think about the alternative. Michael was the only other relative she could trust to love it. The land had to go to someone who would take care of it and nurture it as her father had and his parents had before him.

The doorbell rang and she sighed. Lee would be standing out front, shifting from foot to foot and looking so fucking good she'd want to scream. All through the pain of her absence, the underlying current of pleasure she'd found in her arms remained. There wasn't much left to say though. Lee had made her choice and Cole had made hers. Mending fences should be easy, Cole had been doing it all her life, but this was the one fence that might be irreparable.

"How many times do I have to tell—" Cole froze.

Lee's bright blue-green eyes glistened with hope. She wore dark jeans and a button-down shirt of deep maroon, contrasting the blond shock of hair. A bottle of bourbon was cradled in the crook of her arm along with a bouquet of sunflowers. A tiny gift bag dangled from the fingertips of her other hand. Her smile wasn't tentative or shy, and it was heart-stopping.

"I know, but I'm going to continue to ring the bell and you're going to continue to tell me I don't need to." Lee leaned in and brushed her lips over Cole's. "If I'm still welcome after tonight, that is."

She should have said all the things she'd thought of saying over the last month. Should have yelled or screamed or done something—anything—to show Lee how much her leaving had hurt, but she couldn't. Lee was here and her heart drummed just as hard as it did the first time. Her pulse jumped and her clit twitched just like the first time they'd been alone together. She took a step back and motioned her in, then took the items and set them on the entryway table. Before she had time to change her mind, she took Lee by the shoulders and stared into the depths of her eyes, drowning herself in the warmth of them.

"I should be angry." She glanced from Lee's eyes to her mouth, to the indentation of her throat where the skin was so soft and sweet it reminded her of ripe fruit that yielded to her teeth, making her mouth water. Cole returned her gaze to Lee's eyes, and the desire in them moved her to action. She pressed her against the door, captured her mouth, and tried to convey how very much she'd missed her in the scorching intensity of the kiss.

Gasping, Lee turned her head. "Oh God." Her body trembled.

Cole pressed her thigh between Lee's legs. "I'm not God, but having you here makes me feel like I'm in heaven." She backed away. "But first, I need to hear what you came to say." It took every ounce of concentration she had to pick up the bottle and flowers and move toward the kitchen. Kitchen tables were deep discussion territory. Two miniature mason jars sat at the ready. Sensing rather than hearing Lee behind her, she took the time to find a vase to settle her body from reacting as it always did when they were together. No matter what Lee had to say, she had every intention of taking her to bed, consequences be dammed. She'd already paid the price of loving Lee. That love was bought and paid for. She wouldn't feel guilty for having a part of Lee for selfish reasons. This time, Cole would brand Lee's skin with her touch and Lee's gaze would be tattooed on her heart forever. She set the flowers on the table in the same spot Lee had placed the wildflowers the day they buried Dixie. Funny how every detail came into focus without even trying.

Lee opened the bottle, poured, and remained silent until Cole sat down. "I fucked up. Big time." She held her jar aloft.

Cole waited. What good would it do either of them to hurl accusations and angry words? Lee had done what she thought she needed to do, and no magic in her collection of wishes would turn back the clock. They could only go forward, and forward was the only direction she had any interest in. She raised her drink. "To today," she said, and threw back the burn without blinking an eye. She'd gotten good at ignoring pain.

Lee took a modest sip. "When I found out you were selling the garage, I couldn't believe it. I thought you loved what you were doing." She started to protest, but Lee raised her hand. "I thought I loved what I did, too. I still do. But it's different from when I arrived in Inlet. *I'm* different." Lee moved to the edge of her seat, fight or flight radiating off her. She lifted the bottle and poured herself another inch. "When my parents threw me out, I knew they couldn't love me for being who I was. They loved the idea of an obedient daughter they could be proud of. And when I went to college, I thought I'd found love with a woman in my dorm, but she didn't love me. She loved the sex I provided and the fun we had together, but she didn't love *me*." Lee downed the last of her drink. "After graduating, I got an apprenticeship in a construction firm. I enjoyed it because I could take something, tear it apart, and make it look beautiful. It made me feel useful, capable, like what I did mattered. For the first time in my life, I was successful and financially secure, and I learned to live my life the way I wanted." Lee went quiet, her hand around the jar, deep in thought.

"I think you were successful before that," she said. Lee was troubled by a shortcoming that existed only in her head. "Not many teenagers would have done what you did and survived, and you've more than survived, you thrived."

"You're kind to say so. The truth is I ran, and I've never really stopped. I ran from my parents, my friends, my lovers. Whenever I felt insecure, I was gone. It was easier than asking the questions I didn't want to know the answers to." Lee downed another shot and coughed hard. "How can you drink this like it's water?" Lee asked once she could talk.

Cole laughed. "Hardy stock? No sense? Who knows?" She poured a ridiculously small amount in Lee's cup and filled hers halfway. "To being afraid of the unknown." Lee tapped her glass and they drank. The fireball hit her stomach and she grimaced. She really needed to eat something. "I'll be right back."

She went to the fridge and found a block of cheese and snagged a box of crackers. She wanted to fill the empty places inside of her, too. The places no woman had been interested in filling.

She felt her nearness before Lee wrapped her arms around her waist and kissed the side of her neck. Her lips were warm, soft, and Cole relaxed against her, unable to deny how much she'd longed for Lee's touch and her firm body against hers.

"You feel so good. Smell so good." Lee dragged her teeth along the length of her neck, sending a shiver down her spine. Her hand moved upward and stopped before it reached her breast. But the intent was clear, and Cole's heart galloped in response.

She turned in Lee's arms. "I'd be lying if I said I didn't miss you. All of you." She placed a light kiss on Lee's chest where her shirt lay open. She wanted more and yearned for the connection they once shared. "Let's have something besides alcohol, shall we?"

Lee searched her face, as though looking for answers she wasn't sure she had, then backed away. "Okay." She picked up the board and carried it to the table.

She took a slow breath. There were questions that needed answering and she was determined to get them. Before joining Lee, she grabbed a couple of waters, then eased onto the chair and snagged a piece of cheese. The sharp bite helped clear her head. "I get why you ran from your parents, but why did you run from me? I thought we had something."

Tears glistened in Lee's eyes. "We did. I was terrified I couldn't love you the way you deserved. I don't have a great track record. I'm not even sure I know how to love myself, let alone someone like you."

"Like me?"

One corner of Lee's mouth lifted. "Kind, generous, strong, sexy, fun, beautiful, loving. Should I continue?"

"You make me out to be someone who's perfect." She picked up a cracker, trying to focus on taking her time instead of quickly forgiving and heading to the bedroom, and forced herself to remember what the heartache had felt like. Still did.

"That's just it." Lee threaded her fingers with hers. "You *are* perfect...for me. You challenge me. You've seen things no one else has ever bothered looking for. It took being away from you to realize how much I want another chance, Cole. I want to show you how desperately I want that, even though I know I'll fuck up sometimes. Even if you tell me to leave right now, I'm going to stick around and try to convince you we're meant to be together. Please let me show you?"

"You're staying in Inlet? For me?"

"For us. This place has grown on me. I didn't think it would, but things change. Please give me a second chance."

"You'll talk to me if you get scared? If you feel the urge to run again, I have to know we'll sit and discuss it, and work things through."

Lee kissed her hand and pressed it to her cheek. "I swear."

Cole swallowed hard. There were still so many unanswered questions. So much she wasn't sure of. What was that old saying? *Be willing to take a chance because you never know how perfect something could be unless you do.* She wanted that, and she wanted it with Lee. Right now what she wanted most had nothing to do with unanswered questions and everything to do with the heat of passion and desire she could so easily read in Lee's eyes. She stood and brought Lee to her feet, then led her to her bedroom.

"It's not just sex I want from you. I want your promise of tomorrow."

"Tomorrow isn't promised, but waking up knowing you've given me another chance is something to aspire to." Lee brushed her knuckles along her jaw. "I know it's not just sex, and I want more of all of you."

Cole ran her hands over Lee's shoulders, then moved her thumbs to trace her collarbones before contiuing down her bulging arms, the muscles twitching beneath her touch. "I didn't think I'd ever get to feel you again." Lee's breasts lifted with her rapid breaths, and the strain of holding back was evident on her face. Cole couldn't imagine not sinking her fingers deep inside her. Lee's body trembled and she grinned nervously. "I want you, too." She cupped Lee's full breasts, blew a warm breath over her nipples, and watched them tighten.

"I'll never say no." Lee's mouth twitched into a small smile as she pressed forward. "But I hope you'll let me fuck you, too. Easy. Hard. Whatever you want, however you want it."

Cole shivered as the vision formed. She hadn't ever considered there was a side of her that wanted someone to command her body, until Lee had shown her there was nothing wrong with giving in to the desire of being taken care of or being the receiver rather than the giver. She made Lee gasp as she squeezed and tugged the puckered peaks. Her eyes burned with naked need that inflamed Cole to take what *she* wanted. At least, she hoped that's what she saw.

Lee pulled her down on top of her until their lips met. Cole held her hip and moved over her flat stomach, slipping her hand under the material to her downy covered mound, gliding her fingers through her excitement, and Lee's hard clit pressed against her palm.

"Take me."

She groaned and pushed into Lee as she spread her legs wider to invite her deeper. Slick and tight and hot. She needed to inhale her and taste her, wanted her in every way possible. She would brand her and lay claim to her. Cole wanted to be unforgettable. Every time Lee closed her eyes, she wanted to be the only woman she ever saw. She outlined Lee's lips with her tongue as she pulled away before stripping to her underwear. Her fingers trembled as she removed Lee's clothes, tossing each piece to the floor while she let herself become lost in Lee's gaze.

Cole settled over her and pressed into Lee's center. "I want you so bad." She kissed her hard, and a sense of urgency unlike any she'd ever felt, electrified every fiber of her being. She moved her hand between them to capture the hard, swollen knot and tugged. Lee moaned. "Will you come for me, love? Fill my hand?" As she circled her, slippery moisture covered her fingers, and Lee's hips thrust upward for more contact.

"Yes. God, yes."

Cole pressed deeper. She held still, enjoying the tight space, and kissed her as she began to move in and out, the pace carefully timed. Lee tried to meet her, but she held her down with her body. Lee's pupils contracted and her eyes darkened, clouded with desire. Buried inside her, Cole thumbed Lee's surging clit. "Look at me while you come." She pulled back, entered her hard. Once, twice.

"Coming." Lee gasped, her fingers digging into Cole's shoulders.

Lee shook beneath her. Muscles flexed as her abdomen became a hard plank. She was beautiful, and when her body tried to crush her fingers, Cole wanted her again. Wanted to experience that surge of power as she guided Lee's body toward the edge of oblivion. After she came, Cole yearned for more. Her insatiable need drove her on. But this time Cole wanted to taste her and when Lee's eyes fluttered open, Cole brought her fingers to her mouth and sucked them. Lee's unique flavor was familiar, salty and sweet. Her tousled hair had a freshly fucked look. She was gorgeous and perfect in the ways that mattered most to Cole.

"Do you have any idea how hungry I've been for you?" She kissed her gently. "Not just in bed, and not just for sex. For *you*, Lee. For you." Her vision blurred and she tried to blink the tears away. "I thought I'd never see you again."

Lee kissed the wetness on her cheeks. "Baby, I'm here." Lee held her face. "We can just hold each other. I want to feel your body next to mine. I've missed you, too. More than I can say."

The idea of snuggles was tempting, but tomorrow held no promise, and she'd be damned if she wasn't going to take everything Lee had to give. "Maybe later, but right now I'm going to feast on you." She pushed Lee's thighs open and settled in. With her tongue flattened, she licked the length of her in slow motion. Once. Twice. Three times. Her cheeks were slick with Lee's essence as she buried her face in her pussy and pressed her tongue into her hot entrance, wanting to consume her. Lee grabbed a handful of her hair.

"God, you make me feel so good," she said, her voice rough.

Lee's legs began to shake. She held the throbbing length of her clit in her mouth, loving how it swelled as she gently sucked. Lee's strangled cry and surging hips drew her gaze upward. Strong, sexy Lee was sobbing as her orgasm washed over her. Having her fill, Cole climbed up beside her and pulled her into an embrace as the last vestiges left Lee's body limp.

Cole kissed her chest. Her face. Her lips. "It's okay, love, it's okay." Because it was. Lee had given herself completely, and that's how she wanted to love Lee. Totally and completely. She maneuvered until Lee was half on top of her and smoothed her hands over her warm body. Lee mumbled against her chest, some incoherent apology. "Shh...rest now." As Lee's breathing evened into the steady rhythm of sleep, doubt crept in. She'd asked for a second chance without saying the words Cole most needed to hear. If Lee couldn't tell her she loved her, she wasn't sure she could trust the future.

❖

"God, I'm a mess," Lee whispered against Cole's breast.

"It's okay. You're a beautiful mess."

She used every ounce of strength she had to move over Cole and rested her weight on her forearms. "Nice of you to say, but if I remember correctly, you wanted me to show *you* how much I wanted another chance."

Cole smoothed her palms along her shoulders, down her arms. "You did. You gave yourself over to me. You trusted me. You let me see your vulnerable side."

She captured her mouth and kissed her slowly, tenderly. Denying she wanted to give Cole everything she had to give would have been futile. She may have fucked up, but that ended here by showing Cole how much she cared for her. How much she loved her. Yet, she couldn't bring herself to say the words. They were on the tip of her tongue right along with the fear she'd waited too long to say them out loud.

While she argued with herself to tell her, she didn't fight the need to touch her, and moved her hand over the outer curve of her breast, and used her thumb to massage the softness in such contrast to the rest of her lean, muscled form. Her mouth watered as she watched Cole's nipples tighten. "I really need to touch you."

"You won't hear me object," Cole said as she lightly dragged her nails along her sides.

Cole's warm, smooth skin felt amazing against her palm. Beads of moisture clung to the soft, dark hair between her thighs, and her slick center begged for attention. The urgency coursing through her told her to hurry, and she fought against it.

Lee mapped Cole's body, memorizing the peaks and valleys. The firm places and the incredibly soft ones. She finger-walked along the lines, noting when Cole shuddered, or moaned, or sighed. Cole hadn't actually said there was a chance for them, though their physical attraction remained intact. For the first time in her life, physical wasn't enough. Lee wanted the emotional connection she'd never had and so desperately wanted. Cole stilled her hand.

"Tell me what you were feeling when you left. While you were gone." Cole flipped onto her side and faced her.

"Now?"

"Right now." Cole rested her head on her hand. Watching. Waiting.

Of course, Lee couldn't blame her. She blew out a breath. She'd never been good at facing what made her uncomfortable. Hated it, actually. She was used to the yelling, angry kind of discussions, when words were meant to hurt and degrade and shame. What she said in this instant mattered and she fought to find the right words. "I'm not going to make excuses. After we made love, I was open, vulnerable, but I was also content." Cole listened while looking at her with such intensity she almost broke eye contact. Almost. "You were laying in my arms, relaxed. Satisfied."

"I remember."

She nodded, refocused on her thoughts and feelings, not Cole's. "When you said 'I love you,' I was sure I'd made it up in my head and I was terrified. I almost left right then, but I couldn't."

"Why not?" The tenderness in Cole's voice made her want to cry. Cole's fingers twitched, as though she wanted to touch her.

"Because no one had ever said it before." Her gaze flicked away for an instant. "Because I loved you too, and the thought of leaving you when you were in my arms…" She shook her head, tears threatening. Cole's fingers brushed her jaw, directed her back.

"Leaving because you were afraid is one thing. Moving away and not even returning my calls broke my heart." Cole's voice was soft, no anger or judgment, just the truth. Just…Cole.

She pulled in a shaky breath as her vision blurred. "I never meant to hurt you. I wasn't afraid of your love. I was afraid of mine. I've failed so much, and I didn't want to fail you."

"Why would you think you'd fail me?' Cole moved closer, the heat of her body like a warm blanket wrapped around her.

"Because I don't deserve your love."

"Why not?" Cole took her hand.

"I've never loved anyone. There were lots of times I didn't even like myself." There. She'd said it. Her greatest fear was out there on the proverbial table. In that moment, Lee hated herself. Hated the walls she'd built and all the things she'd been denied because of them.

Cole shifted to prop herself against the headboard. "I think you're being awfully hard on yourself, but I won't lie to you. I'm worried. It wasn't the first time you've run, and I have to be able to trust you won't leave if things get tough, because they will. That's life. But I also believe if we face the future together, there isn't anything we can't handle." Cole kissed her softly. "Are you sure this is what you want?"

"All I've thought about is us, about you. Christ, I've done nothing but think. I've been miserable without you."

Cole ran her fingertips down the center of her chest, leaving a trail of heat. Mostly though, Cole's touch reached her heart. She broke out in gooseflesh.

"I'm not sorry about that." A wry grin appeared on Cole's face. "I've been lost in the void. One minute you're here, the next gone."

"Fuck. This is why I had to come back. Because I need to face what I've done and apologize." She moved her hand to find Cole's. "An apology will never be enough, but it's what I've got."

Cole took a deep breath and let out a long sigh. "I'll accept your apology on one condition."

"Anything. Whatever you want."

The corners of Cole's mouth twitched. "Make me come."

She kissed her long and hard. "Whenever you want."

❖

Cole cried out as she climaxed and pushed away any lingering thoughts of having her heart broken again.

Lee had proven life served up highs and lows, an ebb and flow. And while tides were predictable, the landscapes they touched were ever changing. There were other parts of life, though, that Lee helped her find, and she needed to focus on them. A space to be comfortable in being herself, whenever and however she wanted. She'd shown her a way to share grief and sorrow without words. How to enjoy the simple gift of giving to someone who hadn't been given much in her life without a price attached.

"Are you okay?" Lee asked.

"Yes. No. Maybe?" She tried not to laugh at the panic in Lee's expression. "It's okay, baby. Just a lot going on in my head."

"Then I've failed you." Lee cupped her breast and gently squeezed. "You shouldn't be able to think at all when I'm making love to you, except that you're going insane with need."

"Oh, I couldn't think. Not until right after the world came crashing back." She cupped Lee's face. "I love you."

"I love you, too." Lee brushed swollen lips over hers. "Tell me what's going on in there." Lee lightly tapped her forehead.

"Stuff. Where do we go from here and how do we get there? Are you coming back to me or is this a long-distance thing? And while I love having you around, you need more than me in your life."

"Wow."

"Yeah. Lots of stuff."

"Then we should talk more."

"We will, but not tonight. I just want you to be in my arms until the morning light wakes us."

"That sounds wonderful." Lee tucked her body close with an arm over her stomach.

She was tired of thinking. Tired of worrying. Lee was here and that's all she needed to be sure of for tonight. "Just a minute." She untangled their legs and engaged the lock on her bedroom door before slipping back under the covers."

"Why did you do that?" Lee asked, as she readjusted.

"In case you want to bolt. I'm hoping the lock will slow you down enough that I can catch you."

Lee slapped her stomach. "You think you're funny, don't you?"

Cole caught her hand, brought it to her lips. "Not at all, just planning ahead." She wanted plans that included Lee. They still had work to do and details to iron out, but they'd come. She was sure of it.

CHAPTER TWENTY-SIX

The coffee pot beeped. Lee took in all the modern conveniences in the kitchen and smiled. For as much as Cole boasted about being small town, you couldn't tell from the fancy culinary gadgetry she'd discovered while hunting for the coffee pot and fry pans. She let the brew steep for a couple of minutes and broke a half dozen eggs in a bowl. Once she had them whipped smooth, she added milk, a touch of vanilla and cinnamon, then sank a thick piece of homemade bread into the mixture. The built-in griddle was a nice feature on the massive stove top, and she planned on using it as often as Cole let her. She would also make a point of exercising every other day if she were going to eat like this. With the sausage sizzling in the pan, she began humming as she moved around the kitchen.

"You're awfully chipper this morning. What are you doing up already?" Cole leaned against the island, her silk robe open to reveal she wore nothing underneath. The smile on her face suggested she knew exactly what effect her wardrobe, or lack of, would have on her. Cole sauntered over and lifted her chin with her index finger, as though to close her mouth. "You'll catch something you don't want in there if you aren't careful."

"You don't play fair."

After pouring coffee and adding cream, Cole turned. "Who says I'm playing?"

She moved so fast she surprised herself, but the wide-eyed expression on Cole's face was well worth it. "If you play with fire, you're going to get burned." She growled low in her throat and pushed her fingers into Cole's wet entrance. "Is this what you want for breakfast?" Lee slid out and pulled at Cole's swollen clit. Cole's legs trembled, and making her weak kneed made them on even ground.

Cole leaned against her. "Maybe, since whatever you're making is burning."

Lee glanced over her shoulder. "Shit." She pulled out, grinning quickly, then grabbed the pan of sausage and shoved it onto a cold burner. Glaring, she turned her attention on Cole. "This is your fault."

Cole's brow raised. "I hardly think so. I didn't invite you to sink your fingers into my pussy."

She pursed her lips. "Oh, now I need an invitation?"

"You've been practicing," Cole said as she ran her index finger along the edge of her jaw. "We're debating meaningless points like a long-suffering couple."

"If you expect to get anything that's not burnt, I suggest you close your robe, otherwise you might *be* breakfast."

"Mmm. Tempting, but I'm ravenous." Cole refilled her cup and fixed a second before taking a seat at the island. She tapped the stool next to her. "Come have your breakfast, baby."

"I'm good here." She stood on the opposite side and slid a plate in front of Cole.

"Don't be silly. You cooked. Relax while you eat, and I'll clean up."

Lee shrugged. "I don't want to." When Cole's brow wrinkled, she confessed. "I can't look at you if I'm next to you. I've missed your face."

Cole's gaze softened. "Babe, come sit. I promise you can still see me."

She huffed before moving around and taking her assigned seat. "Hold on." She held her hand up before Cole picked up the jug of maple syrup. She reached around and brought the material together, then tied it. "As much as I love your body, I can't eat breakfast and not want you." She brushed her lips over Cole's.

Cole shared a mischievous smile. "So, what's on your agenda today?"

"Unpack the truck first."

Cole's fork was halfway to her mouth. "Wait. What?" She blinked several times.

"Didn't I tell you? I quit my job. I'm here for good."

A kaleidoscope of emotions flashed in Cole's eye before she jumped up and hugged her, nearly knocking her off the stool.

"When were you going to tell me?"

"Last night, but…well, other things took precedent, and I didn't want to steal your thunder."

Cole play-punched her. "My thunder could have waited." She resumed pouring an outrageous amount of syrup on her French toast. "So, where—" The doorbell rang. "Jesus. Who could that be on a Sunday morning?" Cole jerked her robe tighter.

She jumped off her stool. "I'll get it, if you don't mind."

Cole harrumphed. "You better or I may look for a weapon."

Lee hid her smile by turning away. She opened the front door and stuck her hand out. "Hi, I'm Lee."

"Nice to meet you. You sure about this?" Michael glanced at his feet.

"Definitely. I cleared it with Betty."

Michael picked up the box. "You're a fast learner. I'll see you in a week. Enjoy your time."

She accepted the package from him. "I owe you big. I promise you won't be sorry."

"Go, before she shows up with a gun."

"What is it with guns in this family? Should I be worried?"

Michael cocked a smile at her. "Only if you keep her waiting too long."

"Got it." She turned and headed for the kitchen, praying all the plans she'd made weren't for naught.

"Who was that?" Cole asked around the last bite. Even though the sausage was a bit crisp, breakfast had been delicious. She'd been a little surprised by Lee's skills in the kitchen until she remembered Lee had been doing for herself for a long time.

Lee set down a big box with a red bow. "Delivery."

"From whom?"

Lee shrugged. "If it was December, I'd say Santa Clause. Open it."

Cole knelt and pulled the lid off. A German shepherd puppy was curled up inside on a big, fluffy blanket, sound asleep. She gasped and looked up. "Did you? Is it for me?"

"I did, and of course she's for you." Lee crouched down by the box. "I have it on good authority you've been thinking about getting a dog, and...well, a pup is always best. You get to teach them all the stuff they can and can't do right from the start."

"What's her name?" She scooped up the round ball of fluffy fur, making her whimper and open her sleepy little eyes.

"That's up to you."

Cole thought about a name. It had been so long since she'd had a puppy. "Is her color going to change?"

Lee pulled out her phone. "I've got a picture of her mom."

The adult's back was mostly black, and she had caramel brown brows, chest, and forelegs. The pup was an exaggerated copy. "Luna. Is that okay?"

"You're not mad?" Lee looked worried.

"Baby, I think she's a wonderful surprise. Thank you." Cole kissed the frown from her forehead.

"Good. There's going to be times when I'm gone for a while and I didn't want you to be alone. I want her here to protect you when I'm not around to."

Dread rose up, churning the contents of her stomach. "What do you mean for a while? You've just come back."

Lee appeared sheepish. "Another surprise. Your cousin, Michael, offered me a job with his crew. He said they travel a lot, sometimes for weeks, which will fucking kill me I'm sure, but reunion sex is great, so there's that." She smiled.

"Again with the curveball. When...?" It didn't really matter how Lee had made it possible to return, and get her a dog, and find a job. All of those wonderful things solidified Lee's words as true. Lee wanted their relationship to work, and she'd gone to great lengths to try to make it happen. She could find out how later. There was just one detail she wanted to clarify. "Are you moving in?"

Lee blushed. "I don't want to crowd you. You want to do something different. I get that. I'll support you and be by your side no matter what. Uncle Dan said he'd be happy for me to stay with him again. I'm going to be busy on a job and you're going to do whatever you've decided to do after the garage."

"Look around. This place was never meant for one person. There's plenty of space. If you annoy me too much, there's always the barn, or the shed."

Lee looked stricken before shaking her head. "Are you considering becoming a comedian?" She pulled her close to hug her. Luna whimpered. "You wouldn't mind if I moved in?"

Cole gently set Luna on her blanket. "I'll help you unpack. Let's go." She hadn't been this keyed up about anything in a long, long time.

"Babe?"

"Yeah?"

"You might want to put something else on."

She glanced down and giggled. "I'm a little excited."

Lee held her face and kissed her slowly. "So am I."

"I'll be right back."

❖

Lee was rambling. She couldn't help it. They carried the last of the boxes into the hallway and stacked them on top of the others next to the staircase. "I don't know what to do with my furniture. I don't want to throw it out, it's like new. I guess I could leave it for a while."

Cole handed her a bottle of water before sitting on the stairs. "They're your things. I think we should go get them."

Lee thought for a minute about logistics, something else she'd discovered she was good at. There were other rooms in the rambling home she hadn't even seen yet. "Okay. So we rent a van and road trip it to get my stuff. Overnight, because it's like seven hours one way."

"What about Luna?" The puppy was investigating her new space, wandering from place to place, her tail wagging constantly.

"Luna comes with us. She's part of the family. Our family." She held Cole's gaze. "It will be a great way to acclimate her to traveling and bonding."

"We'll have to get supplies. I don't have anything for her."

She picked up a large shopping bag among the pile of her things and handed it to Cole. "The rest of your present." Inside was puppy food, chew toys, a collar, harness, leash, and an array of other likely useless items, but she'd been so wound up she grabbed one of almost everything that caught her attention.

There were tears in Cole eyes. "Have I told you I love you?"

"Maybe a time or two." She grinned.

Luna looked between them, yipped once, and then proceeded to pee on the tile floor. Cole snatched up her still peeing pup and beelined out the door. When Lee got to the porch, Cole was kneeling in the grass, having a heart to heart with Luna and telling her the rules about not peeing or pooping in the house. That she and Lee were going to love her and show her what a great place she'd come to live in. She couldn't agree more. Luna yipped and circled, fell over, bounced back up and did it all again. Cole's laughter was light and joyful.

"Luna, come." Cole hand-gestured and Luna tumbled behind her. She tried to leap up the first step, but she was rounder than she was tall, and flopped onto her back. Cole reached down for her. "I guess it's carrying you till your legs grow." Luna licked at Cole's face. "Ugh. Puppy breath."

Lee stepped close, but Cole backed away. "I'm pee covered. A shower would be really good right now, but I'm not sure we should leave her to explore."

"Just a sec." She grabbed a chew toy from the bag. "We might want to get her a crate, but I didn't know how you'd feel about that. If we give her something to keep her busy, we can take her in the bathroom with us."

"I've always liked the way you think."

After a long, sensual shower, occasionally interrupted by puppy yips, they got out and toweled off. They discussed travel plans and how some of Lee's furniture would mesh with Cole's, especially a piece or two in her soon to be revamped massage room.

Lee watched Cole and Luna playing on the grass, and she could barely breathe, her contentment overwhelming. She'd never pictured a life of love in a small town, but in her heart, there was no question that this was where she belonged—at Cole's side, living and loving through hot sultry days, and equally hot nights. For the first time in her life, she looked forward to tomorrow with euphoric anticipation.

EPILOGUE

One year later...

Cole's phone pinged, announcing a text. She finished changing the sheets on the massage table before swiping her screen. The displayed message made her smile.

Two hours away. God, I've missed you.

Sighing, Cole shared the sentiment. Luna lay in the doorway and raised her head. "Lee's coming home, girl." Luna sat up and whined, her tail wagging. She scratched behind her ear. "I miss her, too."

The front door opened, and Dan Burke walked in. Luna went to greet him. "Hi, Cole. Hello, Luna." He petted Luna's head after receiving a thorough sniff. "How is everyone?"

"Good. I just heard from Lee. She'll be home after we're done. You're welcome to stay. I'm sure she'd love to see you."

"After six weeks, I'm fairly certain she would rather have you all to herself."

"I'm hers." She held up her ring finger. "Forever. I think we can control ourselves for a visit with our favorite uncle."

"I've always liked you, Cole. I like you even more knowing how happy you've made Lee. You both deserved to find a home for your hearts...and your desires."

Cole blushed. She and Dan had a bull session late into the night during one of Lee's out-of-town jobs. They'd gotten a little drunk and confessed a little too much. She'd inadvertently shared a bit more than she should have about how much pleasure Lee gave her. Dan never mentioned the details of that conversation, but from the look on his face she'd been quite descriptive.

"Go on in, Dan. I'll be there shortly." He nodded, smiled, and closed the door. Dan was her last massage of the day. When she'd heard Lee was coming home, she'd cleared the rest of her Friday schedule. They'd celebrate her return for the entire weekend.

Cole sat on the bench they'd brought back from the storage unit. Her customers all knew to just come in, and the memory of Lee standing outside whenever she'd come over made her smile. If the door to the massage room was closed, customers settled in to wait their turn. If Luna wasn't out running in the fields, she would greet them and keep them company until she or Lee appeared.

"Go play for a while, girl. I'll call you when I'm done."

Luna licked her hand and padded off to the back door. Lee had installed a doggie door in the mud room once Luna had been trained to stay on the property. She washed her hands in the half bath off the foyer, then knocked on the door and stepped through.

"How's your body feeling? What can I do to help you feel better?" she asked, closing the door behind her.

After hearing what muscles needed the most attention, she began the massage while soft music played in the background. When she got to the practical part of her training, it surprised her to find how similar working on the human body was to cars. Each one was different. Each one needed special attention to one part or another. Sometimes her touch needed to be soft, coaxing the part to relax and let go. Other times they needed a firm hand to manipulate the desired change.

Lee still occasionally mentioned missing the slightly rough pads of her fingertips. Cole made up for whatever sensation she longed for in other ways. God, how she loved that woman. During one of their post-orgasm chats while they lay in each other's arms, she told Lee she'd found her balance. Her outward presentation of androgynous butch, for all intents and purposes, was who she'd always been. However, in the bedroom, she was happy playing with presentation and not always having to be in control, or dominant, or whatever label it might have. Lee loved all of her sides, and all of her quirky, kinky, playful moods. That's really all that mattered. Lee loved and wanted Cole, the whole person.

Seventy-five minutes later, Dan emerged after redressing. His relaxed posture assured her she'd done what he insisted he pay her to do. The same as all of her customers. She handed him a bottle of water and waved him to follow her to the kitchen. He dropped onto a stool as she fixed a pot of decaf. The plate of cheese and fruit she'd prepared earlier sat on the island, along with a variety of flat breads and crackers.

"Help yourself. Lee will be home soon."

"I should go." He started to get up.

She put her hand on his arm. "She misses you. I can't tell you how many times she's told me she didn't know what she would have done if you hadn't welcomed her into your home. Into your heart." Memories of the first glance, their first touch, warmed her. "You're the reason we met and fell in love."

"I'm prejudiced, but I think she's pretty easy to love."

"I happen to know you're right."

Luna came bowling through the doggie door and skidded to a stop in front of her with her tongue hanging out her mouth.

"What?" Luna turned in excited circles and chuffed, stamping her feet. Dan raised a brow. "Lee's home." Luna dropped her head to her paws, ass in the air, and whined. "Okay. Go to the door." Luna jumped up and disappeared. Dan laughed. "Is Lee prepared to be knocked over?"

"Luna won't jump on her. She's not allowed, and she knows it. Especially not now. I think she senses there's something different with Lee. Come on. Let's give her a family welcome."

❖

Lee pulled the truck to a stop as her mind settled into the familiar calm that always enveloped her when she arrived home. Cole would be waiting with open arms, and Luna would impatiently sit until she was acknowledged. The SUV parked off to the side was an unexpected treat and she jumped out, taking the stairs two at a time, then opened the door. She'd gotten over the feeling of not belonging pretty quickly once she'd moved in.

"Welcome home, love." Cole folded her arms around her and kissed her. Luna whined.

"Hi, babe."

"How are you feeling?"

"Great, especially now that I'm home." She hugged Cole again before letting go. "Uncle Dan, what a nice surprise. It's good to see you." She hugged him and he gently returned her embrace.

"I was going to leave you two to your reunion, but Cole insisted I stay."

"I'm glad she did."

Dan looked over her shoulder and chuckled. "I think someone's ready for her greeting."

Lee turned. Luna sat with a paw raised, trying her hardest to rein in her enthusiasm. "Luna, come." She jumped up and trotted to her before circling her legs and leaning into her. "I've missed you, too, girl." She rubbed Luna's side and scratched her head. She glanced at Cole. "Please tell me there's coffee."

Cole laughed. "Of course. Decaf."

She groaned. "I'll be glad when I can have the real thing again. Come on, Uncle Dan," she said as she wrapped an arm around Cole's waist and rested her hand on his shoulder. "Tell me all the latest town gossip. Cole never gets the details." She hugged her wife tighter.

Lee poured her coffee and inhaled the rich aroma. She loved working with Michael, but Cole still made the best coffee in the world. One of her guilty pleasures. While she snacked, Dan told her about old Mrs. Perth, the town busybody, and the latest dirt she was spreading. When the laughter died down, Dan became serious.

"So, how long are you going to keep working?"

"I'm barely beginning to show. The doctor said I could work as long as I feel well."

"With the exception of heavy lifting in her last month," Cole chimed in.

She kissed Cole's head. "Yes, love, I remember." If someone had asked her a couple of years ago if she would ever have children she'd have vehemently scoffed at the notion. That was before Cole had helped her understand they had so much they could give to their child and that they would never have to do it alone. They did, indeed, have a village to raise their son or daughter. The reality that Cole couldn't carry their baby had been devastating for Cole, and Lee had done some reassuring of her own. Carrying their baby had been an easy decision. She would have done anything to wipe the sadness from Cole's beautiful eyes.

Dan stood. "I'm going to leave you two to have a proper welcome home."

Lee hugged him and promised to drop by for lunch during the week. When Cole returned from seeing him out, she kissed her hard.

"Dan's right. We need a proper reunion. God, I've missed you." Cole took her hand.

"Do you want to show me how much after a nice warm shower?" Lee asked.

"Sounds pretty perfect to me. I'd like nothing better than to show you every minute of every day."

Lee smiled. It sounded perfect to her, too.

About the Author

RENEE ROMAN lives in upstate New York where she embraces the change of seasons. She is passionate about cooking, entertaining, and writing lesbian romance and erotica. Her works include her debut novel *Epicurean Delights*, *Bonded Love*, and most recently, *Body Language*.

"Hard Body" was her first solo erotic short story.

Renee is writing her seventh novel, *Escorted*, and has several more ideas taking form. Rest assured; this is *not* where her stories end.

You can find Renee on Twitter @ReneeRoman2018, and Facebook at https://www.facebook.com/renee.roman.71/ or you can contact her at reneeromanwrites@gmail.com

Books Available from Bold Strokes Books

Busy Ain't the Half of It by Frederick Smith and Chaz Lamar Cruz. Elijah and Justin seek happily-ever-afters in LA, but are they too busy to notice happiness when it's there? (978-1-63555-944-6)

Calumet by Ali Vali. Jaxon Lavigne and Iris Long had a forbidden small-town romance that didn't last, and the consequences of that love will be uncovered fifteen years later at their high school reunion. (978-1-63555-900-2)

Her Countess to Cherish by Jane Walsh. London Society's material girl realizes there is more to life than diamonds when she falls in love with a non-binary bluestocking. (978-1-63555-902-6)

Hot Days, Heated Nights by Renee Roman. When Cole and Lee meet, instant attraction quickly flares into uncontrollable passion, but their connection might be short lived as Lee's identity is tied to her life in the city. (978-1-63555-888-3)

Never Be the Same by MA Binfield. Casey meets Olivia and sparks fly in this opposites attract romance that proves love can be found in the unlikeliest places. (978-1-63555-938-5)

Quiet Village by Eden Darry. Something not quite human is stalking Collie and her niece, and she'll be forced to work with undercover reporter Emily Lassiter if they want to get out of Hyam alive. (978-1-63555-898-2)

Shaken or Stirred by Georgia Beers. Bar owner Julia Martini and home health aide Savannah McNally attempt to weather the storms brought on by a mysterious blogger trashing the bar, family feuds they knew nothing about, and way too much advice from way too many relatives. (978-1-63555-928-6)

The Fiend in the Fog by Jess Faraday. Can four people on different trajectories work together to save the vulnerable residents of East London from the terrifying fiend in the fog before it's too late? (978-1-63555-514-1)

The Marriage Masquerade by Toni Logan. A no strings attached marriage scheme to inherit a Maui B&B uncovers unexpected attractions and a dark family secret. (978-1-63555-914-9)

Flight SQA016 by Amanda Radley. Fastidious airline passenger Olivia Lewis is used to things being a certain way. When her routine is changed by a new, attractive member of the staff, sparks fly. (978-1-63679-045-9)

Home Is Where the Heart Is by Jenny Frame. Can Archie make the countryside her home and give Ash the fairytale romance she desires? Or will the countryside and small village life all be too much for her? (978-1-63555-922-4)

Moving Forward by PJ Trebelhorn. The last person Shelby Ryan expects to be attracted to is Iris Calhoun, the sister of the man who killed her wife four years and three thousand miles ago. (978-1-63555-953-8)

Poison Pen by Jean Copeland. Debut author Kendra Blake is finally living her best life until a nasty book review and exposed secrets threaten her promising new romance with aspiring journalist Alison Chatterley. (978-1-63555-849-4)

Seasons for Change by KC Richardson. Love, laughter, and trust develop for Shawn and Morgan throughout the changing seasons of Lake Tahoe. (978-1-63555-882-1)

Summer Lovin' by Julie Cannon. Three different women, three exotic locations, one unforgettable summer. What do you think will happen? (978-1-63555-920-0)

Unbridled by D. Jackson Leigh. A visit to a local stable turns into more than riding lessons between a novel writer and an equestrian with a taste for power play. (978-1-63555-847-0)

VIP by Jackie D. In a town where relationships are forged and shattered by perception, sometimes even love can't change who you really are. (978-1-63555-908-8)

Yearning by Gun Brooke. The sleepy town of Dennamore has an irresistible pull on those who've moved away. The mystery Darian Benson and Samantha Pike uncover will change them forever, but the love they find along the way just might be the key to saving themselves. (978-1-63555-757-2)

A Turn of Fate by Ronica Black. Will Nev and Kinsley finally face their painful past and relent to their powerful, forbidden attraction? Or will facing their past be too much to fight through? (978-1-63555-930-9)

Desires After Dark by MJ Williamz. When her human lover falls deathly ill, Alex, a vampire, must decide which is worse, letting her go or condemning her to everlasting life. (978-1-63555-940-8)

Her Consigliere by Carsen Taite. FBI agent Royal Scott swore an oath to uphold the law, and criminal defense attorney Siobhan Collins pledged her loyalty to the only family she's ever known, but will their love be stronger than the bonds they've vowed to others, or will their competing allegiances tear them apart? (978-1-63555-924-8)

In Our Words: Queer Stories from Black, Indigenous, and People of Color Writers. Stories selected by Anne Shade and Edited by Victoria Villaseñor. Comprising both the renowned and emerging voices of Black, Indigenous, and People of Color authors, this thoughtfully curated collection of short stories explores the intersection of racial and queer identity. (978-1-63555-936-1)

Measure of Devotion by CF Frizzell. Disguised as her late twin brother, Catherine Samson enters the Civil War to defend the Constitution as a Union soldier, never expecting her life to be altered by a Gettysburg farmer's daughter. (978-1-63555-951-4)

Not Guilty by Brit Ryder. Claire Weaver and Emery Pearson's day jobs clash, even as their desire for each other burns, and a discreet sex-only arrangement is the only option. (978-1-63555-896-8)

Opposites Attract: Butch/Femme Romances by Meghan O'Brien, Aurora Rey, Angie Williams. Sometimes opposites really do attract. Fall in love with these butch/femme romance novellas. (978-1-63555-784-8)

Swift Vengeance by Jean Copeland, Jackie D, Erin Zak. A journalist becomes the subject of her own investigation when sudden strange, violent visions summon her to a summer retreat and into the arms of a killer's possible next victim. (978-1-63555-880-7)

Under Her Influence by Amanda Radley. On their path to #truelove, will Beth and Jemma discover that reality is even better than illusion? (978-1-63555-963-7)

Wasteland by Kristin Keppler & Allisa Bahney. Danielle Clark is fighting against the National Armed Forces and finds peace as a scavenger, until the NAF general's daughter, Katelyn Turner, shows up on her doorstep and brings the fight right back to her. (978-1-63555-935-4)

When in Doubt by VK Powell. Police officer Jeri Wylder thinks she committed a crime in the line of duty but can't remember, until details emerge pointing to a cover-up by those close to her. (978-1-63555-955-2)

A Woman to Treasure by Ali Vali. An ancient scroll isn't the only treasure Levi Montbard finds as she starts her hunt for the truth—all she has to do is prove to Yasmine Hassani that there's more to her than an adventurous soul. (978-1-63555-890-6)

Before. After. Always. by Morgan Lee Miller. Still reeling from her tragic past, Eliza Walsh has sworn off taking risks, until Blake Navarro turns her world right-side up, making her question if falling in love again is worth it. (978-1-63555-845-6)

Bet the Farm by Fiona Riley. Lauren Calloway's luxury real estate sale of the century comes to a screeching halt when dairy farm heiress, and one-night stand, Thea Boudreaux calls her bluff. (978-1-63555-731-2)

Cowgirl by Nance Sparks. The last thing Aren expects is to fall for Carol. Sharing her home is one thing, but sharing her heart means sharing the demons in her past and risking everything to keep Carol safe. (978-1-63555-877-7)

Give In to Me by Elle Spencer. Gabriela Talbot never expected to sleep with her favorite author—certainly not after the scathing review she'd given Whitney Ainsworth's latest book. (978-1-63555-910-1)

Hidden Dreams by Shelley Thrasher. A lethal virus and its resulting vision send Texan Barbara Allan and her lovely guide, Dara, on a journey up Cambodia's Mekong River in search of Barbara's mother's mystifying past. (978-1-63555-856-2)

In the Spotlight by Lesley Davis. For actresses Cole Calder and Eris Whyte, their chance at love runs out fast when a fan's adoration turns to obsession. (978-1-63555-926-2)

Origins by Jen Jensen. Jamis Bachman is pulled into a dangerous mystery that becomes personal when she learns the truth of her origins as a ghost hunter. (978-1-63555-837-1)

Pursuit: A Victorian Entertainment by Felice Picano. An intelligent, handsome, ruthlessly ambitious young man who rose from the slums to become the right-hand man of the Lord Exchequer of England will stop at nothing as he pursues his Lord's vanished wife across Continental Europe. (978-1-63555-870-8)

Unrivaled by Radclyffe. Zoey Cohen will never accept second place in matters of the heart, even when her rival is a career, and Declan Black has nothing left to give of herself or her heart. (978-1-63679-013-8)

A Fae Tale by Genevieve McCluer. Dovana comes to terms with her changing feelings for her lifelong best friend and fae, Roze. (978-1-63555-918-7)

Accidental Desperados by Lee Lynch. Life is clobbering Berry, Jaudon, and their long romance. The arrival of directionless baby dyke MJ doesn't help. Can they find their passion again—and keep it? (978-1-63555-482-3)

Always Believe by Aimée. Greyson Walsden is pursuing ordination as an Anglican priest. Angela Arlingham doesn't believe in God. Do they follow their vocation or their hearts? (978-1-63555-912-5)

Best of the Wrong Reasons by Sander Santiago. For Fin Ness and Orion Starr, it takes a funeral to remind them that love is worth living for. (978-1-63555-867-8)

Courage by Jesse J. Thoma. No matter how often Natasha Parsons and Tommy Finch clash on the job, an undeniable attraction simmers just beneath the surface. Can they find the courage to change so love has room to grow? (978-1-63555-802-9)

I Am Chris by R Kent. There's one saving grace to losing everything and moving away. Nobody knows her as Chrissy Taylor. Now Chris can live who he truly is. (978-1-63555-904-0)

The Princess and the Odium by Sam Ledel. Jastyn and Princess Aurelia return to Venostes and join their families in a battle against the dark force to take back their homeland for a chance at a better tomorrow. (978-1-63555-894-4)

The Queen Has a Cold by Jane Kolven. What happens when the heir to the throne isn't a prince or a princess? (978-1-63555-878-4)

The Secret Poet by Georgia Beers. Agreeing to help her brother woo Zoe Blake seemed like a good idea to Morgan Thompson at first…until she realizes she's actually wooing Zoe for herself… (978-1-63555-858-6)

You Again by Aurora Rey. For high school sweethearts Kate Cormier and Sutton Guidry, the second chance might be the only one that matters. (978-1-63555-791-6)

CPSIA information can be obtained
at www.ICGtesting.com
Printed in the USA
LVHW031552050821
694493LV00003B/254

9 781635 558883